T0365684

THE AD MAN

A MOROCCAN AFFAIR

Timothy Dickinson

authorHOUSE

AuthorHouse™ UK
1663 Liberty Drive
Bloomington, IN 47403 USA
www.authorhouse.co.uk
Phone: 0800.197.4150

Published by AuthorHouse   08/12/2016

ISBN: 978-1-5246-3462-9 (sc)
ISBN: 978-1-5246-3461-2 (e)

Contents

The End

I have not been sleeping very well recently. If I get five hours of sleep, I feel lucky; two or three hours has been the norm for the past month.

We argued again last night. Well, it was more a disagreement than an argument, but we do seem to be having more disagreements these days. I have nothing more to give her. Since we got married, our love seems to have faded slowly away. This beautiful woman lying next to me used to fill my mind, my soul, and my heart. Here she is, breathing peacefully and uttering sexy little grunts in her sleep, but the grunts are not for me. Her back is towards me; she never faces me anymore. If I want a hug, I wrap my arms around her and press myself against her. My hands fall naturally on her breasts, and if she is in a good mood, she will let me caress them. If she isn't, I get sent packing.

There is no point in my opening my eyes; the room is in complete darkness. The bedroom balcony looks out over the sea. The only light outside comes from the moon. The sea this morning lies lifeless and lightless. The only sounds are from the street cleaner at the front of the apartment, the first tramcar rolling past, and the wild dogs knocking over the trash cans behind the restaurants down on the corniche. It must be two thirty in the morning.

My mind is fully activated. My body is still fired with passion, with lust, with desire, and I have nowhere to release it. Here I am, lying next to this smooth, tanned body twenty years younger yet unable to make contact with her. She tosses and turns in her sleep. I move to the edge of the bed, saved from falling out by a thin, twisting yarn that circumnavigates the mattress edge. I turn just in time to narrowly avoid being cracked across my face by her flailing arms responding to yet another nervous twitch. Finally she lies still. I know she is awake; she can only lie still when she is awake. The cold air rushes in as she throws back the duvet and inconsiderately leaves me cold and coverless. I listen to her groping her way down the unlit corridor towards the kitchen. *I would love a cup of tea*, I think, *but experience has taught me that she will only make one cup, one cup without sugar for herself.*

We row about nothing. The most insignificant discussions turn into anger and frustration – man's logic versus woman's passion. We are both stubborn people and refuse to give in. Eventually she starts insulting my manhood, my hygiene standards, my cooking ability, and my age. I have no answer for this kind of onslaught. So I shut up; she chalks this up as a win and adds it to her list of insults. What is the point? We used to make mad, passionate love every night. After an argument, it was tremendous; it made the argument worth having. But now she turns her back on me and pretends to be asleep. I can hear the kettle boiling, and now she is stirring in the milk. There is silence. What is she doing now? I don't have a clue.

It seems like an age passes. Maybe I fall asleep for a few minutes, or was it an hour? Now there is a single shaft of light breaking through the curtains; the sun is coming up. I can hear her coming back to bed. She will be cold; maybe she will cuddle up to me for warmth. That would be nice. I sense her enter the bedroom and through half-open eyes watch her walk towards the bed. She is holding something out towards me. Has she brought me a cup of tea? Should I speak or pretend to be asleep? As she raises her arm, I realise it isn't a cup in her hand but a knife – a kitchen knife. Its long blade flashes in the dawning light as she kneels on the bed beside me and thrusts it down towards my chest.

'Oh my God!'

In the Beginning

The back streets of Casablanca are just a blur; I am running for my life. Sweat is pouring down my face, stinging my eyes. How can an innocent morning walk around the city end up with me running for my life? My only escape from this madness is to reach the souk, the oldest part of Casablanca. The labyrinth of the Derb Ghalef neighbourhood, I hope, will offer me protection. This huge souk is not for the faint of heart; with luck I can lose my attackers amongst the small shanty shops and stalls. The alleyways between the stalls are no more than several feet wide. Some double as drainage ditches with rainwater gushing down the centre gully. From there I can find my way back to the Sheraton Hotel.

I glance over my shoulder and to my horror see the man who claims I insulted him, leading a gang of twenty or more men. All are shouting and screaming and waving sticks in the air. Panic floods through my entire body, but running out of breath and stopping due to exhaustion is not an option. If these guys catch me, they will rip me apart. I make it into the chaos of the souk; my progress is slower now amongst the shoppers. The sellers step in my way and show me their latest wares. These guys are the masters of negotiation. Every successful sale is concluded with enthusiastic shouts and screams. Insults and rude gestures are the norm if you don't buy. When they see me pushing my way through the crowds, they don't see a frightened man; they see a rich English tourist. I have to push them aside as they stand in my way waving jewellery, pots and pans, radios, and bedding in my face. As I pass I hear them shouting obscenities, and some are even joining the chase.

I can hear the shrill squeak of a police whistle. *Is this my escape, to give myself up to the authorities?* I might have to spend the night in the police station filling in reports, but that would be better than being beaten up by this mob. I reject the thought as the stupidest idea I have ever had. Not for one minute would the police be on my side.

The alley ahead is the fashion area of the souk; I can see thousands of dresses, blouses, and skirts blowing in the breeze, hanging from racks held on by bent-wire coat hangers. Every type of garment imaginable is there, from brightly coloured dresses to long white *thobes*. Maybe I can hide amongst them and move silently from one stall to the next until I lose my pursuers and they tire of the game. *Could this be my escape?* I finally sink to the floor in the corner of one such shop and hide behind a rail of black *abayas*. I can hear the men shouting in the alley, banging their sticks on the support poles holding up the canvas stalls. My breath is loud and sharp. I stifle a cough. The sand, the dust, the grime, and the sickening pedestals of smoking Arabian Oud have penetrated deep into my lungs, and I am gasping for air.

I was simply walking across the city square, taking in the sunshine and the sites like all the other tourists to the city, when a middle-aged, casually dressed man offered to be my guide, to show me the sights, and to educate me on the history of his beloved city.

'You want a guide, sir?' he asked. I was not in need of a guide; I was doing very well on my own, thank you very much, reading the tour book as I went. He would not take no for an answer and refused to go away. His English was good and his manner polite, so I invited him to walk with me for an hour. We eventually paused at a pavement cafe; he suggested we stop for a croissant and coffee, as this was his cousin's coffee shop, and he would only charge me half price. So we sat and talked for about an hour. But with the sun at its height and no shade to be had, it didn't take long for my scalp to turn a bright tomato red. I made this my excuse to leave.

I paid for the coffees, which I thought were rather expensive, and thrust a five-hundred-dirham note into his hand. I had given a great deal of thought as to the amount I should tip him. I decided five hundred dirham, worth forty-five pounds, was a reasonable price for two hours of his time, during which he had done very little except drink a free coffee. Goodness! If he earned this every hour, he would make two hundred pounds a day. I only make two hundred pounds a day as the creative director of a Middle Eastern advertising agency, and for that my day is sometimes twelve hours long. I was taken by surprise, to say the least, by his negative reaction. As I stood to shake his hand and thank him for his company, he started screaming like a lunatic – I guess in Moroccan Arabic. The few words I did recognise made it quite clear he was insulted at the amount. According to him, an American would have given him two thousand dirham, and even a Canadian would have given him a thousand – *and* bought him lunch, cigarettes, wine, and a glass of brandy. My five hundred dirham was an insult to his intelligence, his pride as a man, and his status as a father of five children. For that he was going to kill me.

I hadn't realised that life was so desperate in Morocco and that so many people were out of work and their children so hungry. Life looks upbeat on the street, but apparently Morocco is going through a very disruptive time. The government has promised to improve the economy, but the only thing on the way up is the number of unemployed men, like my guide, struggling to feed their families. Established factories, which have been the source of income for a hundred years, are losing contracts to a new breed of forceful, ruthless businessmen and being forced to close. Most of these new companies are from China, but many are from America and Europe. The French are seen as one of the leading disruptive countries in this transition of power.

Anyway, his ranting escalated into violence. As I tried to make a sharp exit, he started throwing cups and teapots at me. His chair broke into many pieces as he kicked it towards me. I clutched my bag and maps and started to run down the street, hoping the waiter and his cousin would calm him down. They didn't. In fact, they were making matters worse, nodding in agreement to his reasoning. I glanced back and saw to my horror that all three were throwing tableware at me. Another cup flew past my head, and I realised how lucky I was that it wasn't a bullet. I was running for my life and took a sharp right down the nearest alley; I had no idea where I was or where I was going.

That is how I find myself hiding in the souk, shaking with fear and praying the angry mob of men chasing me will give up. A mangy cat is sitting with me; it looks rather annoyed at having to share its corner. It hisses as I eventually shoo it away, only for it to be replaced by a small boy who pushes his way through the garments to join me. Apparently he has been watching me for several minutes. He holds out his hands and puts ten fingers up to his face. I get the message; he wants ten dirham for his silence. I place a coin in his palm and pat him on his head. He seems pleased with his ill-gotten gain and runs off to catch the cat. There are no signs of my guide and his mercenary army. The souk is returning to normal, with women thumbing through the racks of clothes and the sellers verbally bombarding them with words of encouragement to buy. I crawl out of my hiding place and head towards the end of the alley. At the main road the stench of the market's drainage system changes to the smell of diesel fumes as black, acrid smoke clouds out of the badly maintained buses and trucks. The chatter of the excited women shoppers has changed into the clatter of donkey carts on the cobbles; which insist on splashing my shoes with gutter water as they rock 'n' roll past me. I hail a taxi and take a deep sigh of relief. 'To the Sheraton, please,' I gasp as I squeeze into the back seat of a very small, dirty, dilapidated red Fiat Uno, trapping my foot in the door as I slam it shut. The pain is not important.

'You English?' asks the driver.

All I can do is grunt, but it seems to satisfy his curiosity as to why I am rubbing my leg. We accelerate off towards the Sheraton, down Beir Anzaran left at the lights and along the corniche. To go the shortest way is a rare occurrence; I am usually taken on a tour of the town first.

'Have you enjoyed your day?' asks the pretty receptionist in the hotel lounge, her tight white blouse gaping open provocatively at the fourth button. I can just see her name badge, which is partially hidden behind the lapel of her dark blue jacket.

'Hello, Maryam. A most enjoyable day, thank you.' Lying doesn't come naturally to me, especially when I am distracted by thinking how nice it would be to cuddle up with her. Right now I am in desperate need of some comfort.

My room is immaculate. Fresh flowers have been placed in the vase on the coffee table and fruit arranged in the bowl. The bed is perfectly wrapped up in crisp white linen and looks very appealing. I spread eagle myself on it, burying my face into the pillow, and then I start to shake. The flight of the day has scared every nerve in my body, and I am exhausted. I fall into a deep sleep. There is no way I am going out again today. My love of Casablanca has taken a big hit; it will take a miracle to change my opinion.

It is dark when I awake. Cool air is blowing in through the partially opened window. Along with it comes the sound of the evening street, the squealing of the trams, the honking of the taxi horns, and the excited screams of the young revellers making their way to the night clubs and bars. I take dinner in the hotel restaurant. I have experienced enough of Moroccan culture for one day, so I order steak, fries, and salad (so very British). My waiter suggests I enjoy my coffee in the lobby and relax with a brandy. I agree with him. I especially like the idea of a brandy. I search the lobby for a table, but all thirty tables are occupied with a pretty girl sitting alone. The nearest table is in front of the large revolving street door, the rest spiral around the piano, under the staircase leading to the elevators and across the front of the bar. I squeeze between them, thinking what a peculiar coincidence this is and hoping one might come available as I pass. Suddenly a chair is pushed in front of me, blocking my path.

'You can sit here, sir. This table is free.' I look down into the blackest of eyes, down the longest of black hair that cascades over the smoothest of chests and down to the sexiest of knees, which she crosses, uncrosses, and crosses again when she sees me admiring them. Just to remove all need of imagination, she hitches up her skirt a couple of inches. I hesitate for a second, feeling rather embarrassed, and glance around the room. All the other girls are watching my every move. My gaze shoots from dark eyes to long, dark hair and from heaving chests to sexy knees. Every girl is identical. This is sexuality cloned to perfection, with long, straight black hair, golden suntanned skin, pouting lips, and seductive eyes. The waiter, who has been following me around the lounge, places my coffee on the table. The decision where I am to sit has been made for me; I sit down and smile at her.

'Could I buy you a drink?'

She bends towards me, displaying her wares.

'I'll have a dry martini,' she whispers.

'Shaken or stirred?' I joke. Now she is looking at me as if I am stupid; obviously James Bond has never stayed at the Casablanca Sheraton.

The waiter needs no prompting and is already on his way to get one. He is on a mission to please me in the hope of gaining a generous tip.

Conversation is slow and difficult. She must have guessed I am British, as her invitation to sit with her was well rehearsed. The rest of her vocabulary is not as confident. I am sure her invites are equally polished in French, German, Arabic, or whichever language is required to make the hit. She is definitely a smart lady. I can tell she is sophisticated, cool, and confident as well as being so very beautiful. She doesn't need to know any more English, her eyes, her body, and her legs do all the talking for her. It only takes half an hour of her company for me to be relaxed and refreshed. Unfortunately, she asks me what I have been doing during the day. My memory of the day brings me out in an ice-cold sweat, and memories of the city guide throw up many questions. Will this girl charge me for her company? If so will it be by the hour, by the trick, or for the night? Oh my God, this is déjà vu. I hope she doesn't ask me to give her what I think she is worth. Images of me being chased by thirty Sheraton girls, out into the Place de la France, across the railway station, and into the heart of the port spring into my head. I can see myself hiding amongst the containers all night. They are probably full of fashions for the bazaar.

I have had enough; I excuse myself and make a dash for the elevator. *'Cinquieme étage, s'il vous plait.'* I have no idea why French is coming out of my mouth; the elevator attendant speaks English fluently.

'Floor five, sir,' he announces.

Nagano: It's In Japan, Do You Know

Room 542, room 544, room 546 – where is room 545? Oh! It's across the hall. I fumble at the lock and escape into the sanctuary of my room. It takes several minutes to find the TV remote. The screen bursts into life, and the main feature is the Winter Olympics from Nagano, which I later learn is in Japan. *Thank goodness for such an interesting programme,* I think to myself. *I will be quite content watching this all evening, even if it is in French.*

I lie on my bed for over an hour and try to concentrate on the downhill slalom, but my mind keeps recalling the last twelve hours. The day has been a nightmare. I recall the chase across the city and escaping by rolling up like a pussycat behind a pile of women's clothes. Then there was being solicited by a Moroccan hooker and leaving with my dignity and my wallet still intact.

There is a knock on the door. I freeze. Is it the man with the gun? The hooker? Is it the hotel manager or even the police?

'Who is it?'

'Room service.'

Room service? I haven't ordered anything.

The voice is that of a young girl, light and shaky. She sounds Moroccan with a possible hint of French. I open the door, and standing there is a pretty little girl with a beautiful, innocent smile. She tries to explain her presence, but I can't understand. Like most people learning English, she is speaking too fast and not moving her lips. Small and slightly dishevelled, she pushes me out of the way and walks around the bed. I stand and watch her. She could be new at the job. She seems to be nervous, but it might be because I am watching her. She plumps up the pillows and folds down the sheets. It is going to be a long night for her. She still has fifteen more rooms to service on this floor alone. Eventually she returns to her trolley, takes a chocolate from a box on the top shelf, and places it on my pillow. With a little curtsey and a faint *'Bonne nuit, Monsieur'*, she heads for the door.

'Wait!' I call after her. Taking a two-hundred-dirham note from my pocket, I thrust it into her hand.

'Shukran, kind sir.' She in return grabs a handful of chocolates from the trolley and arranges them delicately on my dressing table. The day is ending on a high. I feel better and more in control. For the first time today I am positive about tomorrow.

The Olympics is turning an otherwise boring evening into an interesting one. The four-man bobsleigh is my favourite. Their skill and technique is superb. No one can beat the Americans. The Norwegians come close, being only point eight of a second behind them. The British team must have an engine failure; their sleigh seems stuck in third gear. They have come twelfth out of the thirteen teams competing. Just as I am fumbling for the remote to turn it off, there is another knock on my door. I search for my mobile to check on the time. It is 1.56 am.

'Who is there?' I ask, leaning in close to the door so I don't have to shout at this unearthly hour.

'It's Khadija, sir. I tided your room earlier.'

'Did you forget something?' I am so naïve at times.

'I am bringing you more chocolates, sir. Let me in. I can get into trouble for doing this.'

I unlock the door, and she quickly slips in under my arm.

'Quickly, close the door, sir. The floor walker must not see me.' I hurriedly push the door until it clicks shut and check that the lock has taken hold.

'You are beautiful. I didn't recognise you out of uniform.' She is wearing the prettiest lightweight printed summer dress. It is patterned with bright-coloured flowers, and the V neckline buttons neatly across her chest. I just catch a glimpse of her small, white breasts, which look like young children playing in a field of flowers. They are unsupported and very, very appealing.

'I know you kind man. I need kind man to care for me, and this is for you.' She places a handful of chocolates onto the bedside table and tugs at the loop of her belt, which is hanging loosely around her waist. Her dress opens, and she slips it off her shoulders. Standing naked before me, she is flawless and oh so young. After being confident of my approval, she pulls back the duvet on the bed, picks up two pieces of the chocolate, and throws one over to me, which I fumble but catch. The other piece she places between her teeth and sucks slowly between her lips. She giggles and pats the mattress beside her.

I am excited to say the least; she is so full of fun and play, so energetic, and far too lively for me. Explorative and explosive, she climaxes time after time, more from her own enthusiasm than from my touch. The world is hers for the asking.

We lay wrapped around each other, panting and sweating. Her hand is exploring my body and her tongue teasing my nipples. Wow! Casablanca is proving to be quite a delight.

'Khadija,' I whisper, 'can you stay with me all night?'

She laughs. 'Me go at five. I serve breakfast. Sleep now.' I take a deep breath, stroke her tousled hair, and congratulate myself on a job well done. 'You not know me, okay?' she says, suddenly sitting up, her breasts quivering above my face.

'Who are you, anyway?' She laughs, then collapses across my chest and closes her eyes.

I don't know how long I have been asleep. I have no idea what the time is, but it is still dark. At first I don't even know why I have awakened. Khadija is still lying there, so I assume it isn't five o'clock yet. Then I hear the tapping on the door. My first thought is, *It must be someone visiting a room down the corridor.* But no, there it is again, and it is definitely on my door. I slip out of bed and drape a towel around myself. The tapping is louder this time. I try to look through the door lens but can see nothing more than the blurred shape of a woman. I unlock the door and open it a couple of inches.

'Mr Collinwood?'

'Yes!'

'It's me. You left so quickly, and I was worried about you.'

The pungent smell of stale perfume fills my nose as I recognise the hooker from the lobby. She pushes her way into the room.

'You can't come in here. What do you think you are doing?'

'Don't be silly, darling. It's your birthday, and I am your birthday present.'

Khadija sits up in bed. 'Who is this?'

The two girls stare at each other, both recognising the other but not quite knowing from where.

Then the fireworks start.

'I know you! You are the room maid.' Swinging round, she tries to slap me. 'You left me for a simple room maid?'

Khadija is equally outraged.

17

'You have me then order her?' She jumps out of bed and grabs her dress. I take time out. For the next ten minutes the two of them scream and shout insults at each other as only Moroccan women can do. Then their attack turns to me.

I open the door wide and point to the corridor, ordering them both to leave. I have no clue as to what they are saying; it is just vile outrage. If I were to hazard a guess, it would be 'You'll regret this, you won't get away with this.' I close the door and listen to the insults until they fade down the corridor. They are probably the best of friends by now, their insults being aimed at me. I can't even be bothered to put the light on; I just climb back into bed and lie there in a daze. What can possibly happen next?

The door rattles again, not a gentle tap this time but a firm, determined knock, I am furious and open the door expecting it to be the girls.

'This nonsense must stop once and for all. Ohh!' A man is standing there; he is enormous and fills the doorframe.

'I am the hotel floor walker. Everything that happens on this floor has to have my approval.' His stare is frightening. 'You have entertained two girls tonight. That is two thousand dirham or I will have you evicted from the hotel immediately.' Behind him two more grotesque men appear to add meaning to his message. When he says he will throw me out, I believe him. So I hand over two thousand dirham.

'Thank you, Mr Collinwood. If there is anything else that you require, I am at your service down the corridor. Enjoy your stay in Casablanca.'

A Bed to Myself

This is one of those times I need a bed to myself. My love of women has always been my weakness. Like most men, I can't say no to a pretty girl who is offering herself to me, nor can I resist a chase for a girl who is playing hard to get. However, my feeling towards women has just taken a second knock. The first was when my wife left me after twenty years for a younger man. Anyway, times have changed. The rule of one man for one woman, which I understood to be gospel, doesn't seem to apply here in Morocco. In fact, it doesn't apply in England anymore.

So is my production manager at the agency in Jeddah correct when he explains his attitude towards dating? It was during a simple question-and-answer conversation about his forthcoming visit to London that he asked, 'So, if I meet an English woman and take her to see a West End Show, lavish her with gifts, and treat her to an expensive dinner, is it okay for me to take her back to my hotel, or should I rent a back street apartment?' His focus was on the acceptance of the hotel, not on the agreement of the girl.

'Would it be acceptable practice?' I laughed. 'What makes you think she will want to sleep with you?'

'If I spend money on her, she has to,' he replied.

I honestly thought there was only one woman for each man. I actually believed in love. I am still hoping to feel the chemistry again, to find a magic spark and enjoy love everlasting. That is why I come out in a sweat when I think of my ex-wife and get excited looking through our photo album. I would be interested to question a newly married couple on their expectation of a long-lasting relationship, as 20 per cent of British marriages last less than three years and 60 per cent end in divorce. Anyway, here I am in Casablanca taking in the sights, meeting the people, and experiencing what I can only describe as sex. I am still looking for the woman who can restore my belief in togetherness, but in the meantime …

With that thought, I fall asleep for the third time tonight, but I am not at peace. My brain is trying to sort out the world and my nervous system is actively twitching, but my body is exhausted.

I decide to take breakfast in the VIP suite; it will be safer than the public breakfast hall. I don't relish the idea of having black coffee thrown over me first thing in the morning by Khadija. My decision proves to be the right one. There are only four guests seated at the elaborate tables, so the five waiters on duty have time to pamper us. The atmosphere is peaceful and civilised. I am surprised to see that one of the guests is a woman, as this is very much a man's world. It is quite fortuitous that I am topping up my orange juice at the same time she is. My previous observations of her also prove to be correct. In her mid-thirties and single, she is obviously a morning person, as she is immaculately dressed and groomed in a tight black suit and high heels. She must have been awake very early to look this perfect. By my watch it is still only seven fifteen. Oh yes! And she is French, the clue being her newspaper.

I find her very intriguing. The fact that she is on her own proves she has confidence and charisma, unless her husband or father is hiding behind the curtains. She does not play-act; her body language is simple and dynamic, purposeful yet natural. She is very happy with herself. I get a good feeling from her. She smiles at me. Unfortunately, due to a lack of concentration she floods the juice over the top of her glass. Wow, what a fuss this has created. The waiters rush to her aid. One removes the glass from her hand and offers her a clean white serviette with which to dry her arm. A second waiter pours her another juice, and the third holds her arm to steady her as she rocks on her high heels. I also rush to her aid.

'May I help you back to your table? I have a free hand, and I could carry your juice.'

'Merci beaucoup!' And with that she thrusts her glass into my hand.

I follow her back to her table like a little puppy dog on a leash and wait for her to be seated before rearranging her cutlery.

'Enjoy your day!' I wish her well as I return to the sanctuary of my own *petit déjeuner*. In my head, up pops the tab 'Challenge'. I laugh at my silly thoughts. I hope no one heard the starting pistol going off in my head.

The waiter comes over to top up my coffee, 'Thank you for helping,' he says.

'Helping! What did I do?'

He nods his head in the direction of the woman.

'For helping her to her table. She is a very difficult and demanding woman. She makes our lives a misery.'

'Tell her to get a life of her own and to leave you alone.'

'We can't do that, sir. She is Madame la Chapelle, Adeline la Chapelle. Her brother is the Ministère Des Affaires Étrangères et Européennes, the French Minister of Foreign Affairs, and her great-grandfather was the high priest of the Basilica of the Sacred Heart of Paris, known to you as Sacré-Cœur.'

'Does this mean she is a virtuous, religious lady or a political rogue?'

'Like all women, it depends on the time of the month.'

'Whooo … you are a brave man even thinking that.'

'Be careful, sir. There are easier challenges out there.'

I slip him a hundred-dirham note; he touches his forehead and goes to ask if she is in need of anything more.

A Big Mac, Cheap at the Price

The day is going to be hot. There isn't a cloud in the sky, and the rising dust from the street is already polluting the air. There is only one place to go: the corniche. I will take my book to excite my imagination, my iPhone to keep in touch with reality, and a thousand dirham for food, probably a coffee and a Big Mac meal. If I were to be mugged, robbed, or killed, which after my experience yesterday in the city is a possibility, my adversaries will not get more than a thousand dirham out of me. My only hint of wealth is my Breitling wristwatch, which is in fact a real one, a magnet for a poor Moroccan boy on the prowl for riches at any cost. It isn't unusual for me to accidentally stray down the back streets or into a sultry bar. I hate shops and shopping, and to escape them I usually take myself away from the main tourist routes. I also take a bus or the tram, never a private taxi or chauffeured car. I enjoy touching the city first-hand.

Sometimes it works in my favour, like the time I had to travel across Paris from La Gare du Sud to La Gare du Nord. Instead of a taxi or the Métro I took the bus. It cost me eight francs and took ninety minutes, during which time I had my own personal guide, a Madame Simon who sat next to me. I don't know why; there were many vacant seats. She was a sophisticated, elderly lady whose delight was to stab me in the leg with her umbrella every time she wanted my attention. But she was great company. When she told me I was a perfect gentleman and that the English were her favourite lovers, I liked her even more, until she explained that she was only comparing us with the Americans. Anyway, I gathered from our conversation that she must have slept around in her day. She knew every famous man from Monet to Charles De Gaulle. But unfortunately, on this occasion I had a train to catch. I know it doesn't take an Englishman long to make love, but this time I didn't have time to make her day.

Today it is my intention to lie low. After the fiasco down the back streets of Casablanca yesterday I think this strategy best. It takes only five minutes to reach the corniche. At this early hour the sea front is practically deserted. The incoming tide is crashing over the barriers and cascading over the row of open swimming pools. By lunchtime they will be full of bathers. I want to sit at Miami Plage, a sea front coffee shop with tables overlooking the water. Here I can feel the breeze of the sea on my face and watch everything that happens along the shore. I have a choice of ten tables along the front edge. I chose the one on the end. Here I will have my back to the road and be able to watch everyone who comes and goes. I can also watch the sea coming in, which is spectacular. Only two other tables are occupied.

Sitting at the first is a middle-aged man and a woman who I guess is his wife. They are shouting at one another, but that doesn't mean they are arguing. Moroccans and most Arabic people converse by shouting. Their body language and the tone of their voices are always angry and forceful. But the longer I watch them, the more certain I am that they are arguing. Their voices rise even higher. He stands up to leave and then sits down again. She is ranting the same words over and over again, and he is being stoned to death by words. The first he manages to avoid, but as they keep coming, one after another after another, he falls silent. His head slumps into his hands, and he just stares at her. Her attack is serpent-like; she hisses and sprays him with venomous spit, shaking her fingers and pulling at his shirt. It is obvious he is planning her death, or maybe his own. Eventually they both stand up and storm off in opposite directions. The waiter chases after the man, waving his bill; he must have decided he was the most approachable.

My attention is focusing on the second table. There are two young women taking their time drinking coffee. In fact, it must be cold by now. But as long as there is a drop in the cup, the waiter will let them stay forever. One girl is Moroccan, the other slightly fairer, possibly French. Her eyes are green compared to the Moroccan's black. They too have been watching the gladiatorial battle, and I guess they were supporting the woman. They give her a big smile as she passes them. Our gazes meet. I gesture a slight wave and return to my book, which I have not yet started to read.

'Bonjour Monsieur, excusez-moi. S'il vous plait, avez-vou le feu?' The girl fingers a cigarette between her lips, asking for a light. Moroccan girls are never slow at coming forward. She is so close I can smell her perfume on the breeze; it turns the salt spray into rose petals. I shake my head and gesture back that I don't smoke.

'Parlez-vous Anglais?' I ask.

She turns to face her friend. 'English?'

'English?' The other girl repeats the word in a questioning voice.

Well! They seem to have understood that I think to myself, but instead of ignoring me they come and sit at my table. The Moroccan girl brings over their cold coffees and perches herself opposite me. Well, at least they are pretty, which is a great improvement on my guest yesterday.

It takes two hours to establish that my name is Tim and their names are Linah and Roxanne. Roxanne is French, as I had predicted, but Linah is from Casablanca and by far the more confident of the two. She is a touchy person, patting my knee consistently and blowing cigarette smoke into my face from her deep red, heart-shaped lips. Two more hours pass, after which time they know more about me than I know about them. They know my hotel, how long I am staying, what I do, and that I live in Saudi Arabia. I know they are both very beautiful, do not have a job, and are bored most days. That is not a lot, really, but it is easier for me to talk to them than to understand what they are saying. We laugh a lot at our clumsy conversation and my exaggerated hand movements as I try to explain the simplest of stories. The afternoon costs me two Big Mac meals, which I feel is a reasonable cost for the enjoyment of their company. It is five o'clock when they leave; I plunge back into reading my book, which is still open on page one.

The First Date

T he day in the sun has taken its toll. My face is bright red and my forehead sore; even my ears are burning. I look at myself in the mirror and give out a gasp. I spread a jar of after-sun cream on my face and arms and pray this hideous tomato colour will calm down before dinner. I plan to eat at the Sheraton; I have endured enough excitement for one day and definitely had too much sun. I sleep for three hours. The sea breeze has cleaned out the dust from my lungs and revitalised my blood. When I wake, my skin is returning to a natural golden brown. A shower stimulates every nerve in my body. I don't usually take long showers; I never have the time. But today I deserve a treat. I just start at the top and let the soap run down my body. I follow it down, rubbing and scrubbing. By the time it reaches my feet, I am done. But this time it has taken thirty minutes, possibly longer. Even after the small tablet of hotel soap has completely dissolved, I let the warm water ravish my body for another few moments.

What to wear is not important. I intend to eat alone, watching and listening. Hopefully I might enjoy an innocent chat with an interesting guest or two. So I pull on a pair of jeans and a white shirt laundered by the hotel, my favourite black leather shoes, and a black jacket, which gives me the classic look. I don't really need the jacket, but the pockets are useful for my wallet, passport, and spectacles. When I first started travelling, I hated eating alone; I felt so self-conscious. I once took a book to the restaurant but remembered it was bad manners to read at the table. Now people eat with their mobiles stuck to their face or twitch to the latest music through their headsets, which I think is even ruder. I enter the dining room feeling calm, confident, and hungry.

'Good evening, Mr Collinwood. Have you had a nice day?' My waiter from breakfast is on restaurant duty.

'Very nice indeed,' I respond. 'I met two very interesting people at the corniche.' I hope he doesn't delve any deeper into who they were.

'Excellent. Let me show you to your table.' He leads the way around several guests already eating; the food looks and smells delicious.

'I will enjoy exploring the menu and possibly trying something Moroccan this evening.'

'Very well, sir. I will return to take your order in a couple of minutes.'

'Mr Collinwood!'

I turn to see who has called my name. It is Madame la Chapelle.

'Excuse me for knowing your name, but I overheard the waiter welcome you. I just wanted to thank you for your assistance this morning. It was very kind of you.'

I blush.

'I am pleased I could be of service. I hope you have had a pleasant day.'

She ignores my statement. 'Are you dining alone?'

'It does appear so, unless I meet a beautiful woman during the evening.'

She laughs at my joke. 'Would you care to join us? We are in need of some light conversation.' She is sitting with two over-groomed businessmen. The table is littered with champagne glasses, and the waiter is standing by with yet another bottle in his hand, ready to uncork it.

'I would be delighted, Madame la Chapelle.' She is taken aback at me knowing her name. 'You see, I also have done my homework.'

She laughs again. She is even prettier when she laughs. This challenge is going to be even easier than I first thought, especially as my two competitors sitting with her have never laughed in their lives.

The two men stand as she introduces me. 'This is my brother, Jean Claud, and my cousin, Abel Lafleur.'

'Pleased to meet you. I hope I am not interrupting anything.'

'You are not! Please join us.' They answer in unison, which I think is a little too orchestrated.

'The French Minister of Foreign Affairs and his accountant,' whispers the wine waiter into my ear. The cork bursts from the champagne bottle, and I sit next to Madame la Chapelle, tasting the finest shower of bubbles France can offer.

'Call me Adeline,' she begs.

'And I answer to Tim, but don't tell your brother.' I wink at her, and she giggles.

Conversation flows awkwardly. Only an occasional joke with Adeline breaks through. Eating oysters isn't helping me relax either; I have never eaten oysters before, and I have no idea what to do with them. I watch intently as each in turn prises one open with the oyster knife and parts the flesh from the shell.

'This is called shucking,' Adeline informs me.

'It looks pretty shocking to me,' I reply. She slaps my hand and continues to demonstrate the technique by squeezing lemon juice over it before lifting it to her lips and letting the flesh slide into her mouth. She is good. This girl has style. And just to add a touch of magic to her performance, she makes a little slurping noise as she sucks it in. Whatever next? I stare in hormonal passion as her tongue comes out and runs around her lips. She gives me a wicked smile.

'You see, Tim? Now it is your turn.'

'To lick your lips or swallow an oyster?'

'To swallow the oyster.' She reaches out, and with her finger she touches my lips.

I would be lying if I said I enjoyed the oyster, but the T-bone steak is grilled to perfection, and the individual lemon soufflé is divine.

During the conversation I briefly describe my job, which is creative director of publicity. I advertise and market anything from international products to services and even countries. If my client has the money to support it, I can make it a success. But I am taken by surprise when Lafleur leans towards me over the table and suggests I meet them in their office at ten in the morning.

'We have not been completely honest with you, Tim,' he says. 'We know more about you than you think and have followed your career over the last few years with great interest.'

I can feel my mouth drying up and my shirt sticking to my back. 'We are impressed with your success, and we feel you are the right man for a task we have in mind. But we can't talk here. Meet us at the French Embassy tomorrow. Come alone, and introduce yourself at reception as Jacques Giger, a Swiss banker. All will be explained to you there.'

They don't give me time to refuse. The three of them stand to leave, shaking my hand as they turn to go. I hold on to Adeline a couple of seconds longer. 'I was hoping we might share a nightcap in the bar,' I whisper to her.

'Not tonight, Tim.' She falters. 'Another time.' I am disappointed; my only joy is watching her trim ankles waver as she climbs the stairs out of the restaurant. The seams of her stockings are an invitation to go where no man has been before, disappearing under her skirt and ravaging my imagination. This girl knows how to impress. Seamed stockings are a thing of the past. Yet when worn correctly they represent style and sophistication, and Madame la Chapelle knows how to wear them. I just sit in dreamland. Her lingering appearance excites my entire body as I plan an expedition into the source of the seam.

The waiter saunters over and joins me. 'You appear to be very pleased with yourself, sir. I hope you had an enjoyable encounter.'

'I am hoping the enjoyment will come later. But it was certainly an interesting encounter, very interesting indeed.'

He stands over me. 'They paid the bill, didn't they?' I ask, as it suddenly occurs to me that I have not seen any settlement for the meal?

'Oh yes, sir, Madame la Chapelle has an account with the hotel.'

'Thank goodness for that. Just for a second I thought I had been—'

'Set up!' He laughs. 'A nightcap, sir?'

'No thank you, I don't drink alone. I will turn in and savour the chocolate on my pillow. Good night. And, err, thanks for your help this evening.'

'Just doing my job, sir. But be careful.'

The evening has passed so quickly. I glance at my watch as I slide my key card down the door slot. The time is 12.18. My room is immaculate, with fresh flowers on the coffee table. The bed has been folded down and looks very beckoning. Ah! Yes, and on my pillow are not one but three pieces of chocolate.

There is a light on in the bathroom. I must have been left it on by mistake. I can't wait to get into bed. I will be asleep in minutes. Yet there is something not quite right with the room. I have a strange feeling someone has been through my things. I place my hand on the bed to feel if it is warm. It is. The TV is also warm, and ouch! The wall light over the bed is hot. I search the bedside drawer to see if anything is missing. Then, just as I am about to open my suitcase, I catch a movement in the mirror. From behind the curtains there is a face. I turn, not with anger but with shock. I haven't a clue what to do.

In fact, I do nothing; I simply freeze.

'Come out and show yourself! You have been caught red-handed. I am calling the police.'

What a pathetic thing to say. They might have a gun or a knife. What if there is more than one? The long drapes part, and out steps a small, sexy girl, wrapped only in a bath towel.

'Please don't hurt me, sir. I wanted to surprise you. I have been waiting for you for over an hour. I am Khadija, your maid.

'You stupid girl, you scared me to death. What are you doing here?' *Another stupid remark.* It is obvious what she is doing here. She lets the towel drop to the floor and throws her arms around my neck.

'Are you expecting anyone else tonight?' she whispers, her lips brushing my cheek.

'Well, as a matter of fact, I am not. My diary is clear until ten in the morning.' We interlock tongues and fall onto the bed. I pin her down by her arms and raise myself above her. 'How old are you?'

'Sorry, sir, me not understand.'

'Oh forget it. It doesn't matter anyway.'

The Advertising Brief

I wake to find that Khadija has already left to serve breakfast. As I take my place by the window, she gives me a neat curtsey and politely asks if I require tea or coffee. No one would guess that she has just got out of my bed. They would think we have just met for the first time and we are complete strangers. I suppose that is what we are; I know nothing about her.

'Jacques Giger', I announce as I walk into the palatial reception lounge of the French Embassy and stand in front of a glass and brass desk. The receptionist looks up and smiles. The room is out of this world. The walls are tiled with unique Italian ceramics. Beautiful Moroccan tapestries are draped in front of them from invisible hangers. There are three large pieces of carved furniture in the room, each one strategically positioned to achieve the greatest effect. Again typically Moroccan, each one is heavily carved with hundreds of tiny cameos of warriors, hunters, farmers, and lovers. I am sure each must be telling a story. I wish I had the time to understand them. Four marble columns stand on sentry duty at the extremities of the room, they must reach forty feet into the air before finally arching into the centre of the ceiling. A narrow wooden walkway circumnavigates the domed glass skylight. I'm glad I don't have to clean that. My name echoes around the pantheon.

'Welcome, M'sieur Giger. The Ministère is expecting you. I have been instructed to take you up to Monsieur Chapelle the moment you arrive.' I follow her to the elevator, which is hidden behind one of the columns. The glass doors slide effortlessly apart, and we are whisked to the third floor in silence.

'M'sieur Chapelle,' she announces as she ushers me through the large wooden doors. 'M'sieur Giger has arrived.'

Jean Claud rises to his feet and steps towards me, his arms outstretched as if we are old friends.

'Welcome! I will call Abel Lafleur. He also wants to be present.' My attention is distracted as a door to the right of his massive bookshelves swings open and in walks Madame la Chapelle. She is dressed this time in a long kaftan, its brightly coloured silks shimmering in the sunlight streaming in through the stained-glass window. The gold embroidered waistband exaggerates her slim, attractive body. Her femininity is outrageous, her beauty extraordinary. She holds out her hand for me to kiss, which I rudely make a meal of. She laughs at my eagerness.

'A pleasure to meet you again, Mr Collinwood, or should I say, M'sieur Giger.'

'The pleasure is all mine. You look stunning.' Stunning? What sort of a description is that? I must stop using these Yorkshire-isms if I am to be a Swiss banker.

Abel Lafleur marches into the room and immediately takes command of the meeting. He arranges three chairs in a semicircle in front of the desk and indicates that I am to sit to his right and Adeline to his left. Jean Claud leans forward from his leather chair, and his smile changes into a frozen frown.

'Tim! You approve of me calling you Tim?' I nod in agreement. 'We are investing billions of Euros into Morocco. The potential is enormous. Morocco is a country waiting to happen, and we are going to see that it does. We are going to develop a car industry here, an aerospace industry, a computer industry second only to Silicon Valley in Northern California. We are going to give the Japanese and the Chinese a run for their money in the scientific and technological future of our planet, and we are going to beat them.

'Morocco will become the fastest-growing country in Africa. The people will be rich, real estate will rocket in price, and construction will outstrip that of the Middle East. Casablanca will be the biggest port in the world, it will be the link between the Middle East and America via the Mediterranean and the Atlantic. Europe and Africa will be connected by a new road and rail network. Do you understand our dream?'

I nod like a silly schoolboy lost for words. 'I once built a brick wall a few years ago. I could be useful on the construction projects.' They all laugh at my pathetic joke, but only for a second.

'You can be a lot more useful than that. We need the people of Morocco to love us, to admire us, and have faith in us, because without their participation our investment is doomed. We want you to create the PR campaign of your life. We need you to sell the idea that France is not only a great country but also their friend, and we want them to trust us passionately. PR will only be one part of your task. As each part of the project progresses and each industry expands and develops, it will be your creative ideas and imaginative campaigns that sell the products and opportunities, first to the Moroccan people and then to the rest of the world. That is how impressed we are with your work and how confident we are in you succeeding. Now, have you any questions?'

Are these guys serious? If they are, I am overwhelmed. I stand for a second in awe, eventually realizing they are waiting for me to say something, I do. 'I have two questions. The first is who is financing you. And the second is far more important: what is in it for me?'

'You come straight to the point, don't you, Tim? I like that. You don't need to know who is behind us just yet, but as time goes by all will be revealed. We can tell you what is on the table for you. We are sure you will be pleased. You have a free rein to do whatever you feel is necessary to achieve the goal; the bank vault door is open to you. As for your personal gratification, you can name your price. Whatever you desire is yours, as long as you succeed. Any other questions?'

I look at their three faces in turn. The smiles have gone.

'What are the negatives?'

'There are no negatives, just targets to meet.'

'Such as what?'

'The five main industries must be up and running this summer. For that to happen, the people of Morocco must be totally supportive of our projects.'

'And?'

'And we have to make our presentation to the investment consortium and our bankers in three weeks.'

'What will the presentation consist of?'

'Your entire plan of action and your timeline, of course.'

'In three weeks?' I ask in dismay.

'Yes, on 24 June, at eleven in the morning.'

'At this moment in time, Tim, we cannot tell you any more, not until we are sure you are with us. Do you need time to think about our offer? We are running out of time, and we hope for your acceptance very soon.'

'I need twenty-four hours to get my head around this. I will only accept if I am sure I can deliver. If I believe I can do it, then you have found your man. If I can't, you have a problem, because nobody else can.'

Abel Lafleur grabs my hand and shakes it. 'Call me at nine in the morning. If your answer is yes, be here at ten for a full briefing.'

By the time I have reached the street, I am in a daze. I need fresh air. I need to be able to think clearly. I need to be able to think this thing through. The corniche is the obvious place. The one thing I don't need are the two girls I met yesterday. Unfortunately, they are sitting at the café and zoom in on me like a pair of Exocet missiles.

'Linah and Roxanne.' I greet them by pointing at one and then the other.

'Nearly! Roxanne and Linah.' They laugh.

'Do you spend every day here? Do you have a job, a husband to take care of, a wedding to organize? You are both very beautiful. Moroccan men must be flocking to court you.'

'Oh yes, there are plenty of men.' Both girls answer simultaneously. 'A few are handsome, but none are rich enough. They have no money and no job. The young Moroccan boys play football all day on the beach. The men queue all day at the construction sites begging for work. The lucky ones are driving trams for the new city transit system, but it doesn't pay very well. The old men, like our fathers, sit playing dominoes at the pavement cafes, drinking cheap black coffee which rots their teeth and sours their breath. When they come home our mothers shout at them and insult them, calling them lazy and useless. Life is tough, scary, and not much fun.'

'You two are pretty and intelligent. There must be job opportunities for you two.'

'Our only chance is to meet a young European or an Arab, impress him, and hope he will take us away from here or at least support us. They know our desperation, so they take advantage of us. They have a good time with us and usually leave us with a baby. It is a risk we have to take.'

Linah is practically crying. 'Look what you have done now! We have come here for a laugh, and all you do is make me cry.'

'I'm sorry I don't understand. Let's have an ice cream sundae. Waiter, your ice cream dessert menu, please.'

The menu is tatty and sticky, but we aren't eating the menu. If the desserts taste as good as they look in the pictures, they will be amazing.

I don't get a chance to think about my job offer. The afternoon takes a turn for the better, and by five o'clock the girls and I are the best of friends. I don't want to say good-bye. I will come back tomorrow, confident that they will be waiting for me. By nine thirty I am pushing pieces of chicken around a tagine in the Sheraton's restaurant. The weight of decision is taking its toll. I have been doing this for nearly an hour. I eventually stand and head for the lounge, where I hope to relax. It is fascinating watching the call-girls at work. Two of them will be paying their rent tomorrow; the rest will go home disappointed after sipping only empty promise cocktails. I thought selling sex would be easy, but apparently it isn't. The girls are tired and dejected and start to leave. I can't tell one from the other. How men choose amazes me. The chemistry of physical attraction must be prevalent even for a f--k. The lounge is almost empty now; only the two girls with clients remain.

'You look as if you have the weight of the world on your shoulders, M'sieur Giger.'

'Maybe I do.' I turn to see who is speaking to me.

It is my dry martini girl from the previous evening. Just as beautiful, even sexier, she leans toward me. Her breasts practically fall out of her dress as she almost overbalances.

'Would you care for a massage?' she whispers. 'To ease away the strain of the day. I have been watching you all evening. You are in need of some tender loving care.'

'Well, you are right there, that is for sure.'

'Come with me. Tonight I am offering you my skills for free. We will use the back stairs to avoid the floor walker. Any decision you have to make will be easier in the morning.' It is an offer too good to miss.

'I accept, but I insist on paying.'

'We'll see.'

'And by the way, what happened to your sexy French accent?'

'Der French accent perts up the price, you understand.'

'You are bad.'

'If that is what takes your fancy.'

It isn't easy bypassing the floor walker. We hide until he steps into his office, which is next to the staircase marked 'Fire Exit'. But by the time I have my card key in the slot, he is racing down the corridor towards us. He stops short.

'Oh it's you, Mr Giger. I didn't recognise you for a minute. I hope you had a pleasant day.'

What is he on? Surely there is money to be made here. We step into the room. 'Good night, Milady. Sleep tight.' I look at her in amazement. She laughs.

'You see? He recognises a good woman when he sees one.'

'I'll tell you later if you are good or not.'

She is good; the strain of the day is disappearing fast. A head massage followed by a spine search leads to fast, furious sex. It is so energetic I think we are going over the balcony at one point. That would have been a first, making out on top of a car parked beneath my window. She absorbs it all and comes back for more. The room is trashed and the floor covered in clothes, lamps, and bedding. We lie there exhausted, sweating, and breathless on the bare mattress.

'You're good.'

'You're not so bad yourself.' I flip her over onto her back and wish her a good night's sleep.

A Moment of Indecision

I wake with a stinking headache. My vision is blurred, and my mouth tastes like a drain. Whatever did I drink last night? This is definitely not the condition required to discuss the job of a lifetime. As events slowly come back to me, I recognise the trashed room.

'God! This is going to cost me a fortune.'

There is a crash in the bathroom.

'XXXXXXX! Shit!'

I understand the last word and guess the rest; the expression of pain is the same in English and Arabic. Martini Dry limps out into the bedroom.

'Be careful when you use the bathroom. There is f------ glass all over the floor.' She holds up her foot to emphasise the point. Blood is seeping out of a cut.

She sits on the bed and holds her foot out for me to stem the flow. Looking up her body from kneeling between her legs is a nice way to start the day. She lets the towel gape open and touches herself.

'Stop it! I have an appointment. I have to go. Anyway, thank you for last night. You were just what I needed. How much do I owe you?'

'It's on the house … with one condition.'

'And what is that?'

'We do it again, tonight.'

'There! The bleeding has stopped. Now you had better go, or I will be late. What is your name, anyway?'

'Anything you like. What do you want to call me?'

'Oh, I don't know. Err, Tony.'

'Tony? That's a man's name. Are you queer or something?'

'Okay, Tony with a C.'

'How do you pronounce that? Ctony.'

'No! Silly, you put the C at the end. Tonic.'

'Tonic? Mmm, I like that. I am a tonic for you, aren't I?'

'You are indeed. Now go.' She slips on her dress and squeezes her foot into her heeled shoe. Just as she opens the door she says, 'Oh, by the way!'

'What?'

'Your little slut came round in the night, about three o'clock.'

'Oh God! What happened?'

'I told her to f--k off as you were busy.'

'And she went?'

'Eventually, but not peacefully. I heard the floor walker dragging her down the corridor. She was screaming obscenities until he pushed her into the elevator.'

'No breakfast for me then?'

'You don't have time, or so you said.'

Goodness, she is right. It is five minutes to nine. Where is that phone number? I try to format my brain into some sort of order: 1) Job offer. 2) Decision. 3) Can I or can't I do it? Of course I can. 4) Paper. 5) Phone number. 6) Where did I put that number? I put it in my wallet. where is my wallet?

'Get me 0 66 44 69990.'

'0 66 44 69990, yes sir?'

'And hurry.'

The phone is answered immediately.

'Bonjour, M'sieur Lafleur's office.'

'Mr Lafleur please.'

'I am afraid M'sieur Lafleur is in a meeting. Can I give him a message?'

'Yes, tell him Mr Col—' I stop myself just in time. 'That M'sieur Giger called and that I will be with him at ten.'

'*Merci beaucoup*, I will tell him.'

'*Merci beaucoup* to you too.'

The only thinking I have done during the last twenty-four hours is during my conversation with Linah and Roxanne at the corniche. My heart went out to them. They need all the help they can get, as does everyone in Morocco. I know the Moroccans are hardworking people; they just need a bit of luck. I was also made aware of their pride. They would not relish the idea of working for the French. My job will be to persuade them that France was actually helping Morocco and they would be working towards a better life. All I have to do is make them aware of the opportunity. So to help Linah, Roxanne, and their families, I have decided this is a mission I cannot refuse. As for the element of difficulty, those mountains I will climb as and when I reach them.

The Five Pillars of Success

Monsieur Abel Lafleur doesn't smile very often. As for laughing, I think that is an impossibility for him. He is direct, determined, and totally focused.

'Tim, I don't have to tell you that this is top secret. It is so secretive that signing a piece of paper is a complete waste of time. We are putting our lives on the line here. You and I will not exist if things go wrong. We will get no support and no acknowledgement. Our very being will be denied. The next ten years of Morocco's development must appear to be happening naturally. Are you still in?'

'Gulp! I'm still in,' I stutter.

'Then let me give you the first five steps of the plan.'

I take a pad of paper out of my case.

'Tim, no notes. Nothing is to be written down. Just listen and absorb. The first thing you need to know is why. Morocco has been a French territory for over two hundred years. We, the French, have invested not only time but also billions of Francs and millions of lives in its defence and its development. It is payback time. But as you know, France is part of the EU. We don't intend to share anything related to this project with our European partners. Do you understand?'

'Yes.'

'That's where you come in. It has to appear to be happening naturally. Do you understand?'

'Yes.'

'Okay, these are the big five industries we have to have under our control by the end of the summer. It is a simple list. You will remember them easily. Do you understand?'

'Yes.'

'You have to remember them in your head and keep it to yourself. No talking in your sleep or boasting to get your wicked way with film stars or street girls. Okay?'

'Okay.'

'Then this is the master plan. The first industry is oil. Two is electricity. Three is banking. Four is import and export. Five is sex.'

'Sex? You are joking, aren't you?'

'I don't joke, Tim. We have to attract business. And as Morocco has the prettiest and most streetwise women in the world, that's the carrot we are offering. Now, my time is up. I have a meeting to attend. Get your head around it and meet me back here this time next week, and have some answers. Here is your passport. Here are the keys to your new apartment, owning an apartment classes you as a resident of Morocco. My receptionist will give you the address. Here are your credit cards, cheque book, bank account numbers, and on-line banking codes. Your account has been credited with ten million dollars. As you spend, it will automatically top up to ten million. Now I must go. Don't let us down.'

'I need a secretary and a car. I need researchers.'

'Tim, it's your show. Buy what you need and employ who you want. See you next week.'

With the address of my new apartment in my pocket, I cross the street to hail a taxi. But the aroma of a Costa Coffee catches my nose. As I missed out on breakfast, I surrender to the smell and order a large Americano with milk, accompanied by a blueberry muffin. Desperately in need of energy, I empty three, four, five files of sugar into the coffee. Good heavens, whatever have I got myself into? I find an empty stool at the bar that runs around the window. After resting my feet on the foot bar I stare out onto the street, sip the coffee, and crumble the muffin between my fingers. I used to sit regularly at Nero's coffee shop in Trafalgar Square. I loved watching the red buses pass and hearing the tourists laugh as they explored the streets and statues. Boris bikes were everywhere increasing the vigour of the street. London used to be a polite place, but it is changing. The car horns are prolific, and tempers rise quickly now. To be honest, it is just the same as Casablanca.

A Mercedes has knocked over a handcart loaded with melons. Boy is he angry and quite rightly so, his livelihood is rolling down the street. A screaming match evolves right in front of me. The Mercedes is a large, black, chauffeur-driven car, and the driver has to restore his credibility as one of the city's elite by blaming the street trader and pushing him about. The cart man is not giving in. He comes back with his fists flying. He can see today's earnings rolling away; someone has to pay for this. I grind my muffin into bird food as I watch the show develop. I am fascinated.

The rear door of the limousine opens, and out steps the most gorgeous pair of legs I have ever seen. The shoes are designer, the light tanned stockings shine in the light, and the seams run perfectly up the centre of her legs. It is Madame Adeline la Chapelle. She walks up to the cart puller and pushes a wad of notes into his hand, slaps her chauffeur across his shoulder with her newspaper, and steps back into the car. Wait! There is someone else in the back of the car, another woman. I only catch a glimpse of her face as the door slams shut, but I could swear it is Tonic, the girl who has just stepped out of my bed. Surely not. Of course not. All these girls look the same. It could be one of a thousand girls. The Sheraton lobby is full of them every night. Wow, this coffee is strong. Or is there something in the muffin?

I let the image of Tonic slip from my mind and call a taxi. In my sweating palm I find myself squeezing the card on which is written the address of my new apartment. I have no idea where it is. I am relieved when the taxi driver nods and tells me he knows where to take me. We race down to Le Gare du Port, sidestep the late arrivals rushing to catch the Marrakech Express, turn left onto the corniche, which passes the Hassan II Mosque, and swing into the New Marina Gateway. I look up at the recently completed apartment block that looks out over the beach and the stimulating waves of the Atlantic. My apartment number is F4.19.24. Apparently that means: front 4, floor 19, door 24.

The keypad on my apartment door is something from outer space; it looks like a crystal ball in the shape of a doorknob.

'Just put your hand on it so all your fingers wrap firmly around it,' instructs the concierge who has accompanied me. I put my hand around it, its red glow turns to amber, and then to green. 'It's reading your handprint, all five fingers and your palm.' The door utters a soft click and swings open.

'It has been designed to swing open on its own because most people are carrying things and don't have a hand free to push with. Clever, isn't it?'

'How did it recognise my hand? I have not been here before.'

'A woman from your office arrived an hour ago and fed in your print. She said she wanted to make sure everything was perfect for you.'

I scratch my head in disbelief.

'Welcome home, sir. I hope your apartment is to your liking. Call me if you need anything.' And with that he steps back along the deep red carpet towards the waiting elevator.

Inside, the apartment is total luxury; the far lounge wall is one large piece of semi-circular glass reaching from the floor to the ceiling. It glides at a touch, opening onto a balcony, which overlooks a bay of golden sand. On the balcony is a table already set for lunch, and to the right, two bright yellow leather loungers invite me to relax. This place is amazing. Inside, on the walls above a traditional brown leather suite, are prints of my favourite French Impressionists; even the books in the bookcase are my chosen favourites. A twenty-seven-inch iMac is flickering the latest stock market news in the corner; on the table an iPad, Apple laptop, and iPhone wait for me. I close the door behind me. I need privacy, time to explore, admire, and think.

'Welcome home, Tim. I hope you like your apartment.'

The voice comes from the balcony. I push the massive glass wall to one side. It moves with ease, and I step out. Adeline la Chapelle is pouring out a Gewürztraminer; I recognize it by its floral aroma.

'Come, let us celebrate your arrival.' She holds out a glass towards me. 'I have spent many hours trying to make it homely for you. I hope you like it?'

'You have certainly done your homework. And my palm print – how did you get that?'

She laughs.

'That was the easy bit. From the prints on your wine glass when we had dinner together the other evening.'

'Good grief! Is nothing sacred?'

'As far as you are concerned, I'm afraid not. We are risking everything we have in you. We could be even risking our own lives.' She is looking straight into my eyes, her glare challenging mine. God, she is beautiful!

'And what about you? Are you sacred?'

She leans across the table and touches my lips with her outstretched finger.

'Me, sacred? Don't be silly, of course not.'

I grab her wrist and yank her out of the lounger; her wine glass shatters to the floor. I pick her up and pin her to the wall. If anyone from the adjacent block is watching, they are in for the performance of a lifetime. Her legs wrap around me. Her tight skirt rides high above her stockings. A garter zings open and hangs between her thighs. I grab the cheeks of her arse and dig my fingers into her soft flesh. She yelps like an excited dog. My tongue is down her throat. She has pulled my shirt over my shoulders, and her nails are biting into my back. My body automatically reacts, lurching forward and trapping her tighter to the wall. My hands are free to ravish her as I want. I rip open her blouse. She is bra-less, her breasts perky and her nipples extended. I bite each one in turn. She is slowly slipping down my body. Soon we will be impaled together, locked in passion, sweating and glued together. Our eyes are staring into each other's as we wait for the moment.

Her mobile vibrates and shuffles across the table, terminating her screams of delight. She reaches out and catches it before it falls over the balcony. 'It's Jean Claud. I have to go.'

'Now?'

'Now.'

She drops to the floor, forces her feet into her shoes, and arranges her dress as she makes a dash for the door.

'I hope you will be very happy here.'

'I am sure I will.' With that she is gone.

Shame about the wine glass, but the bottle is still half full. I take a slug straight from the bottle and feel the aromatic juice run down my throat. If this is how it is going to be, then I am in.

Knowledge Is Power

I t is only a short walk from my new apartment at the Marina Complex to Miami Beach, where my favourite coffee shop overlooks the outdoor swimming pools and the ocean. The sea air is superb. The sun is scorching, as you might expect in Morocco at the start of the summer, but the westerly breeze brought in by the incoming Atlantic Ocean refreshes and cools. My skin tingles as my sweat evaporates instantly. The finest of sand particles are blowing off the beach with the breeze, lodging themselves in my eyebrows and my hair. A shower will be a necessity when I get back to the hotel. My clothes are still at the Sheraton; I will sleep there this evening and move everything into the apartment immediately after breakfast. I laugh when I think of breakfast. Whether I take breakfast or not depends on Khadija and to what degree her dignity was injured last night. Being dragged along the corridor and thrown into the elevator could be the last straw. I will know how angry she is by the number of chocolates she puts on my pillow. Wow! A woman-ometer – how useful is that, to know the mood of your girlfriend before you meet her?

As I had hoped, Linah and Roxanne are sitting at their usual table, but their faces are full of thunder. They ignore me as I sit with them and continue to chatter childishly about a group of boys they met last night. I stand to walk away. They stop me.

'You have come back, then?' I turn to face them.

'Are you pleased to see me?'

'You didn't come yesterday.'

'I had an important meeting. It took all day. Did you miss your free ice cream?'

'We don't like ice cream.'

'Only when it is bought for you, I suppose.'

They were like children, sulking. I saw two spoilt, pretty poodles with their heads on their paws. 'So what did you do last night?' I ask.

'Just hung.'

'Just hung out the washing? Just hung the lounge curtains?'

'Ha ha! We just hung around doing nothing, as usual. And you! What did you do?'

'I moved into my new apartment in the Marina.'

They suddenly light up, and their mood changes.

'You live at the Marina?'

Now I have their attention back. I will take advantage of their interest.

'Would you like to see my place?'

They pretend not to be too enthusiastic.

'If you like,' Linah mutters.

'Okay! I will take you tomorrow. Now tell me, where do you go shopping?'

I have to find out as much as I can about the lives of the Moroccan people, specifically about the buying of petrol, and these girls are typical subjects. The magic word 'shopping' does the trick. I can't stop them talking. Apparently there are four supermarkets in Casablanca and one mega-mall, none of which sell petrol. Petrol stations are far and few between and are usually in a terrible condition: old pumps, unreliable measuring implements, dirty. The few stations in the city all break the most basic of safety and fire regulations. They tell me that more mugging and pick-pocketing takes place on the forecourts of petrol stations than at any other location in the city. Whilst drivers are struggling with the antiquated equipment, they are easy pickings. Only on the new expressways out of town are the stations modern and attractive, yet to travel on these roads you have to pay a toll. Linah and Roxanne have no idea of the petrol brands, but they are sure it is not important. Their fathers are always so relieved to find a station that the brand is irrelevant.

I change my questioning to the cars their fathers own. Price is the major factor; company cars are unheard of. In exotic parts of the city like the new Marina, expensive cars fill the car parks. But for most Moroccans, a small Fiat, Peugeot, or Kia is the only choice. Road safety and rules are non-existent; maintenance and vehicle security are unheard of.

'Just observe the traffic at any major intersection,' butts in Roxanne. 'We have cars, trucks, donkey carts, buses, and handcarts, all in the same queue at the lights. It is chaotic. It takes exactly the same time to drive across town in a Mercedes as it does to ride in a donkey cart.'

Linah and Roxanne are incensed with the unfair opportunity and division of wealth. The city is building new apartment blocks and hotels for rich Middle Eastern, European, and American visitors. Property prices are rocketing through the roof, leaving local Moroccans in the old, crumbling apartments that make up the inner suburbs, as this is all they can afford.

My fact-finding mission is in full swing; the girls are brilliant. After three hours I understand the complete history and social status of Morocco. We have even discussed the thinking and attitude of the people. With all this information, I know I can turn this country around. All I need now is my magic wand.

We walk down the corniche. It is proving to be not only an informative morning but a beautiful one. The corniche is a delight. At the stand we wait for a tram destined for 'centre-ville.' I kiss them both as they step aboard and find myself holding Linah's hand for a couple of seconds before she pulls away. How did that happen? I wave as they find a seat and wave back at me through the glass.

At the Sheraton my room is unmade. The bed is just as I had left it. The bath is still full of water, the soap mark forming a ring around the sides. My first instinct is to pick up the phone and complain to the hotel manager, but I know this is Khadija demonstrating her anger. I check my watch. It is six o'clock. She should be on the corridor by now. She isn't difficult to find; I just head for the slamming doors, flushing loos, and howling vacuum cleaner.

'Khadija, I am sorry. Listen to me.' She completely ignores my plea. 'Listen, I am sorry. Let me explain.'

Goodness, she is so stubborn. I pull the cleaner's power cable out of the wall socket, and the motor falls silent.

'There is nothing to explain. You used me and had me thrown out when you'd had your fun. You are a horrible, selfish man. I hate you! I am going to tell my brothers to teach you a lesson.'

I laugh. 'You told me you didn't have any brothers and sisters.'

She picks up the vase of flowers off the window table and throws it at me. Luckily it misses and shatters against the wall behind me.

'Enough.' My patience has dissolved. 'You will lose your job. Now clean up this mess and come to my room. I have a present for you.' She just stares at me with murder in her eyes.

I have no idea what I have for her. I just made it up on the spur of the moment. I don't see myself as being selfish, and I can't leave her upset. My male ego has taken a hit. It never enters my head that she is playing with me and that she has been with many guests before and played the very same trick of giving herself to a man and then making him feel so guilty that he gives her everything she wants. Goodness! Even last night she might have slept with the Italian in room 512 or the Kuwaiti in room 539. I sit on my unmade bed and wait for her.

I wait, and I wait. One hour passes before she eventually arrives. She stands in the doorway.

'Well! Where is my present?' she asks.

'Come in and close the door.'

'I am busy. I have a job to do.'

I reach out and pin her arms tight to her body.

'Stop being so difficult. The woman in my room last night' – I have to think quickly.–'is my cousin's wife. Yes, she is a hooker, and no, he doesn't know. He drives taxis all night, so she comes to the Sheraton to make a little money for herself. We were just talking and fell asleep'

'You must think I was born yesterday,' she squeals.

'It is true! There is nothing between us. We were simply discussing a family problem.' I softened my approach. 'Come to me tonight. I will be waiting for you.' As an afterthought, I take a two-thousand-dirham note from my pocket. 'And go buy yourself a new dress. You can wear it when you come to me later.'

She snatches the money from my hand. 'I will have to think about it.'

I hear the vacuum start up; I can relax now. Inviting her back to my room was probably a very stupid thing to do; I should have let her go. Women and my ego are a disastrous combination!

I shower and change for dinner. I wonder who I will meet this evening?

One thing is for sure: I decide to give the Sheraton a miss. I saw a fish restaurant this afternoon down near the port that looked exciting and upbeat. I envision fish soup and sardine tagine washed down with white wine, with possibly a tiramisu cheesecake if I still have the appetite. I sneak out of the Sheraton, avoiding the lounge full of hookers by darting from pillar to pillar until I eventually reach the street door. I can see Tonic on one of the middle tables; she already has a man staring into her eyes – or, to be more accurate, staring at her gaping blouse. She looks hot; I must admit I am very tempted to stay.

The restaurant is full. The maître d' is full of apologies as he doesn't have a free table.

'We have a celebration party in this evening, sir. All the tables are taken.'

'But there are two seats over there at that corner table.' I point to show him where.

'I doubt the two gentlemen already sitting there will agree to sharing it with you.'

'So what is the celebration? Maybe I am a part of it.' He looks me up and down.

'I doubt it, sir. You are British.'

'Swiss,' I correct him. 'Anyway, what has that got to do with it?'

'The French shipping line GoFrance has just been awarded the contract to enter the port with two container ships every week from China. The Chinese are not very happy about it. The incumbent company Shanghai Line say the French … well, let's just say they cheated.'

'Ha! I thought everyone cheated.'

'This is cheating big time.'

'Ask those two guys if I can sit with them. Tell them I am a Swiss banker and would like to congratulate them on their success.'

The maître d' is putting on a tremendous performance, and it is only a matter of time before their shaking heads turn to a nod of agreement.

'I told them, sir, that you are a Swiss banker and a representative of BCGE, one of the banks financing their shipping line. They don't know about banking; they just know about loading and unloading.'

I follow him to the table. The two gentlemen stand to greet me.

'Oh! By the way, what does BCGE stand for?' I whisper to him.

'Banque Cantonale de Genève.'

'How do you know that?'

'The director eats here regularly.'

'Good evening, gentlemen. Thank you for sharing your table.'

They grunt politely and sit down, continuing their muffled conversation.

The restaurant is in high spirits, with lots of chatter and laughter and lots of wine being drunk, including a whole crate of Champagne, which I doubt is Champagne. In acknowledgement of a few short speeches in French, which I barely understand, I applaud with everyone else and toast the success of the company by slurping the wine on the table. The soup meets all expectation, and the sardine tagine tastes great but is very messy. I always have a problem with the little bones.

The maître d' interrupts. 'Excuse me, sir, there is a lady to see you. She says she is your secretary. Shall I bring her to your table?' As I don't have a secretary, I look over his shoulder to see who she might be. It is Tonic. Everybody is staring in her direction, not only because her gaping blouse is heaving like a ship in the ocean due to her being out of breath but because she is the only woman in the room.

'I will come to her at reception.' I stand and excuse myself from the table.

'Please explain before I call the police.'

'Sir, I saw you leaving the hotel. I was worried about you.'

'I am a big boy now, Tonic. I can take care of myself.'

'No, sir, you do not understand. This is a very dangerous place. You must leave with me now, this moment. Tell them you have an important meeting. There is no time to lose. I will wait for you outside.'

'Tonic, you are being very silly. Go back to the hotel and do what you do best.'

'Sir! If you don't come with me now, I will take all my clothes off and lap dance every man in the room.'

'No, no! That is not necessary. I will come.'

I return to the table and explain my departure. They laugh when I tell them Tonic is my secretary. If I had told the truth, that she was my lay, they would have accepted that far more willingly.

There is a crash at the door; shards of glass shower everyone. A motorbike roars into the restaurant, knocking over the Maitra d', who stupidly was trying to stop it. The man on the back throws a grenade into the centre of the room. The bikers, dressed in black leather and wearing black helmets and goggles, disappear as quickly as they arrived. The explosion is deafening.

One Survivor, Seventy Dead

My head is a mush; I can't think. I have no idea what is happening or where I am. I can hear people crying and shouting. I can hear police sirens and alarms shrieking. I can sense the ceiling crashing down on me. There are wooden beams and ceiling tiles all over me, and the air is full of thick black smoke and dust. I can't breathe; my chest won't work. I am sure my eyes are open, yet I can't see anything, just blackness. Someone is trying to lift me and force water into my mouth. It's as if I am floating, being carried on a cloud. Then there is nothing. My body has collapsed, and my brain has accepted death.

I don't know how long I have been unconscious; it could have been days or only a matter of minutes. I open my eyes, but all I can see is a bright blur. A white ceiling with long fluorescent tubes of lights flashes past me. My brain is trying to make sense of it. Unable to move due to the pain in every muscle,

I scan my body with my mind. I start with my toes and wriggle them. Then I bend my knees and my arms. I cannot move my left hand. What is wrong with my left hand? Do I still have a left hand? Do I still have fingers on it? I am too scared to look.

'Welcome back, Tim. We were worried about you.' It is Madame Adeline la Chapelle. She is holding my hand tight. I can feel her now; the warmth of her caressing fingers is penetrating through.

'Where am I?'

'You are in the Clinique Aftal, a private hospital in the Oasis district of Casablanca. You are the luckiest man in the world right now.'

'Why?'

'You were unfortunately in the wrong place at the wrong time. You somehow have survived a massacre. You managed to hide under a table just before the grenade exploded.'

My head is starting to clear. I remember throwing myself across two chairs. I can remember rolling onto the floor and the table coming down on top of me.

'Yes, I remember the motorcycle. There was an explosion.'

'Well, as I said, you are very lucky. You are the only survivor from inside the restaurant Sixty-three personnel of GoFrance died in the bombing. The dining room was full; every chair was taken, and there was nowhere for the others to hide. You were seated next to the only free seat, and you were the only person who had the opportunity to get under the table.' I stared at her in disbelief. Then suddenly it all came back to me.

Tonic! Tonic was also there. It is all coming back to me. 'Is Tonic okay?'

'If you mean Amina, well, she is alive, but you must forget about her.

'What do you mean, forget about her?'

'As she left the restaurant, the motorcycle knocked her to the ground. Before she could get up, they ran over her again whilst making their escape. Her back is broken. She will never walk again. She is paralysed from the waist down.'

'Good God, she saved my life. If it had not been for her, I would be dead also. Is there anything we can do for her?'

'Everything that can be done is being done. Now you have to rest. We want you back on the job as soon as possible. You have a presentation in two days with Jean Claud and Abel. Time waits for no man, or so you English keep telling us.'

As the day progresses, I feel myself gaining in strength and read the local newspaper. Well, I look at the pictures, as it is in French. The bombing is front-page news. The police are blaming the Chinese gangs and the drug barons in their fight for supremacy. But I know the truth; it isn't going to be as easy as I first thought to sell the French takeover of Morocco. If the French intend to move in, then they have to persuade others, like the Chinese, to move out. And it appears they don't intend going quietly. Apart from the shock, I am unscathed. It is four o'clock, time for me to go. I ignore all medical advice and sign myself out of the hospital and return to the Sheraton. As I enter my room, the real world becomes a priority. The scribbled note on my pillow reads, 'Yu bastard, yu ar not getin awaw with this.'

Khadija! I had forgotten all about her. She was coming to me last night. There is no way she will understand why I wasn't waiting for her, unless I can get her to read the newspapers. Even then, it doesn't have a picture of me in it. Oh God! How can I persuade her I have just been blown up?

A crazy idea comes into my head. I dash back to the clinic to find the nurse who cared for me and explain my predicament to her. She is about the same age as Khadija and is sympathetic with my dilemma. She says she totally knows what Khadija will be thinking and agrees she will be very angry.

I leave the hospital with my arm in a sling and a bandage on my head, which is so big it looks like a turban. When I enter the Sheraton this time there is a gasp of disbelief from the reception staff.

'M'sieur Giger, are you okay?' Two girls rush over to help me into the elevator.

'It's nothing, really, just a slight cut.'

'Mr Giger, you are so brave. We know you were at the port last night. Just call us if there is anything we can do for you.'

I wonder if they could speak to Khadija and explain to her why I wasn't in my room and that I am lucky to be alive. But I decide against it. They probably don't even know her, and for me to be sleeping with the floor maid would not help my street cred.

'M'sieur Giger, M'sieur Giger!' I wake with a start, expecting the door to be knocked off its hinges.

It is Khadija. It is two in the morning, and I have been asleep for nearly eight hours. I sit up in bed and make myself look as sick and as pathetic as I can. I straighten my turban and stick my bandaged arm out above the duvet. 'Who is it?' I quake.

'M'sieur Giger, M'sieur Giger, let me in. It's Khadija.'

'You will have to let yourself in. I cannot get to the door. Use your key.'

I hear her key rattling in the lock. 'Oh 'M'sieur Giger, M'sieur Giger, whatever did they do to you?' She is shocked to see me all bandaged up.

'Is that your new dress?' I quake.

'Yes!' She stops and gives a twirl. 'Do you like it?'

'You look amazing.' She bursts out crying and wraps herself around me. Wow! This is just what I need.

'Why did you go to the port? Why did they attack you? Why did you not call me? Why –?'

'Stop, stop. I am okay. I escaped. It is a thing of the past. Let me look at you.'

She stands in front of me and twirls again. Her dress swings out, revealing her beautiful legs. Her hair is tied up in a bun, but with one shake it cascades down her shoulders. Then she picks up the hem of her skirt and yanks it over her head. She has nothing on underneath. This girl certainly knows how to dress. I tear off my turban and throw away my sling as she dives into my arms.

'You are not hurt? You are teasing me.' She starts to slap me all over. 'I am so happy,' she squeals.

'Ouch!' I scream as she hits a tender spot on my chest. 'I do have a few sore parts.'

The Mosque of Inspiration

I need time to get my head around this campaign. Time is running out, and my week of planning is nearly over. I have to find a place where I will not be interrupted, where I am not known, where my mobile phone will remain silent, and where I can sit in silence and think the campaign through.

'I know where you can go,' boasts Khadija.

'Okay, clever dick, where?'

'The Grande Mosque on the corniche.'

'I love you, you clever girl.'

'You love me? Did you say you love me?'

I freeze. 'Did I say that?'

'I knew it! You don't love me, you bastard.'

She slams the door and leaves. I let her go. I will only dig myself into a bigger hole if I try to explain that I love her, but I am not in love with her.

It will not be easy for a fair-haired Christian to gain access to the mosque, so I buy myself a plain brown djellaba with a big hood and a pair of turned-up-toe slippers and slither my way across the corniche towards the Hassan II Mosque, hopefully disguised as a Moroccan. This phenomenal building is the world's third-largest mosque and was designed by Michel Pinseau, a French architect. He was King Hassan II's favourite architect and was invited to build the mosque to celebrate the king's sixtieth birthday. The minaret is seven hundred feet high and overlooks the Atlantic Ocean. The prayer room occupies twenty thousand square metres, and the roof can slide open to enable prayers free access to the heavens.

My disguise seems to be working. The guards are not paying attention. They don't even turn a head as I walk past them amongst a group of Moroccan men on their way to prayer. I have to follow them because I don't know where to go or what to do. After removing their shoes, they head for a space in the centre of the mosque and kneel cross-legged on the floor. I follow their every move. I like to think that I am praying for guidance in my task to help these people succeed and to enjoy a happier future.

France intends to make a lot of money out of Morocco. I can also see quite clearly how Chapelle and Lafleur will make millions and become the most powerful of men. I feel it is my responsibility to focus on the Moroccan people, making sure that their sacrifice and hard work are rewarded in both benefit and opportunity. This will only be possible if the new wealth is invested back into the kingdom. I kneel in silence for a further three hours, listening to the silence. The only sound is the faint rustle of clothing as men rise and fall on their knees in the completion of their prayers. Yet there is another sound. No, it is not a sound. It is a vibration coming up through the floor. It is the pounding of the Atlantic Ocean against the mosque's sea wall. It is like a heartbeat; I can feel its force through the floor. Its power is awe-inspiring, penetrating concrete four feet thick to stir my body and stimulate my mind. I stay with my thoughts until the sun disappears.

It is essential that I understand the Moroccan people in order to create this iconic advertising campaign. What are their dreams? What makes them tick? What are they good at, and equally as important, what are they not so good at? I need to know what Morocco has achieved and what it has to sell. In advertising terms, what is its unique selling point? What can Morocco offer the world, and what does Morocco expect of itself? I make a list in my head of Morocco's top five industries:

1. Arable farming (crops and fruits).
2. Livestock farming (cattle, sheep, and chickens).
3. Phosphate mining.
4. Tradition- and culture-related goods (fashion, leather goods, arts and crafts, cuisine, foodstuffs).
5. Tourism.

Then I make a list of Morocco's top five attributes.

1. Enthusiasm.
2. Good work ethic.
3. The pride of the people.
4. Its African, Arab, and European cultural mix.
5. Its need of inspiration and investment.

I ease myself into an upright position. My bones creak and my head aches, but I feel positive. I know I am capable of taking on this mammoth task and succeeding. I stop by the corniche to reward my thinking with an ice cream. Linah is sitting there all alone.

'Bonjour!'

'Hello! Where have you been?'

I decide not to tell her. She will start asking questions that I don't have answers for.

'Just sorting out the apartment.'

'You said you would take me to your apartment.'

'I will.'

'Now?'

'Where is Roxanne?'

'She can't make it today. Her baby is sick.'

'I didn't know she was married.'

'She isn't. The father lives in Muscat. He visits her twice a year.'

'Are you married? How many children do you have?'

'No, and none. Let's go. Show me your apartment.'

I reluctantly get to my feet.

'Okay, let's go.' I hail a taxi and give him the address.

Linah is impressed, to say the least, as the door crystal dances in my palm and the door swings open. To be honest, so am I. The place looks amazing. And when the blinds roll up and the curtains glide back automatically, the moonlight reveals the majestic beauty and energy of the Atlantic Ocean.

'Gosh! This is so beautiful. I have never seen an apartment as luxurious as this.'

She is so excited that she throws her arms around my neck and gives me a big kiss.

'Oh, I am so sorry. I forgot myself. Please forgive me.'

'I forgive you. So you are impressed?'

She nods until her head nearly falls off.

'So am I. You kiss pretty good.'

'Don't get any ideas. I am very hard to get. I just forgot myself.'

'I understand totally. I too am very hard to get.'

Now she shakes her head until it nearly falls off.

'You are a man. I can crack you in two minutes.'

'Oh no you can't.'

She laughs and rushes out onto the balcony. 'So why are you still living at the Sheraton?'

'I simply have not had the time to move.'

She dashes inside and stops in front of the computer. With a tap on the screen it blinks into life. She presses a few keys and looks at me in expectation.

'What?' I ask.

'Give me the password. I can't get in.'

'Why do you want to get in?'

'To see how much these apartments are selling for.'

'So you know how to operate a Mac.'

'Well, I haven't worked with this latest model. But I have worked on the older version, yes. I used to be the personal assistant of an oil magnate. I practically ran the business, and I definitely ran him. I wrote all his letters, did all his research, re-wrote his speeches, translated his mail, chose his clothes, and kept his wife away.'

'So why did you leave?'

'He got transferred to California, and they refused me a visa.'

'You could have worked for his replacement.'

'His replacement had his own PA. She was younger than me.

'What else have you done?'

'I worked for my two brothers. One ran a real estate agency specialising in offices, factories, and warehouses. The other ran a Citroen agency. But now he is in Dubai, and my elder brother is in Miami.'

'So what are you doing now?'

'Sitting on the corniche talking to you. There are no jobs. Well, that isn't exactly true. There are lots of jobs, but not if you want to be paid for your work.'

'I'm looking for a PA. I don't know how long the job will last. It might be a week or it might be five years. But it isn't an ordinary job; it's a 24/7 job. Are you interested?'

I can see her breathing change into long, deep gulps. She is excited. Her eyes are big and black and sparkle like rare opals.

'Would I be working here in your apartment?'

'Err, no, that would not be a good idea. But you can use it.'

'And would I get paid?'

'Oh yes, you will be paid.'

'When do I start?'

'The password is 2 4 J U N 2 0 1 3.'

'Today's date! That's pretty stupid, isn't it?'

'Who would expect the date to be the password?' She thinks for a minute and shrugs her shoulders. 'And what is it tomorrow?'

'2 5 J U N 2 0 1 3. The password changes every day?'

'At midnight.'

'Cool!'

She types and sighs. 'Four million Euros.'

'What is?'

'The price of this apartment.'

A Partner for Life

'**B**efore you accept this job you must understand the rules. If you need time to think about it, then that is okay. Now sit here and listen.' I pat the sofa beside me, and she sits close, curling her feet up under her.

'You must understand that what I do is not against the law, but we will be working on the very fringes of it. Also, you will be on call twenty-four hours every single day. Some days you will have nothing to do, but when I need you, you have to respond immediately. Do you understand?'

She nods.

'Your first task is to find an office. This office will be your base. It must be plain and low-profile, respectable but not ostentatious. Can you drive?'

'Yes.'

'Your second task is to buy yourself a car, a Golf or a one series BMW – a small but fast car. I will get you a Mac computer similar to this one, an iPad, and an iPhone. We will be continuously connected. You will know what I am doing, saying, and thinking. The only thing you will not have access to is my bank account. Your third task is to find an advertising agency here in Casablanca. It should be preferably Moroccan-owned and definitely not French. If not Moroccan, then it should be British. Set up a meeting so I can check them out.'

'Who shall I say we are?'

I am impressed. She is already thinking.

'Tell them you are on a fact-finding mission for a series of government projects. They will be so excited they won't ask you any further questions.'

'Is there more? I should be writing this down.'

'You must not write anything down. Nor do you tell anyone what you are doing, not even your mother. Your life might depend on it.'

She sits up in fright.

'Did you read about the massacre at the harbour the other evening?' I asked.

'Yes.'

'I was there. I was doing some research. I escaped by the skin of my teeth. I was just in the wrong place at the wrong time. What I am saying is, these things happen when big contracts and big money are at risk. And there is going to be a lot of money and big contracts flying about. So! Are you still interested?'

She sighs. 'How much will you pay me?'

'How much did you get at the oil company?'

'Five thousand dirham a month.'

I guess she probably got three thousand.

'You can start on twenty thousand dirham a month.'

Her arms wrap around my neck for a second time.

'I'm interested. And by the way—'

'What?'

'You look stupid in that djellaba.'

Goodness, I have forgotten I am still wearing a Moroccan djellaba. It is the first thing that I hang in the wardrobe. I send her home and hope she will action the tasks I have set her. She has my mobile number so she can update me with her progress, but she asks me for a hundred dirham to top up her phone. Of course she asks me the most important question just as she is leaving.

'Who are you?'

'My name is M'sieur Jacques Giger. I am a Swiss banker. That is all you need to know. The less you know about me, the better.'

It is obvious that she wants to know more, but I can't risk her telling family and friends. When they see her new car they will be asking plenty of awkward questions. And for her own safety it is best that she knows nothing. I watch from the balcony as she walks across the garden and hails a taxi at the gate. She turns and gives me a wave, Cheeky bitch! She knew I was watching her.

The Marketing Objective

My phone bursts into life with an American police siren. I know it is Lafleur before I even look at it. I have a different ring for every caller. Tonic's call sign (bless her) was tweeting birds. Linah now has a bicycle bell, Jean Claud Chapelle has a church bell, Monsieur Abel Lafleur has a police siren, and Madame Adeline la Chapelle has a lilting harp.

'Good morning, Abel. I—'

He cuts me short. 'Tomorrow at ten, I can only give you twenty minutes, so make your presentation simple and succinct. Don't be late.' My phone falls silent. Lafleur is definitely a man of few words. For me, the fewer the better. For some reason I don't like him.

I arrive five minutes early, yet by the time I reach his office door the hall clock points straight up. He stands to acknowledge my arrival.

'Great! I see you have brought some visual aids. Place your pad on the easel over there, and give it to me fast and straight.'

I raise the easel to my height and reveal the first page.

Introduction

    A. Decide which companies we are taking over.
    B. Action the takeover.
    C. Create the advertising and PR campaign for each industry.

Page 1. Front line takeovers

    A. The oil industry
    B. The power/electric companies
    C. Banking
    D. The kingdom's imports and exports
    E. The sex and escort industry

Page 2. Industries to stimulate

    A. Arable farming (crops and fruits)
    B. Livestock farming (cattle, sheep, chickens)
    C. Phosphate mining
    D. Traditions
    E. Tourism

I explain, 'These are existing industries. They need encouraging and restructuring, rather than having money invested in them.' I wait for a comment, but none comes.

Page 3. Automatic development

    A. Construction
    B. Road and rail transport
    C. Inner city transportation (trams and buses)
    D. Phone and Internet servers
    E. Airport development
    F. Water, both fresh and desalinated

'What do you mean by automatic development?' he asks. Wow, he is listening; I thought he had gone to sleep.

'These industries will develop automatically, you just have to be there to take them over when they do.'

'With or without investment?' he asks.

'That depends, but you will know it is a sure winner.'

Page 4. On success grows success

    A. Retailing industry
    B. Hospitals and health
    C. Security and protection companies
    D. Automobile industry
    E. Shipbuilding
    F. High-tech and computer industries
    G. Insurance companies
    H. Farming and agricultural machinery

'These are new industries, which will expand as the economy grows.' I wait for a comment. Again he sits in silence.

Page 5. Service industries

    A. Cleaning companies
    B. Repair and maintenance companies
    C. Cafes, hairdressers, bakeries, tattoo parlours, etc.
    D. Employment agencies

'And the most important of all—'

Page 6. Education

I write it on the pad as I say it to emphasis its importance.

'This is the most important industry of them all. Not only is it a big earner, but you don't want to be buying skills from outside the kingdom.'

I pause and close the pad. 'As each of these industries comes up for development, we will be ready to market it and advertise it. I estimate this to take ten years. How long do we have?'

Lafleur looks me straight in the eye for the first time and laughs.

'Your estimate is very close. We don't have ten years. We have ten months.' He pauses, but only for a second. 'I am impressed with your marketing structure, but how do we get the people to cooperate?'

'I am pleased you asked this question. You remember the 2012 Olympics in London? Before that the country was on its knees, with no vitality and no work ethic. It was a country drowning itself in depression. You saw how the people came alive and rose to the challenge. There was a complete transformation, a resurgence of energy and enthusiasm.'

I flip over the final page.

Page 7. Pride

A. Make the Moroccan people proud of their achievements.
B. Make the people proud to be Moroccan.

'When you have done that, they will achieve everything. That is my job. I will do that.'

'Great! Get on with it.' He stands and picks up his briefcase. 'I have to go. I have given you longer than I planned. Make it happen, Tim. I love your thinking and the way you have structured it. You have grasped the task. We will all watch your progress. Now I can see why you are so proficient at your job.'

I start to fold up my pad.

'Leave that, please. I need to study it further. We were only thinking of investing in the big five, but you have shown us the true potential of this project. I think we are in it for the duration.' With that he disappears out through the door.

He has left me puzzled and exhausted. 'Ten months' keeps reverberating around inside my head.

I need some TLC. I wonder if the girls at the Sheraton are working this early.

'Where are you going now, M'sieur Giger?' asks Lafleur's receptionist as I head for the street. 'Can I call you a car?'

I laugh and reply in a joking manner, 'I need some relaxation after that presentation, so I thought I would find myself a hot woman for the afternoon. Are you free?'

She blushes and shakes her head.

'I wish I was, but I have to work. But I will send a girl to you. Are you still at the Sheraton or living in your apartment?'

Her response has taken me by surprise; I didn't expect that.

'Errrr!' Goodness, what am I stammering for? 'Let's christen the apartment. I will be at the apartment in fifteen minutes.'

'So will she. Meet her in the foyer of your building. You will have to escort her in.'

'What is her name?'

'You can call her anything you like. If she doesn't please you, tell me.'

As I pull into my apartment car park, I can see her waiting for me. She is tall and slim with long, straight black hair, deep eyes, heart-shaped lips, and a great shape exaggerated by her high-heeled shoes. Her appearance is just like all the other girls on the game, except in her clinging traditional Moroccan dress, she looks taller than most of them.

Kamal is sitting at his desk staring at the security monitors. He stands as we walk in. 'Welcome home, sir.'

'Thank you, Kamal. I am not to be disturbed for the next three hours.' I wink at him as I usher the girl into the elevator.

'Very well, sir. Have a pleasant afternoon.'

'That is exactly what I intend on having.'

The glowing door handle on my apartment door doesn't create the same impression that it did with Linah. This girl is obviously used to such toys.

Can I get you a drink, sir?' she asks, opening my chilled drinks cabinet.

'I'm afraid I haven't had the time to stock it up. We will have to operate cold, as it were.'

She looks at me as if I am stupid and takes out a bottle of vodka and one of Kahlua. 'This will be okay, sir.'

'Oh! I didn't know I had those. What have you chosen?' I ask, pointing at the bottles in her hands.

'Kahlua, sir. it is a Mexican coffee liqueur with herbs and vanilla. I will mix it in your blender with Bailey's Irish Cream, top it up with ice, and splash in two parts of vodka. It is just what you need.'

'Sounds great. I suppose it has a name.'

'Pure ecstasy, sir. That is its name.'

Lost for words, I take off my jacket, sit on the bed, and watch as liquid is poured into liquid, beaten and stirred, and finally presented in two glasses with brightly coloured straws bent over the rim.

'I hope you approve, sir.' She hands me one glass and puts the second to her lips.

'Mmm, it tastes divine. Well done.' She unbuttons her dress and steps out of it, revealing the finest, silkiest, and frilliest of pants and matching bra.

'I'm so happy that I can please you, sir,' she says as both legs wrap around me and she sits on my lap. Her breasts clench my glass as I suck on the straw.

'Err! What is your name?'

'Think of a name later, when you know me better.'

'Okay …'

I don't get chance to think of a name for her. She is 'The One'. Her stamina, energy, and recovery time are unbelievable, and she still finds time to make two more Pure Ecstasys. I am glad of the time out as I watch her create her magic.

The room phone rings.

'M'sieur Giger, it is Kamal on the front desk. I could not stop her. She is on her way up to you right now. She is very angry.'

'Kamal, who are you talking about? Who is on her way up? Who is giving you so much grief?'

'Oh! M'sieur Giger, I am so very sorry. Please forgive me. I did my best to stop her.'

'Kamal, Kamal, who is it?'

'Madame la Chapelle. Warn Aisha.'

The apartment door is rocking on its hinges before I put the phone down.

'Let me in or I will break down this bloody door.'

I grab a towel to cover myself before opening the door.

'Where is she? Where is that whore?'

Aisha peeks out from beneath the sheets.

'Get out, get out now! You should not be here. This is not your trick.' She picks up Aisha's dress from the floor and throws it at her.

Aisha picks up her pants and tries to feed her legs through them.

'Don't bother putting those on. Just get out!' And with that she pushes Aisha half naked into the corridor and slams the door behind her.

She turns to me and looks me up and down. 'God, you stink. Go shower whilst I clean up the room.'

I do as I am told. As I wait for the water temperature in the shower to stabilise, I listen to Adeline giving instructions on the phone.

'Kamal, get a cleaner up here immediately with new bed linen. Kamal, now! Do you understand what *now* means?' She slams down the phone.

From the shower room I hear the doorbell bleep. That must be the cleaner arriving. Ten minutes later I hear the door close. She must have left. Time to make an appearance. The room is immaculate and smells as sweet as a lavender field. Adeline is in my bed.

'I am sorry about that, Tim. Aisha was a mistake. She is a woman possessed. Now you need someone far more gentle and loving. Abel has just taken Jean Claud and myself through your campaign structure. We are impressed with your logic and reasoning. You deserve a reward.'

'Thank you. I am pleased you appreciate my work. Are you, err, into a taste of Pure Ecstasy?'

'Very much.'

A Job Well Done

I haven't spoken with Linah for two days. I am testing her, praying she has the commitment and the determination to make things happen without me. When I give her a task I have to be sure it will be done and done properly. To bring this campaign to a successful conclusion in only ten months, I must be able to rely on her judgment and trust her implicitly. Right now, after two days, I am wondering if she is the right person for the job.

My phone is ringing.

'M'sieur Giger it is Linah, I have done everything you requested. Can I show you?'

I am so relieved to hear her voice.

'Great to hear from you, Linah. Meet me tomorrow at Miami Plage. Be there at ten o'clock. We can take breakfast and spend the rest of the day together.'

'Ten o'clock it is, M'sieur Giger. And M'sieur Giger—'

'What?'

'Bring your chequebook.'

I laugh. I really like this girl. She has a sense of humour as well as determination, two of the greatest qualities anyone working for me must possess.

Where is she? It is ten minutes past ten. I stare at my watch as the hands go round. Punctuality is an obsession of mine. I can see her tripping down the corniche towards me. She looks happy and confident; overnight she has become a dynamic businesswoman, walking with purpose and commitment. I have to smile at her as she approaches.

'I am late. I am so sorry. My mother hung my business suit in my sister's wardrobe, and I couldn't find it. When I did I noticed a button was missing and had to rush to the *bagalla* for some thread.' She eventually stops jabbering to take a breath.

'*You* went to the *bagalla*?'

'Of course not, I sent my sister. I didn't have time—'

I had to stop her; she was in danger of talking forever. 'I suppose she sewed the button on for you as well?'

She looked at me before answering. 'I can sew buttons on, but on this occasion she did. How did you know that?'

'I guessed! Anyway, your suit looks very smart. Well done.' I pause for a second. 'And thank your sister.'

She laughs. I love the way she laughs. It is a hearty English laugh with a hint of French *je ne sais quoi*.

'Can I order you a coffee?'

'Mmm, yes please, and a croissant.'

'Okay.' I raise my arm to call the waiter over, only to realise he is standing behind me.

'*Oui M'sieur, tout de suite,*' he responds before I speak.

'So Linah, you are in control of events today. Do with me as you will.'

She blushes and looks at me in a questioning manner. Soon she will understand my English sense of humour. Until then I must be more precise in what I say. 'What is our schedule today?'

'Now I understand you, M'sieur Giger. At eleven thirty we have a meeting with the estate agent downtown. If you approve my choice of office, it is ready for immediate occupation.'

'That is excellent. I can get the computers installed this afternoon.'

'At two we have an audience with the largest Moroccan advertising agency in town. They are excited but cautious. You will need to walk slow. Do you say "walk slow"?'

'Nearly. We say "tread carefully", but it means the same. I promise to be gentle with them.'

'Good! And at five you can pay for my new car. You have brought your chequebook, haven't you?'

'I wondered when you were going to mention the car, what type of car have you chosen?'

'A BMW, as you suggested.'

'Excellent.'

'Have you finished your croissant?'

'Yes, thank you.'

'Then let's go.'

We jump into a petit taxi.

'Tours Jumelles de Casablanca,' she instructs the roughly shaven driver, who responds with a toothless grin. She seems to have totally captivated him. I squeeze into the tiny back seat with her and relax as best I can. I have no idea where we are going.

'We are going to the Twin Towers in the heart of the city. The office is on the fifth floor of the west tower. It is small and bright with a view over the city. For our business it is ideal because within the Twin Tower complex there are conference rooms, apartments, and even a hotel – everything we might need for business meetings and entertainment.'

As we pull up at the impressive front door I notice it also includes a designer fashion boutique.

'Ha! I see it also has everything that you might need.' I point at the sophisticated garments making up the window display.

'I have to look nice for you, M'sieur Giger.'

'You do indeed, Linah.'

There is nothing for me to do but sign the contract. The office is ideal, the location superb, and the facilities perfect. The estate agent hands me two sets of keys, one of which I give to Linah.

'M'sieur Giger, I nearly forgot.' Linah looks at me with a cheeky grin.

'What?'

'I will need a parking space in the basement.' She sucks heavily on her tongue, waiting for my reaction.

I look at the agent. 'Is there a space available?'

'Certainly, M'sieur Giger. I will phone you later with the allocated space number, possibly sometime this afternoon. You can add the electric key for the garage door to your office set now.'

He gives Linah what I can only describe as a miniature glass pyramid. 'Linah, you point the pyramid at the illuminated disc on the door and speak the code into it. The code is 92468. Then you will say your name and your space number, once I have given it to you. After the first entry the security system will recognise your voice, and then only you will be able to enter with this key.'

He turns to me. 'M'sieur Giger, if you ever need to enter the garage, you too must have your own identity pyramid. You will not gain access by using Linah's key.'

'I will need to enter on various occasions.'

'Then here is your key. The advantage is, even if you lose your keys, no one can use them to get inside.'

Linah is impressed with her new toy. So am I.

'I will send my IT team in this afternoon to install our computer system, and we will use our own server. Is that acceptable?'

'The office is yours, M'sieur Giger. You can do whatever you want with it.'

I stand for a couple of minutes gazing out over the city. The Grande Mosque seems only a stone's throw away, and beyond that is the crashing Atlantic. On the horizon a row of French registered container ships are waiting their turn to enter the port. Below is the hustle and bustle of Casablanca's street life. Taxis and limousines are hooting continuously, buses and donkey carts are fighting for space, and young, elegant city girls are shopping hand in hand with their overweight mothers. The modern mixes with the traditional and the rich with the poor. This is what makes Casablanca so charming.

'Let's go visit the advertising agency, Linah. It is already ten to two.'

Two taxis U-turn in response to Linah's raised arm, narrowly avoiding a collision. She beckons the newer and the bigger of the two cars, but there isn't a lot to choose between them. The driver seems to be captivated by her. He jumps out and opens the door for us – well, for Linah. Even she admits that has never happened before.

'We must look pretty impressive,' she whispers into my ear.

'Or rich.' I must admit, she does look amazing; I would open the door for her.

We pull into the grounds of an old Moroccan villa on the outer ring road. It was probably a private hospital or possibly a school at some time in its history, but today it is an advertising agency. The brass plaque in the centre of the door reads, 'Centre d'Invention Bureau de Publicite.'

'Are you sure this is a Moroccan agency? It sounds very French to me.'

'M'sieur Giger, I am sure. The founder was Mohammed Abed Chahid, the famous writer of many books about the workings of the Arab mind.

He died in 1986, and now his son, Mohammed Abdullah Chahid, is the president. It is a full-service agency of great prominence in the city.

Mohammed Abdullah Chahid rushes into reception to greet us. He is possibly the most outrageously dressed Moroccan I have ever seen. A bright blue suit jacket wraps itself around a gold and red striped waistcoat, which in turn contrasts sharply with a green and pink polka-dot cravat bursting out of a pale yellow shirt. It does seem to work with his distinguished silver hair, his silver Jimmy Edwards moustache, and his eyeglass. I immediately take a liking to this guy. He is confident, amusing, and obviously successful, judging by the number of award-winning certificates adorning his office walls.

Our meeting is productive yet reserved. Neither of us wants to give too much away on our first meeting. My major concern is assurance that his creative people are up to the task. I have worked with creative people all my life; they are individualistic, extraverted, egotistical, and usually very sensitive. On my account they will have to take instruction and accept criticism without throwing tantrums. Of course I want their creative contribution, but I have to be in control. They will have to create around my directives.

The agency's marketing and media services are described to me and are second to none; that will be mechanical and not a concern for me. After a tour of the offices in which I am introduced to several leading personnel, I firmly shake the hand of Mohammed Abdullah Chahid and express my pleasure in what I have seen. 'I am impressed and will be back within the week to give you the first campaign brief, along with a deposit of one million dirham up front for your work.'

'I will look forward to our next meeting, M'sieur Giger.'

I believe he will. Giving him payment in advance is not only a goodwill gesture on my part, an attempt to cement our working relationship, but, more important, a strategy to guarantee a fast service and to remove cash as an excuse for any delay. I can't afford any delays.

He in return agrees that I will be the creative director on my own account and gives me the names of the team designated to me. My team consists of a senior art director, four computer designers, and a copywriter. The copywriter is a young girl, new to his staff. I hope she has the ability to think creatively. Anyway, her talent is not my concern; Linah will check and translate everything she writes.

'Are you pleased with me, M'sieur Giger?' Linah asks as we race back into the city centre and head towards the BMW showroom.

'Very pleased. We are going to be a great team. Now, where have you found this little car?'

The young, smartly dressed BMW salesman rises from his desk and dashes through the showroom to meet us. He is relieved to see Linah walking up the forecourt.

'You are late, Linah. I thought you must have changed your mind.'

'Sorry, we were delayed in a meeting. May I introduce M'sieur Giger? M'sieur Giger is my boss and will be buying me the car.'

'You are a very lucky man, M'sieur Giger, having such a beautiful assistant.'

'I think she is also very lucky, don't you?'

'Of course, M'sieur Giger.' He pauses. 'I have asked the mechanic to bring your car to the front of the showroom. It will be here in a matter of seconds.'

A bright red sports car zooms up the slope from the service area and brakes in front of us, missing me by inches.

'Linah, this is not a 1 Series BMW.'

'M'sieur Giger, you said a small, fast car.'

'Linah, this is a BMW Z4 Roadster – top of the range, a millionaire's plaything.'

'I do not understand, M'sieur Giger. It is a small BMW car.' Her face changes to a look of angelic innocence. 'M'sieur Giger, you said you were very pleased with me. I will do a lot more good things for you. You have seen nothing yet. Oh please, M'sieur Giger, I have chosen it for you. We will look good in it together.'

'That is for sure. We will definitely look good in it together.' She wraps her arms into mine and hugs me like a daughter. Her big, black eyes stare through me, her hair brushing my cheek.

'Is everything to your satisfaction, M'sieur Giger?' asks the salesman slightly apprehensively.

'Everything is just fine. Where do I sign?'

We follow him into his office. Two other salesmen stand in politeness as we walk past. I never received this degree of recognition in an English dealership. Then again, maybe they are not recognising me.

'When can we take the car?' I ask.

'You can take it now. It is ready to go.'

'Wow.'

In England we make hard work of buying a car, having to register it, tax it, and have it cleaned and insured. Then we come back for it two or three days later. Here in Casablanca it takes less than thirty minutes. Linah runs out to the car and jumps in behind the wheel. I more sedately sit in the passenger seat as the salesman demonstrates the start-up procedure.

We set off with a jerk. She laughs and flies straight out onto the main road, through the junction at the end of the street, circumnavigating the roundabout at the bottom of the hill twice. Several cars are forced to swerve and brake heavily to avoid us. She screams with delight and fails to be disturbed by the angry gestures from the other drivers. Linah is used to people stopping and letting her pass. Whether they want to or are forced to is of no consequence.

'Where are we going?'

'For a ride, M'sieur Giger. Hold your hair on.'

The ride proves to be my nearest-to-death experience yet. Linah laughs and screams at her own mistakes, narrowly missing a tram, three donkey carts, and four pedestrians. I must admit they are crossing the road too slowly, but still, I would have preferred her to slow down rather than scaring them to death. Many other people on the crowded pavements are stopping and staring in shock and horror. Linah waves at them frantically and continues screaming and laughing with joy. A group of office girls waves back, understanding her delight. The rest wave back in anger.

We screech to a stop outside the Sheraton. Phew!

'Linah, tomorrow your task is not as exciting as your task today. Your computer will be installed by now. Use it to search for the five most impressive and important things that Morocco has created, built, financed, or experienced. It might be the growth of a city, a port, a motorway, a farming venture, or winning a war. Each must be an event or an incident that the Moroccan people are extremely proud of. Can you do this?'

'Of course, M'sieur Giger.'

'And keep in touch,' I shout at her as she slams the car into gear and lifts her foot straight off the pedal.

'Bye!' She disappears, throwing up a cloud of dust as the spinning wheels try to grip.

Is she the most exciting woman on earth or just the silliest? Maybe both.

My phone lights up. It is an unknown number.

'M'sieur Giger, it is Entias, the office agent at the Towers. I have your car parking space number.'

'Hey, great, what is it?'

'It's 21AlphaZooy.'

'21AlphaZooy? What is wrong with one, two, or three?'

'It has to be sound recognizable. There isn't enough definition between one, two, and three.'

'OK, 21AlphaZooy it is. Have you told Linah?'

'No, I thought you should, as you are her boss.'

It's too late to tell her today. I can only see the dust from her car settling back onto the ground. Linah has gone.

'That's fine. I will tell her in the morning.

'M'sieur Giger, it doesn't matter how you spell it, but you must pronounce it twenty-one-alfa-zoi.'

'21AlphaZooy. I understand. I will tell her. Thank you for calling.'

Goodness, this is just to park a car. Why do we make life more complicated than it needs to be?

'9246821AlphaZooyGiger, just to park my car. Whatever next?' I keep repeating it over in my head until I am convinced it will stay there forever.

A Lightning Strike

The headline in this morning's paper is full of promise: 'Big Expansion Plans for Casa Port'.

A shorter feature on page three is not as positive. It announces that a second container shipping contract has been won by the French company Frenchline. This should be good news, but the paper has put a negative slant on it. '1,000 jobs at immediate risk as France rules the waves'. The incumbent Chinese company has announced the immediate loss of five hundred jobs. The report does improve, that is, if anyone reads as far as paragraph six, where it states: 'Better times are ahead and by the end of the year the port will be the pride of Morocco'.

Unfortunately, for the port workers the damage has been done. No one believes in promises anymore. The distraught men are demanding that the French company secure their jobs immediately and that the government apply pressure on it to do so. The French company is promising nothing of the sort.

In fact, quite the opposite; they are stating the entire managerial staff will be transferred from the French port of Marseilles and the only skilled jobs for local men will be on the tractors and the cranes. There will be opportunities for unskilled staff as loaders and sorters, but that will be later in the year when the port is up to speed. Until the expansion is complete, they are planning a considerable reduction in the staff.

Back on page two there is a report of a similar disruption at the power plant. The kingdom's number-one power station is about to be decommissioned. It is old and unreliable. Breakdowns are a regular occurrence, throwing the city into darkness on many a cold night. The power company is an African consortium, and the two new replacement power stations are French-owned. The African community believes this to be a serious social injustice, a bigger plan to rid the kingdom of its African heritage and to replace it with a rich, powerful European work base. It is true that the government is trying to attract overseas investment but not at the cost of its own people.

I have moved out of the Sheraton Hotel and into my apartment. As luxurious as my new home is, I am lonely. I decide to eat out and find solace back at the Sheraton. It is Thursday evening, and the lounge is packed with guests. As usual there is a girl sitting at every table, and they are all fully occupied entertaining clients. The international businessmen will be flying home tomorrow after a week of selling and negotiation. The local salesmen will be driving home to their wives and children for the weekend. This is their last chance for a little fun. I lean against the bar and order a Laphroaig 1977 single-malt Scotch whisky.

'Would you like anything with it, sir?' asks the bartender.

'You must be joking, at 110 euros a squirt.' He laughs and agrees it is rather expensive.

I don't notice the woman sliding onto the stool beside me.

'You know your whiskies, M'sieur Giger,' she interrupts.

I spin round to see a pale, smiling face surrounded by waves of dark brown hair. I don't recognize her; I have never seen her before. My first thought is that she must be one of the guests. She runs her hand through her hair and pulls on her fringe, which flows over her forehead. Surely this must blur her vision. Her petite, shapely body is wrapped in a tight-fitting black dress. Every woman has this little black dress in her wardrobe, but not every woman looks as sexy as she is. She crosses her right leg over her left. With a shake of her foot, her beige, high-heeled shoe slips off and clatters to the floor. Her dress tightens as she bends to retrieve it, revealing a pair of skinny but very sexy knees.

'You have me at a disadvantage. What is your name?'

'My name is Amelia Adelaide Fournier. But, M'sieur Giger, you can call me anything you like.'

That sounds familiar, I think. *I have heard that somewhere before.*

'Hello, Amelia. I am very pleased to meet you. Can I buy you a drink?'

'A dry white spritzer would be very nice. I have been talking all afternoon, so a long drink would be ideal. Thank you.'

'Are you always very talkative?'

She laughs. ' I teach, and this afternoon I have been giving a lecture on the responsibilities of parenthood.'

'Ouch! That sounds scary. You don't look old enough to have any children.'

'I don't. I am not that stupid.' She laughs again, and I find her mirth very infectious. She is great company; the evening slips away. I am surprised when I check my watch to discover it is eleven thirty. It is time to leave. She is disappointed when I bid her *'bonne nuit'*.

'Do I not please you, M'sieur Giger?'

'Of course you please me. You are beautiful.'

'Then why are you going to bed without me?'

'I have a girlfriend. She will not be very pleased if she discovers I have taken you home.'

She laughs again. 'M'sieur Giger, you do not understand. Your girlfriend is Madame Adeline la Chapelle, yes?'

'Well, Madame Adeline la Chapelle is not exactly my girlfriend, but I do know her.' I am puzzled and intrigued. 'Please continue.'

'Madame is in Brussels. She has sent me to you, let me say, to take care of you.'

'Why should she do that?'

'She knows that you are a man of needs, and she prefers to know who you are with.'

'You are right, I do not understand. But who am I to question Madame Adeline la Chapelle?'

'Shall I call us a taxi?' She emphasis the 'us'.

'I am capable of calling a taxi, thank you very much. Will you be warm enough? There is a chill in the air.'

'You can keep me warm, M'sieur Giger.'

It isn't long before I understand why Adeline has chosen Amelia; she is no threat to Adeline. Beautiful as Amelia is, in bed she is just a puppet, extremely submissive to the point of zero innovation. She absorbs everything I say to her and do to her, which is fun in the beginning but soon becomes tiresome. Just a little enthusiasm, a little inventiveness, would be appreciated. Slightly battered, I am ashamed to admit, she finally curls up on my chest and runs her fingers down my face before falling asleep. It is definitely better than sleeping alone. Thank you, Adeline.

'Can I come back this evening?' She looks at me appealingly as she dresses for college.

'I will call you.'

She looks horrified. 'Madame will punish me if I haven't pleased you. Please, sir, I have to come back. Please let me come back.'

I have to think of an excuse – and quickly.

'I can't say just now. I am travelling to Agadir. I have a meeting in Agadir this afternoon and am possibly stopping over.'

'Sir! I will go with you. Agadir is not a safe place for a man alone.'

'Amelia, please leave. I will not be dictated to by you or Madame Adeline. I will speak with her.'

'M'sieur Giger, no! You mustn't speak like this of me. Have pity on me. Madame can be very hard.'

'Please go, I have work to do.'

She runs out and down the corridor. She is crying as she waits for the elevator.

I pick up my cell phone to complain to Adeline, only to realise I never stored her number. It is possibly for the best.

There is a flash followed by a crack of thunder. The weather has changed for the worse. The day started out hot and sweaty, but now there is a wind in the air blowing the first splats of rain onto the balcony. I can see shoppers and tourists running for cover. There is a second fork of lightening streaking across the sky; it splits into three shards before striking the ground along the east side of the city. From my window I watch the weather deteriorate, it is dramatic. In the harbour, where only moments ago the boats were tugging gently on their moorings, now their masts and ropes are slashing into each another. The owners are desperately trying to save their cut-glass wine decanters from tumbling to the deck while at the same time clearing away cushions and towels before they are cast into the sea.

Through the pouring rain I can just make out the main street, which leads up to Old Medina, the original heart of Casablanca. The traffic has ground to a standstill in both directions. The traffic lights are out, causing chaos. I turn on the TV to check on the situation. There is nothing. The TV remains lifeless. My apartment is also suffering a power failure. My iMac computer, still with a small charge left in the battery, is flashing the latest bulletin. Apparently the entire city is powerless. Only battery-operated mobiles and computers are still active, and soon they too will die. An enormous explosion has ripped the heart out of the city's power station. Sky-News is reporting the incident. It shows the station badly damaged. Apparently the storm made a direct hit. A second report states that sabotage has not been ruled out. This is a report from the African management, who will be doing all they can to disprove the frailness of their service.

Wait! There is an official report from a representative of the Ministry of the Interior. He is saying that everything is being done to restore the power and they are expecting reconnection within the hour. He is also talking about the new stations. 'Your government is already in negotiation with the owners of the new power plants to bring forward the opening date. All tests have been completed. Only the price of the fuel remains to be agreed.'

In Morocco the people are prepared for power failures. All over the city private generators are clattering into life, at the hospitals, railway depot, port, and airport. The new hotels along the corniche have been constructed with backup generators, as have many of the government offices. The rest of the city will have to sit in darkness and wait. The people will wait one night, possibly two, but after that they are renowned for losing their patience. Unrest will burst out onto the streets with demonstrations and possible violence. The Moroccan government know this and will agree to any price the French power company puts to them.

Sabotage or storm damage? I will never know unless I go to see for myself. I call Linah.

Storm or Sabotage?

'**D**rop everything you are doing, and come and collect me. Be careful. The traffic lights are out.'

'Don't worry, M'sieur Giger. I know how to avoid the main roads and get across the city around the back streets. I will be with you in twenty minutes.'

'I will be waiting for you in the car park.'

'Okay.'

As my apartment is part of the new Marina Complex, it has its own backup generator. It isn't long before my lights flicker back on and the TV is reporting the very latest scenes from the plant. One corner of the cooling tower has collapsed, and the turbine room is in flames. It is a scene of complete devastation.

Linah screeches her sports car into the car park.

'Why do you always drive so fast?'

'I am a girl in a hurry, M'sieur Giger. Now you are starting to understand why sitting on the corniche all day was driving me crazy.'

'Well, those days are over. Take me to the power station. I want to see for myself what is happening up there.'

We are on the move before I have time to clip my seatbelt.

'The power station is a very dangerous place right now, M'sieur Giger. Something tells me we should stay away.'

'That is why I have asked you to take me, so you can take care of me.'

'I will do my best.' She laughs, but I can sense a hint of trepidation in her voice.

The power station is two miles up the coastal road directly north of Casablanca. On our left is the blue, pulsating ocean. On our right, green farmland stretches out towards the Atlas Mountains. Both sides of the road are home to thousands of electrical power pylons, linked together by miles of drooping cables that form a complex spider's web above our heads. We are definitely caught up in its trap.

Straight in front of us, one mile up the sand-swept road, I can see the massive concrete cooling towers spewing steam into the air. Below them sits the power-generating house, still blazing fiercely. As we approach we can see the fire fighters milling around their machines, connecting hoses onto fire hydrants and dragging them across to the ruined building. 'I thought water and electricity doesn't mix.' I joke with Linah. 'No wonder it is taking so long to get the fire under control.'

'What do you know about fire fighting?' I can tell she is stressed. My humour is lost on her.

'Not a lot!'

Linah pulls the car off the road and parks up on a sandy track overlooking the devastation. From here I can scan the entire facility. Just inside the security gate, men are in dispute. A man with a bullhorn to his mouth is standing on a precarious platform shouting to a crowd of power workers who have assembled around him. I guess he must be the union man stirring up support for his rebellion. Most are chanting and cheering in agreement. TV camera crews are filming and recording everything he says.

In the top corner of the car park, the TV broadcast trucks have formed a circle like the Wild West wagon trains of old. In their centre a makeshift studio has been erected. Reports and interviews are being beamed around the world. There is no shortage of opinion. Everybody is an eyewitness to the explosion, and everybody has a point of view as to what happened and why it happened. Overhead a Sky News helicopter is filming the stricken power house. A second copter, a police copter, is directing the emergency teams on the ground. If it isn't a wall falling down, it's a couple of guys fighting. The police have their work cut out.

Away from the burning complex, several chauffeur-driven black limousines are discreetly parked up. According to their license plates they are French. I recognise one of the dignitaries; it is Monsieur Abel Lafleur. He sees us walking towards him.

'What are you doing here? This isn't the place for an ad man and definitely not the place for a little girl.'

Linah immediately takes offence. 'I don't like him,' she mutters.

I turn my attention to Abel Lafleur. 'What happened?' I ask.

'The lightning made a direct hit on the power house, and the plant exploded, bringing down the corner of the power station.'

'What was in this part of the building?' I could guess, but what was the point when these guys can tell me for sure?

'All the output generators,' interrupts a passing fireman with 'Chief Fire Officer' printed across the front of his helmet. 'Only the main bloody generators.' A hint of a smile passes across Abel Lafleur's face. I take it he finds the man's frustration slightly humorous.

I must admit, assessing the damaged building for myself, I am finding it very difficult to believe a lightning strike caused this carnage. I am not an explosives expert, but the walls have obviously been blown outwards, meaning the explosion occurred on the inside. Fragments of machinery are scattered hundreds of metres in all directions. I can see down the side of the nearest cooling tower a lightening conductor remains intact, still pinned to the side of the concrete wall. Why didn't that earth the storm strike safely to ground?

Monsieur Abel Lafleur shakes hands with his fellow dignitaries who are climbing into an enormous black Mercedes.

'Well done, Lafleur,' I hear one of them say. 'Now you can get the new stations on line immediately.' There seems to be rather a lot of self-congratulating going on. I don't understand. Lafleur walks back towards us. Maybe he is coming to explain.

'This place is too dangerous for you, M'sieur Giger. I suggest you leave immediately.'

'It looks as if the fire department has the fire under control. We will be okay. Thank you for your concern.'

'I don't mean safe from the fire. I mean—'

I fail to catch what he is saying; the noise of the creaking building is making conversation impossible. I ask him to repeat it, but he too fails to hear me. He turns and disappears into his car. He shakes my hand through the open car window. 'I have to go. We have received a request from the king to get the new power stations on line. It is still going to take us several days before we can restore full power to the entire kingdom. Take him home, Linah. You shouldn't be here.'

Then he zaps up the window and taps his chauffeur on the shoulder to go.

'Why is he so concerned about us staying?' I ask Linah. 'It is as if he doesn't want us here.'

Linah agrees that his concern is overwhelming. We watch his car cruise out of the facility and disappear down the road.

'Come on, I want to get a closer look at the damaged buildings.'

I lead Linah through a door marked 'Private'. It seems as good a place as any to start my search. The door opens into a large refectory; food is still on display in the self-service counters. Now the heaters are dead and the food forgotten. The tables show evidence of a mass exit. Plates remain with half-eaten meals sticking to them. The rats have already discovered the free food and are scurrying from table top to table top. The station's cats are watching on, bemused. The rats are as big as the cats, so they are probably thinking twice before chasing them. Holding Linah's hand so we don't fall, I push a couple of dining chairs out of our way before clambering over several serving trolleys. I am heading towards the rear of the kitchen where I have spotted a door marked 'Management Only'. It swings open with the slightest of persuasion.

Inside a group of men are heavily involved in a debate. They stop and stare at us as we enter. Then without warning they attack us, shouting, pulling our clothes, and forcing us to the ground. I feel Linah's hand let go. Taken completely by surprise, I am unable to defend her. The entire room is spinning as I am knocked to the ground. All I can hear are obscene, angry insults.

Hang Him High!

A man is standing over me. Through his legs I can see Linah sitting across from me. She is tied hands and feet. We appear to be in a sand covered arena, a small circus ring. Apart from not being able to move she appears to be okay, Her hair is still groomed and her clothes unruffled. She obviously didn't get the beating that I received.

'You are not getting away with this, you French bastard,' shouts the man towering over me. His horrible, smelly breath is now only inches from my face. 'Do you think we are stupid? We know you have blown up our power station. We know what you are planning. It is you who has put us all out of work, destroyed our livelihood, and ruined our lives for your own gain.' He kicks me as he continues to rant.

I try to plead my innocence. I have no idea what he is talking about. And even more important, I try to explain that I am not French. My screams as he kicks me are unheard against the shouts of anger from the other men. They too are insisting that I should be punished. Their suggestions are absolutely scary; they range from me being hanged to being tied to a car and dragged around the streets for all to see. The guy in my face silences the mob and takes command.

'You! Go get a camera, you! Bring the video recording equipment from the manager's office.' They jump to his instructions. I gather it is his intention to film me reciting a confession as to my part in the destruction of the generator. What they will do with us after that, I dare not think.

The room empties as the men rush out to get the recording and filming equipment. His face comes back into my view.

'You are going to come clean and tell the world what is going on here.' He steps back. 'And if you don't …'

He pulls Linah to her feet by grabbing a handful of her hair and thrusts her head backwards. Then he pulls out a knife and places it on her face. 'Your pretty little girl will not be pretty any longer. People like you must not be allowed to get away with what you are doing to us. Do you understand?'

'I understand I have to do what you tell me to do, but you have got it all wrong. I am Swiss, not French. I have nothing to do with this explosion,' I beg. He isn't listening to what I am telling him and throws Linah back onto the floor.

Linah and I are left alone, tied hands and feet, facing each other from opposite sides of a miniature circus ring.

'Are you all right?' I whisper to her.

She nods.

'Where are we?' I ask.

'I think we are in one of the back rooms of the power station. This looks like a cock fighting ring. I saw one in Fez many years ago. This must be their 'recreation room', for lack of a better term.'

'I thought cock fighting was against the law.'

'Welcome to Morocco.' She pauses for a moment. 'If they participate in cock fighting, they are very cruel men. We must do as they ask. They won't hesitate to hurt us.'

'I suggest we get out of here if we can. These guys appear to be very angry and are capable of carrying out those suggestions. Maybe this is why Monsieur Abel Lafleur was so concerned for our safety.'

'I agree, M'sieur Giger.'

Although we are both tied hand and foot, we are not tied to anything. I manage to get to my feet and hobble over to her.

'It's very hot in here, M'sieur Giger. Is it me or is this room getting hotter?'

Through the bare brick walls we can hear the crackle of the burning building. Gas cylinders are surrendering to the heat and exploding. We can feel the vibration of crashing roof beams and collapsing walls. Linah is right; it is definitely getting hotter in here. We have been alone now for over ten minutes, and nobody has come back. Maybe they can't get back to us. We can hear the fire fighters shouting. They are hacking at beams with their axes, spraying the rafters with water. I try to open the door with my tied wrists, but it has been locked from the outside. Smoke is now billowing in through the cracks in the brickwork, and water is cascading down the walls from the ceiling. The fire sounds to be all around us. Has anyone told the fire department that we are in here? I guess not. Why should they? It was their intention to kill us anyway. With horror we realise that the fire fighters are not trying to get through to us, to save our lives; they are just trying to control the fire. If we don't get ourselves out of here, we are going to be burnt alive.

Scattered around the room are many sharp objects. I guess they must be the tools of recent cock fights. Knives as well as scissors are plentiful. I find an old cut-throat razor and manage to hack through the ropes binding Linah. Now she can release me. The smoke is so thick it is already impossible to see the ceiling. Linah continues to hammer on the door and to scream her heart out. Surely someone on the outside will hear her.

My search of the room for another way out proves fruitless; it is obvious that the only way out is through the locked door. I pick up a plank of wood, possibly a bench stay, and run at the door with all my strength, hoping to batter it down. Ouch! I bounce off it like a tennis ball. My impact has no effect on the door whatsoever, except for the noise it makes and the sound of me screaming as my body reacts to the jolt. Even after three or four more attempts at ramming the door, it remains locked.

Linah is on the ground, coughing and gasping for air. We have almost given up in despair when there is a tremendous explosion. It can only be the second generator blowing itself into oblivion. The room shakes, and ceiling beams come crashing down all around us. It is a miracle that we are still alive. Yet with the roof gone, we can see the sky, and the smoke is escaping upward. We might just get out of here. It takes several minutes for the dust to settle and a few minutes more for us to realise that the door has been blown off its hinges. It is just hanging there, as if God himself had opened it for us. I am expecting to see firemen rushing in to help us, but there is no one. I squeeze through the gap and drag Linah after me. Several bodies are lying over the piles of rocks on the outside. The smell of charred flesh is repulsive. The uniforms of these poor guys are still smoking. Stopping to help them is not an option; all I can focus on is getting us out of here.

Holding hands, we climb over the blitzed remnants of the power station. More fire fighters are heading towards us, intending to save those already inside. Little do they know they are all dead. These firemen are so preoccupied in hacking, screaming, and pulling heavy water hoses through the broken walls that they don't even raise their heads to look at us. Once we are outside in the fresher air, it is apparent what the second explosion was. Both generator houses have totally disappeared. People are being carried to ambulances on stretchers. Others are being attended to on the car park floor. More firemen are arriving, connecting pumps to water mains. It is a scene of chaotic panic. Everybody is rushing to help, but baton-wielding police officers are pushing them back. Too many people are only adding to the confusion. I recognise one of them as the guy giving the instructions in the cock ring. I pause to look at him.

'Keep going, let's get out of here,' Linah screams above the noise.

I don't have to be told twice. I grab her hand as we run through the car park away from the crowd. Only when we reach the car do we stop and look back. The devastation is unbelievable.

Our drive back to the apartment is in silence; we are both shaking and confused. Eventually Linah speaks.

'Whatever have you got me into?'

I shrug. 'I haven't a clue. I thought this was an advertising campaign which would help the Moroccan people and bring success to their kingdom.'

Linah's look says it all. 'Well, the people don't appear to be very grateful to me.'

I don't know if this is her attempt at a joke or not, but it is certainly true.

We collapse onto the sofa and stare at each other whilst sipping a second gin and tonic. We gulped the first one down in seconds.

'Do you want out? I totally understand if you want to leave.'

'Absolutely not. I like being rich, and this is the most exciting thing that has ever happened to me.'

'Exciting! Don't you mean terrifying?'

'I wasn't in danger. It was you they wanted to kill, not me. So for me it was exciting.'

I pour us each a third gin and tonic.

'Do you realise nobody knows we were there? Even Lafleur thinks we left after he told us to.' My brain searches through the last hour of horror. 'In fact, nobody knows who we are. Let's keep it that way.'

'If that is what you want, M'sieur Giger, then it's okay by me.'

'Yes, let's keep quiet about this until we find out what exactly is going on.

'So be it. It shall remain our secret.'

I know she thinks I am stupid, but I need time to work this out. Something is not quite right.

Prepare for Launch

'What have you got for me regarding impressive events in Morocco, not including the destruction of the power station?'

Linah laughs. 'There are many. You have a choice.'

'Then take a shower, freshen up, and let's go downtown to the Cafe du France on the corniche. They will have electricity down there and be open to the public.'

We order French onion soup, followed by pot au feu and crème brûlée for dessert, of course. Her research has resulted in an endless list of events. She talks non-stop throughout the meal, sharing her newfound knowledge with me. She has forgotten about the last eight hours already, and I am relieved to see her so enthusiastic. I want both modern and historic stories, traditional and humorous ones; I want to capture the essence of the Moroccan people and to add a sparkle of innovation and pride into their dreams. Which is difficult when they have just tried to kill us, but we must move on. I choose six articles.

1. The redevelopment of the Casablanca corniche.
2. The construction of the Grande Mosque in 1993.
3. The development of the inner cities, including the new tram systems, city planning, shopping malls, leisure complexes, and entertainment centres.
4. The Casablanca Declaration of 14–24 January 1943, when Winston Churchill, Franklin D. Roosevelt, and General Charles de Gaulle discussed the unconditional surrender of Germany.
5. The formation and action of the French Foreign Legion in 1831.
6. ???

Well, the sixth would be a glimpse into the future, possibly an artist's impression of the new dock stretching as far as the eye can see along the corniche, the airport being built on reclaimed land between Casablanca and Agadir, or high-speed magnetic floatation trains linking the north with the south.

Linah has been so excited, telling me about her work, that she has let her pot au feu go cold. She pushes it around her plate one more time before asking the waiter to take it away. Her crème brûlée does not escape; she devours it with relish and then steals mine. We share the deep red pinot noir, sipping it seductively for as long as we can savour it. I have to call a halt to our fun; we have a meeting with the advertising agency in the morning to deliver the brief for the first of our many campaigns. I will need to be totally energized for this. I have written the campaign theme: 'Be proud of what we did. Be proud of what we do.' I have no idea how this will evolve into a French and Arabic slogan.

The agency director, the art director and the copywriter listen intently to my explanation. I do my best to make it interesting by throwing in as many French words as possible, but they are received as a joke rather than an emphasis. The only success I do have is to make Linah laugh every time I use my hands to describe an action. Apparently I use my head as well. She says I look like one of the nodding dogs that we Brits like on the back shelf of our cars. My performance is over; I am exhausted. My attempt to excite and to stimulate has drained me. It is dark outside now; I have been talking for nearly three hours.

Where Are You?

L inah spins the rear wheels of her little sports car as we accelerate away from the junction of Bir Anzaran and La Rue Fromarge. 'Do you think they understood?' I ask her.

'I have no idea. You will know next week when we attend their presentation.' Then she bursts out laughing.

'What are you laughing at?'

'You, acting like a penguin.'

'A penguin!'

'A penguin. You were flapping your arms like a penguin trying to fly.'

I do see the funny side of my endeavour, but I find it very difficult to raise a smile; everything depends on the agency creating an exciting campaign with dynamic copy.

Linah's driving is getting worse. She is more erratic and unpredictable than usual. She never plans her route but just reacts to the corners by turning at the last minute and even then changing her mind. Her decision to stop or run a red light is not for the faint of heart. On the bright side, the two guys in the Peugeot 208 behind are having great difficulty in following us.

'Do you recognise the car behind?'

Linah checks her rear view mirror for the first time during the entire journey.

'Do you mean the black Peugeot?'

'Yes, it has two men in it. Or is one a woman?'

'Two men, both small and foreign.'

'How do you know that?'

'Their driving is too polite for them to be Moroccan. They are probably Chinese.'

'Now you are just guessing.'

'Do you want to put money on it?'

I ignore her offer. She will probably be right.

'How long have they been following us?'

'Since we left the agency. What have you been up to, Linah?'

'Nothing, apart from being tied up and almost burnt alive with you at the power station.'

'Maybe we were seen and recognized after all.'

'I don't think so, and I didn't see any Chinese there. I have spent the last three days working on the computer, searching the Internet. The only person I have spoken to is you – oh yes, and the commissionaire at the office.'

'Is he Moroccan?'

'No!' she answers, laughing. 'He is far too good-looking to be Moroccan.'

'Then where is he from? What nationality is he?'

'I think he is from Hong Kong or somewhere over that side of the world. So he is probably Chinese with a bit of Arab mixed in.'

'Why are there so many Chinese in Casablanca?'

'They practically run the docks. Most of the imports are from China, most of the ships are Chinese-registered, and lots of the workers on the quay are Chinese.'

'So what would they do if they lost this hold on the kingdom's imports and exports?'

'They won't let that happen. They are too powerful.'

'Mmmmm, I think it already has. Now I am starting to understand. Linah, go home and stay there until you hear from me. Drop me outside your apartment. I will take a taxi from there.'

'Are you sure? I wanted to take you home.' She looks at me with a twinkle in her eyes. 'I love your new apartment. You could invite me in for a coffee.'

'Not today! I want to make sure you are home safe, and I want to find out why these guys are following us.'

'Okay, okay. You be careful. I don't want to lose this job.' She laughs. 'And I don't want to lose you.'

I stand and watch her drive into the dark chasm under her apartment. The garage door rattles and creaks as it lowers and locks to the ground. She is gone.

I hail a vacant taxi across the junction, and as I wait for it to turn and come back for me, the black

Peugeot races past. I can clearly see that both the driver and his passenger are indeed Chinese; they are obviously agitated at seeing me standing on the roadside. They stop fifty yards farther along the road and reverse into a space between two other cars.

I cast a last glance up at Linah's balcony. Her apartment block is nine floors high, and Linah lives on the top floor. I was hoping she would be there to wave good-bye, but the only person I can see is a man leaning out over the glass barrier. He is roughly dressed, wearing a baggy, stained white vest tucked into a pair of brown, dusty trousers. If he is Linah's father, he is either a street digger or a construction worker. Maybe he is looking for her. I know the elevator is old and slow, because she is always complaining about it, but surely she must be in the apartment by now. The man turns and speaks to someone in the room behind him. I assume she has just arrived home.

'To the Sheraton, please, driver.' I have decided not to go to my apartment. I don't want Mr Wing and Mr Wong, or whoever is following me, knowing where I live.

As we turn onto the corniche, the blue of the Atlantic is a sight for sore eyes. Drawn by its appeal, I change my mind yet again and signal the driver to pull into McDonald's car park where it is safe to stop. I will walk the last mile. I have eaten here several times, although I am not a fan of McDonald's burgers. I use the restaurant as a meeting place; it is one of Casablanca's landmarks, second to the mosque. Would I recommend it? Yes, of course I would. The service is fast and friendly, and once you have skilfully manoeuvred past the queue of excited customers without dropping your tray, the outdoor eating area is superb. The tables are arranged around a vast paved arena protected from the wind on all sides by a six-foot-high glass barrier. Wherever you choose to sit, you can watch the sea crashing onto the rocks beneath the cliff. The five minutes it takes to eat at McDonald's is definitely quality time.

Total Recall

I t is a beautiful evening; the heat is caressing my face as I walk down the corniche towards the setting sun. I can see my hotel one mile along the promenade. It will only take me ten to fifteen minutes if I hurry, but I am not in a hurry. The black Peugeot is nowhere to be seen. I start to relax and enjoy the moment. My mind scans through the last twenty-four hours, putting the day's events in an order of priority. Top of the list was spending the day with Linah; she was a delight. I have worked alone for the last few years, but I greatly appreciate her support and enjoy her company. She is a very special girl; I was lucky to meet her.

My brain throws up many unanswered questions. Why me? What am I doing here, and why can't I get Linah out of my head? At first I respond with 'I haven't a clue.' My journey through life has been one of making the most of every opportunity. I set off not knowing where I am going, and at each intersection

I make a decision as to which way to go. I laugh at myself, looking out over the beach right now with the sun slipping slowly behind the horizon. I deserve a pat on the back; I am not doing too badly.

I didn't hate school, but I was always pleased to be on the bus going home. I was a bit of a loner. I preferred playing my guitar after lessons rather than following the school football team and spent my spare time designing and making models. Reading and solving algebraic equations was never on the agenda. During my teens I majored in women, falling in love on sight and failing to understand why they gave me such a hard time. How could I love Sylvia Hollings so much at the age of twelve, and why did she break my heart when she dumped me, just as Pauline, Shirley, Linda, and Barbara had done in the preceding weeks? This facet of my life hasn't changed; I still fall in love at the drop of a hat and never know why they stop calling. So it could be said I left school a failure, which is why I went to art college. If there was one thing I could do, it was draw. After painting I progressed to photography and then to making films and directing TV commercials. By this time I was hooked on creative advertising, selling, marketing, psychology, and social behaviour. With this understanding, I soon became a successful creative director. I won several awards for selling the world's best-loved products, but the greatest award was the joy I got from doing it. Now I can add to my CV working with the richest and most powerful people on the planet. I love my job.

I remember – it must have been five years back – writing a speech for FedEx's marketing guru. He was to announce the company's launch into the Middle East to an audience of five hundred people or more. They consisted of his newly appointed sales team, the company's top management, and the biggest and most influential of Arabic princes and politicians. These men were his target market, and each one had received a personalized, no-expense-spared invitation and gift: a Rolex wristwatch, so they could keep track of the company's delivery time. I paused and re-read my campaign strategy, wondering if the English professor who failed my O-level paper year after year would remotely understand the complexity of what I was writing. I know one thing; he wouldn't believe the five-figure sum I was being paid for creating it.

So from the back streets of a grimy Yorkshire town I find myself walking along the Casablanca corniche. My task is to create a greater, richer kingdom. And if that is not pressure enough, then the responsibility of ten million people depending on me being successful, is. For this I am living in luxury, working with international aristocracy, bedding the most beautiful women, and being paid millions.

My hand is grabbed by a tiny Bedouin girl. She must only be eight years old. She smiles, and her big brown eyes stare up at me through a mass of dusty, tousled hair.

'Gum, sir?' she asks, holding up a stick of Wrigley's.

She practically pulls me over with her insistence. A wash and tidy up would not go amiss, but her beauty and innocence are a beacon of light. I search my pockets and find a ten-dirham note screwed up inside the lining. I hold it out for her. It is gone before I can say 'keep the gum'. She runs off screaming with delight and grabs the hand of a portly German tourist walking in the opposite direction. He is not amused and shakes himself loose of her.

'Shoo, goo awai,' he growls at her.

I wish you well, my little pretty. You already have the charm and the cheek. All you need now is the luck.

So why has Linah got under my skin? Why do I care so much for her?

She was born into nothing and is struggling through life, trying to maintain her dignity in a life-or-death search for something better. I don't think for one minute she has ever begged on the streets selling chewing gum, but there is a similarity between her and the little girl. There is also a similarity with myself. I can recognise my own hopes and dreams. Linah is beautiful; she has massive appeal and somehow has developed a sophistication that I don't see in many of the other girls of Casablanca. Of course she uses her body and especially her eyes to get what she wants, but she also uses her head. She is intelligent, sharp, intuitive, and pretty. She is prepared to work very hard for her living. I must admit I am totally infatuated with her. Apart from that, I am aware that I am the luck she needs. I hold the key to her being a success or a failure. Chance brought us together, and I believe in fate. Let's be honest; I need her as much as she needs me, so I would be stupid to let her go. Adding to my natural instincts of lust and love, I have also developed a fatherly, caring responsibility towards her. I don't have a daughter, so this is something I have not experienced before, but I am sure every father with a daughter will understand. Linah is very important to me; it is more than a duty that I take care of her.

I step out into the road to cross over to the Sheraton. A taxi practically knocks me over, its horn blaring as it screeches past me. He doesn't even attempt to touch the brakes. I am shaken back to reality and reminded that in Casablanca it is every man for himself. For an Englishman, with all the financial support our social aid system offers us, this is a daunting fact to come to terms with.

Back to Reality

I am not surprised to see Amelia sitting at her favourite table in the hotel lounge; she is only doing what a girl in Morocco with dreams and ambition can do. Her client is attentive, listening to her every word. When she sees me she stands up and raises her arm to wave but thinks better of it and sits down again, pretending to arrange her dress. I interrupt their conversation and pat the guy on his shoulder.

'Excuse me, I must have a word with my wife. Our baby is sick.'

He slams his beer down on the table and swears out loud as he skulks across to the bar.

'You bastard! That was a terrible thing to do. I liked him.'

'Shut up,' I whisper in her ear as I kiss her cheek. The waiter is already on his way over to me as I sit opposite her.

'Laphroaig 1977 single-malt Scotch whisky and a dry white spritzer for the lady.'

'You have a good memory, M'sieur Giger. I have been waiting for you to return from Agadir. I knew you would come back to me.'

'So what have I missed in Casablanca during the last two days?'

'I was hoping you might have missed me, M'sieur Giger,' she says cheekily.

'I have, but I am referring to more newsworthy matters.'

'The power station was struck by lightning, and the entire city is on emergency generators.'

'I know about that. What else?'

'A container ship delivering three thousand cars from China has been boarded by the police in the strait. The Moroccan police claimed it was drug running, bringing marijuana into Europe via Casablanca. A French war ship was sent to escort it back to Singapore.'

'Did they find any drugs aboard the ship?'

'No, but it was a Chinese-registered ship. To resolve the incident quickly and quietly and avoid the entire crew being put under arrest, the shipping company agreed to take it back.'

'Were all the cars destined for Casablanca?'

'Not just Casablanca but all of Morocco. The Chinese car manufacturer Woton is growing rapidly in Morocco. The cars were a new model, which was to double their grip on the market.'

'How do you know so much about cars?'

'My father is manager of a Woton dealership. His showroom is empty, and he has nothing to sell.'

'Amelia?' I lean over and whisper to her. 'Did two Chinese men enter the lounge behind me?'

'No one has come in since you did. Why?'

'I just wondered.' I change the subject. 'How is Madame Adeline la Chapelle?'

'She was very angry with me. Her instruction was for me to stay with you and serve you. You got me into serious trouble, M'sieur Giger. I promise to do a lot better tonight.'

'Tonight!'

She slid her skirt higher up her leg, revealing the top of her stockings.

'Please, M'sieur Giger, I promise to do a lot, lot better.'

I can feel her entire body shaking as her knees teasingly part. She is so, so sexy. There is no way I can refuse her invitation; I just have to take her home.

Hong Kong

Three thousand miles due east of Casablanca, a plane touches down at a private airport three kilometres south of Hong Kong. Two men usher the blindfolded girl out of the aircraft, down the steps, and into a waiting limousine. The driver slips it into gear and speeds off before she even has the opportunity to find her balance. She is scared, confused, and hungry, and her wrists are sore and bruised from the ropes that bound her during the seven-hour flight. She can see nothing as they speed down the highway towards Kowloon. The traffic noises sound different; she knows she isn't in Morocco. Occasionally a voice booms from the front seat. She doesn't recognize the language and fails to understand the instructions. He could possibly be Chinese, Vietnamese, or even Cambodian. There is no point trying to work out what he is saying or trying to guess where they are taking her.

The smell of sweet cigarette smoke is sticking in her throat. She has experienced this once before at a party in downtown Casablanca. It was a student bash, and she didn't stay very long. She is at a loss as to what is happening and is too frightened to ask.

Nobody has hit her, nobody has insulted her, and nobody has raped or hurt her. Yet her head hurts like hell, and her stomach is sore and swollen. She retches as she gags on the smoke-filled air; her head is spinning and her eyes burning behind the blindfold. She doesn't know it, but she has been drugged to keep her quiet during the flight. They forced a cocktail of vodka, martini, and sleeping tablets down her throat. As a Muslim girl who has never touched a drop of alcohol in her life, she went out like a light.

She tries to piece together the few clues that she has. The sounds of the street are chaotic; there is lots of clanking and tooting. She hears screeching metallic brakes and whining electric motors. The traffic is on both sides of the car; it must be a very wide road. People are shouting. There are occasional screams, and overhead she hears the howl of an aircraft flying too low for comfort. It is either landing or crashing. Add to this the rain pounding on the car roof, the windscreen wipers swishing back and forth, the wheels splashing over a rutted road, and still that smell of sweet smoke – no wonder her head is spinning.

A sharp turn to the right throws her across the seat. A hand grabs her shoulder and pulls her upright. The car stops, and the rear door is thrown open, letting in the cold, damp air. Her nose welcomes the fresher air as her lungs filter out the drug-filled smog. She is pulled out of the car and held upright as one, two, three car doors are slammed shut. Does this mean there are three men or two and herself? She trips up several steps as they drag her into a back-street tenement block, through a narrow doorway and along a corridor. They then turn right and ascend four flights of steps, turning right on each landing. At first there is a smell of stale perfume, but as they climb higher, the smell changes to rotting wood, damp plaster, grime, and dust. Finally she is seated on a bed and her blindfold removed.

The room isn't as bad as she had expected. She is sitting on a single mattress; there is a wardrobe, a set of drawers, and a mirror. A TV clings to the wall by a metal bracket; its power cable hangs across the ceiling, where it is attached to a hanging bulb socket. Drawn in front of the window is a pair of dirty, flower-patterned curtains. If they meet in the middle it will be more by luck than design. The window is also filthy, on the inside and the outside; only a blurred view of a Hong Kong street is visible through it due to the filth. Outside, dank washing is strung across the alley on an old telephone wire; the dancing garments cling on for dear life. Across the street the windows are similarly dirty, and most are cracked or broken; paint hangs off every rotting window frame. The image is not one of the modern, thriving cities that we see in the travel brochures. The rain-filled gutters are breaking away from the buildings, and the down spouts lean out at all angles. Some are held to the wall with string tied to hooks or nails. The rainwater is cascading out of them, splashing onto the alley floor, where it floods across the cobbles, standing an inch deep in places.

She looks up at the two men standing over her. A third man is holding a tray that holds a glass of milk, a bowl of soup, and a bread roll. There is also some kind of sweet cake, which Linah doesn't recognise either by its appearance or taste. She is glad of the food. She is also glad when all three men turn to leave, locking the door behind them, signalling quite clearly that she is a prisoner.

She wipes the window, hoping to see out. She can hear footsteps on the cobbles below. A door clangs shut, and the voices of the three men slowly fade into the wind as they walk down the alley and turn right when they reach the main road. A dog screams as one of the men kicks it away from its dinner, which is a dead rat gouged open and spread-eagled in the drain. The dog howls again as a second kick sends it rolling across the stones; it picks itself up and limps away down the alley. The men laugh. Linah lies on the bed, covers herself in the blanket, and weeps.

The Games People Play

Madame Adeline la Chapelle and her brother Jean Claud clap and cheer with the forty thousand spectators at the football game. Morocco is playing Saudi Arabia in the Arab League. Compared to the top Brazilian and German teams the game is more like a school playground kick-about. But to the Moroccans this is a game to the death, and at the moment it is 2–1 in their favour.

Neither Adeline nor her brother are football fans, especially fans of Moroccan football. But they are guests of the Moroccan ambassador to France who flew down from Paris yesterday for the game. The ambassador is financing their project and after the game will expect a progress report. He gave them several directives, which, try as they might, they have not been able to incorporate into their plan. If Morocco were to win tonight, it would make their task a lot easier. Their pretence of enjoyment will have to continue for another thirty minutes plus extra time. All the time they are praying that Saudi Arabia does not score an equalizer. It is paramount he is in a good mood.

The ambassador and his entourage of secret police, secretaries, and gofers are in raptures over the game. The third bottle of Johnny Walker Red Label is replaced by the fourth and the ice bucket refilled for the umpteenth time. The remains of several whiskey glasses lie shattered on the floor, flung with excitement against the wall on the far side of the ambassador's box in which they are sitting.

A roar erupts from the crowd. All four thousand Saudi supporters jump to their feet; it's as if the ground is being forced upward by an underground explosion. The Moroccan goal keeper, who has already made several spectacular saves by jumping higher than he has ever jumped before, grabs the oncoming ball from out of the air and brings it down into his chest. Then he falls over his own defender and lets the ball roll onto the foot of the Saudi centre forward, who only has to push it into the net. The Saudi team is chasing each other around the park like children in play; the visiting fans behind the Moroccan goal are throwing hats and bags into the air and screaming like demented hyenas.

Adeline's heart sinks; the responsibility of making the ambassador happy has fallen onto her. She will have to supply her very best girls now, to pacify him, and throw in a few of her lesser-earning girls for his gofers. Her girls will not be pleased.

These guys are not very gentlemanly when it comes to adult play, and the girls will definitely be battered and bruised. Adeline will have to pay them double for their pain, and she could easily lose one or two of them. Still, that isn't really a big deal for her. There are plenty of other desperate, pretty girls willing to join her call centre. It is the loss of money that will hurt Adeline the most.

Her brother throws her an exasperated glance, which says it all: 'What the hell do we do now?'

She waves her hands in a gentle, flowing manner, which says, 'Leave it to me.'

He places his hands on the ambassador's shoulder. 'There is time yet. That was just sheer luck for the Saudis.'

The ambassador doesn't hear him. He is too busy shouting 'Foul, offside, send him off!' and anything else he can think of to get the referee to change the decision.

'Foul, foul!' The referee goes screaming down the field waving a yellow card. There is mayhem on the park. He disappears under a blanket of angry Saudi footballers. Nothing can be heard but the fading shriek of his whistle as more bodies fall on him, reducing his whistle blowing to a faint whine.

The two Moroccan linesmen echo the decision. 'Foul, foul,' they shout, jumping in the air and waving their flags. Then there is silence. Police, officials, and medics run towards the pile of bodies. It takes five minutes for them to calm everyone down. The referee eventually emerges, struts over to the goal, and retrieves the ball. Shoes in their thousands are thrown at him. This is the ultimate insult in Saudi Arabia, to throw your shoe at someone. The next level of disgust is to take off his head. The Moroccan referee will be lucky if he survives the day. It just goes to show what a twenty-thousand-dirham bribe can do.

The anger on the turf is not reflected in the royal box. Here the sentiment is one of relief. The ambassador collapses in his leather armchair and wipes the sweat from his face. He is overweight, to say the least. He is also hairy, sweaty, and distinctly smelly. Adeline looks at him and is nearly sick. He is a disgusting man, and she is afraid of him.

'I was worried about that stupid referee for a minute,' he growls at one of his protectorate.

'You had no need to worry, Mr Ambassador. We had it covered.'

'I am glad for your sake that you had. Now Adeline, let's slip into my private quarters and see what you have to show me.' He laughs at the horrified expression on her face and leans in close to her, his foul body smell filling her nostrils. 'Your chastity is secure today, my precious. I want to hear the plans on our takeover of Morocco.'

He laughs again at his own joke, which no-one else thinks is funny. 'And bring that dithering brother of yours along with you.' Jean Claud jumps to his feet and follows like a little lamb.

The ambassador's lounge at the stadium is palatial. His Moroccan entourage stand at ten-foot intervals around the room. The waiter is laying a silver tray on the central table. It contains every drink the ambassador might desire. The ambassador sinks his body into the deep cushions of the sofa, which is positioned in front of the floor-to-ceiling window overlooking the park. He pats the cushion next to him, and Adeline knows this is where she has to sit.

'Now, precious, tell me about this Jacques Giger who everyone is talking about. Is he to be trusted?' He looks her up and down and places his hands on her knees, sliding her skirt up her legs until her knees are revealed.

'Just to give me something nice to look at, whilst I listen to your report. You understand me, Adeline?'

Adeline understands. 'You are naughty, Mr Ambassador.' She lifts his hands off her legs, but her skirt stays above her knees. 'Of course he is to be trusted, Mr Ambassador. He is the best there is.'

'And does he understand that I am supplying the finance for this operation and that I am your boss and also his boss?' Adeline flinches. 'And I hope you explained to him that his first task is to make me president of the Moroccan Bank.'

'It was the first thing we told him, Mr Ambassador. It is only a matter of time before you own the bank.'

He squeezes her knee. 'Not too long, I hope, Adeline. Now run along. I have to speak with your brother – alone.'

She is relieved to be out of the equation. She knows her brother will tell her everything later. She escapes into the ladies' room and locks the door securely.

Ah! Amelia

Amelia rushes over to the window and peers out through the drapes. The curves of her body send a ripple along the pleats of the curtains, not to mention my spine.

'What are you looking for?' I ask her.

'Nothing, just appreciating the sunset.'

'Amelia, you have never been interested in the sunset before.' I put my hands on her shoulders and turn her body towards me. 'You are as white as a sheet and so cold. I hope it isn't me that is causing you so much anxiety.' I lift her head so her lips are clear of her nose and close in to kiss her.

'Oh no, M'sieur Giger, I am very relaxed with you. I am always very happy when I am with you.'

I feel her kiss come back. Her lips tremble, and then her entire body goes limp as she collapses to the floor. I try to catch her, but she has taken me by surprise. I only just manage to save her head from crashing against the table. Raising her gently in both arms, I carry her to my bed and wrap the duvet around her. She lies there motionless and silent. At first I think she has died. Was she poisoned? Maybe a bullet from a sharpshooter hit her through the window.

My mind is working overtime. There has been no crash, and there is no blood. Has she taken a bad hit or even overdosed? She is beautiful but oh so thin. Her skin stretches tight across her shoulders, and her collarbone protrudes through her flesh. I search for a pulse in her wrist and eventually find one in her delicate veins. I guess she has fainted; maybe through stress or overwork, tiredness, or lack of food. I have no idea.

'Whatever are they doing to you?'

I decide not to call the doctor; she won't thank me for making a fuss. I will give her one hour. She doesn't seem to be in distress, and her body is warming up slowly. I can see a little colour returning to her cheeks. I turn the heating in the room up full, prepare a cup of hot, sweet mint tea, and wait for her to regain consciousness. I have been told that Moroccan mint tea is the cure for all ills, so until I know the reason for her collapse, it is the best thing I can do. Sitting on the side of the bed, all I can think of doing is to stroke her hand. I can feel her body warming up, but it isn't until nine thirty in the morning that she utters her first words and her eyes open.

The sun is streaming into the room and falling on her face. She looks angelic. I slept in the armchair at the side of her bed and held her hand all night, my body aches and I am cold. I covered myself in a blanket just before going to sleep, but it slipped off during the night. The sun is bringing a welcoming warmth to my body.

'Welcome back!' I whisper in her ear. She just stares at me as if I am a stranger, but then a smile spreads across her face.

'Hello, who are you?' She is joking, of course.

'You gave me quite a scare. Whatever are you doing to yourself?'

'What do you mean? What happened? I remember coming home with you and then ... and then nothing. What time is it?'

'It's nine forty-five.'

'In the morning?' She sits up with a start and then freezes as a pain shoots across her forehead.

'Ouch!' She holds her head in both hands and screws up her eyes. 'I have to go. I have an appointment at the ..."

'At the where?' I ask.

'At, er, nowhere. It isn't for you to know.'

'You are with me now, and I am your number-one appointment. I will speak with Adeline. Now rest. I will make breakfast. When did you last eat?'

'I can't remember.'

'Just as I thought. Lie back and rest. Leave it all to me. You are no use to anyone in this state. Is bacon and egg okay? I do believe a full English breakfast is called for here.'

'With coffee, toast, and strawberry jam,' she adds.

'Of course.'

'I have never eaten an English breakfast before.'

'Then it's time you did. You are in for a treat.' I must admit it has been a long time since I cooked an English breakfast, but it comes back to me when I smell the bacon frying.

She lays back and closes her eyes. The sound of the sea, the gentle rattle of the window blinds and the sizzle of the bacon is so therapeutic. When I add the aroma of the coffee, her recovery is faster than I expected.

'So what are you doing to yourself to cause such a collapse?'

'The Moroccan ambassador in Paris is in town. He is a close friend of Adeline, and he always wants her best girls. We attend to his needs in twos and sometimes threes and fours, mostly for our own protection. He is a disgusting man, and his idea of fun is not in the joke book. Do you know him?' I have to admit I have never met the guy. And from the sound of it, I don't want to.

Her mobile on the pillow chimes. It is the 'Avon calling' door chime. 'It's Adeline. I am in big trouble.'

'Do you want me to answer it?' I ask her.

'No, I'll take it full on the chin.' She picks up the vibrating phone and puts it to her lips.

'Adeline, I was just about to call you.' I can hear Adeline screaming at her but not what she is saying.

'I am with M'sieur Giger. I cannot be in two places at once.'

Adeline is relentless. After ten minutes Amelia finally puts down the phone. 'She is right, of course.

I should have told her if I wasn't going to make the appointment. The other two girls could be in trouble. They had to serve the ambassador without me, and Adeline hasn't heard from either of them this morning.'

'Will they be all right?'

'I would guess so. He can't risk any bad publicity. But they will have been roughed up a bit. That means Adeline will have to rest them for a few days. Nobody wants to be entertained by a girl covered in bruises. This man is cruel. Just the thought of going to him scares me to death.'

'So what is Adeline thinking of?'

'He pays her big bucks and tips the girls well. It's unbelievable what girls will do for his kind of money.'

'Another coffee?'

'No thanks, I'd better go. I am so sorry about last night. I am supposed to be taking care of you, and you had to care for me.'

'You frightened me, Amelia. I am concerned.'

'I am a big girl now, M'sieur Giger. I can take of myself.'

'I am not so sure. Be careful, and I will call you later.'

Amelia smiles and closes the door gently behind her. I just have time to clear away the breakfast pots before my mobile clatters into life and falls off the table due to the vibration.

'It's Adeline!' she bellows down the phone even before I can wish her good morning. 'What the hell was going on last night?'

I don't know if I should tell her the truth or not. There is a silence.

'Well?'

I decide that she should know and blurt out the sequence of events. 'That's all I need, a girl who cannot take the pressure. My girls are the best-paid girls in Casablanca. They live in luxury apartments and drive fast cars, and this is how they repay me? She will have to go.'

'Adeline, slow down.' But the damage has been done; Adeline isn't handing out any sympathy today.

'Your presence is required at our office. Be here at eleven sharp. You are to meet the Moroccan ambassador to Paris, who just happens to be our partner and financier. We wanted to protect you from the politics of our project, but he has specifically requested to meet you. Be prepared to answer questions as to your progress. But more important, listen to what he has to say. Keep quiet and don't answer back. We will discuss his contribution to the project when he has gone. Don't be late.'

The phone falls silent; I stare at it in my hand. It seems to have a nervous twitch all of its own. Then I realise it is my finger trembling. This is the very same guy that Amelia is frightened of, and it sounds as if he has the same effect on Adeline. What in heaven's name does this guy have? A man who can turn such confident women into dithering wrecks must be a dignitary of immense power. Anyway, in one hour I will find out what makes this guy tick.

My phone flashes into life again. Maybe it is Adeline apologising. I should think so, too.

'Is that M'sieur Giger?'

'Yes, this is he.'

'I am sorry to call you, but I am Linah's father. I believe she is working for you.'

'Yes! We are working on a project together. Is she ill?'

'I don't think so. It's just that she didn't come home last night, and her mother and I – we were wondering if she was with you. We are concerned.'

'No, she isn't at work just yet, but I am expecting her to arrive within the next ten minutes. I will tell her to call you as soon as she steps into the office.'

'Thank you, sir. We would appreciate that.'

Now I am also worried about Linah. Why was he so concerned? His voice was trembling. I definitely got the impression that he knew more than he was letting on. Surely she is old enough to stay out all night if she so wishes. She must have stayed out before. Besides, where the hell was she? I watched her drive safely into her apartment's basement car park. Why did she not arrive at her apartment? Where did she go? Who did she meet?

The Power of a Bear

Adeline pounds her brother's chest. 'Tell me what he said. I have a right to know. If you are plotting against me I'll kill you myself. Tell me before he arrives. Tell me now!'

'Adeline, we don't have time. All will be revealed when M'sieur Giger arrives and the ambassador goes through his plan. But I will tell you this: I am not expecting anything new.'

'Well, I am expecting a life of luxury for the rest of my life. If that has changed he has a big problem.'

'And so you will, my dear sister. You will enjoy a life of luxury.'

'Monsieur Chapelle, The Moroccan ambassador in Paris,' announces the secretary. 'Shall I show him in?'

The words are wasted as the ambassador pushes the secretary aside and bursts into the room followed by Monsieur Abel Lafleur.

'Good morning, Monsieur Ambassador. It is so good to see you.' Chapelle's sentiments are not shared by his sister; she sets into him immediately.

'Where are my girls, Mr Ambassador? What have you done with my girls? If you have hurt them, then I—'

'Then you will what?' he scoffed. 'I asked for three girls, and you sent me only two. They had to work extremely hard, and this morning they are taking a well-earned rest at the embassy.'

'Are they okay? Did you hurt them?'

'Well, I must admit my security team got a little enthusiastic. But they will be fine in a day or two.'

'I will send a car for them immediately. I want them under my care.'

'Adeline, you couldn't care for a kitten if it came in a basket. I will return them when I think fit.'

The large black oak doors to the office creak open again, 'M'sieur Giger has arrived,' announces the secretary.

'Good, show him in,' answers Chapelle.

I walk in to silence. Chapelle and Monsieur Abel Lafleur are seated in armchairs at either side of the large stone fireplace; the cinders are prepared but not lit. Adeline perches herself on a high chair and crosses her legs uncomfortably. The Moroccan ambassador is pacing around the centre of the room. He is exactly as described: fat, smelly, and sweating. As he sucks on a cigarette and blows the smoke out through his nose, saliva runs from the corner of his mouth.

'M'sieur Giger, I presume.' He laughs at his own little mimic of the Livingstone joke. 'I have heard so much about you. I hope you are going to deliver all that you have promised.'

I cast a glance towards Adeline, who gives a little shimmy of her head, telling me to stay calm and quiet.

'I am the Moroccan ambassador in Paris and a close friend of Chapelle.' He turns to face Chapelle. 'This is correct, isn't it, Chapelle?'

Jean Claud nods in agreement. 'This entire project and your employment are due to me. It is my power, my money, and my influence and business connections that are making it possible. Therefore, M'sieur Giger, I am your boss. As you are probably aware, given my position in European politics I cannot be seen to be manipulating the markets and the industries of Morocco, which is why I have employed Jean Claud to front the project. Do you understand so far?'

I express my understanding.

'Now, I can sit here all day and listen to your plans. But this will bore me and take too long, so I am going to tell you the priority of your tasks. How you achieve them is up to you. All I will say is, time is of the essence.'

'Should I be taking notes, Mr Ambassador?'

'Good grief, no. You are a doer not a writer, aren't you?'

I nod like a little schoolboy.

'Your number-one task is to establish the new Bank of Morocco and me as the director general. Once I am in command of the finances, I can take control of all the other industries. Now did you need to write that down?'

'Of course not, Mr Ambassador.'

He laughs again. 'Simple, isn't it? Now, the only other thing I want to stress is the timeline. You have six months from today. Do you understand?'

'I understand, Mr Ambassador.'

'Excellent. And by the way, you will need to get yourself a new assistant. Linah is out of the country at the moment. She is safe in my care, but should you fail in your task I will put her to good use. And I have changed my mind about your girls, Adeline. Send a car for them. I don't see why I should have to feed such skinny, half-starved wenches. Next time I ask for three girls, I advise you to send four, just in case one decides she fancies a night off. My coat, if you please, M'sieur Chapelle.'

'I believe you left it in the outer office. My secretary will get it for you.'

'You are quite right, I did. I will take my leave and call on you again next time I am in Casablanca, when I expect good news of serious progress.'

'You can rely on us, M'sieur Ambassador.'

'I wish I could.'

With that Jean Claud helps the ambassador into his coat and leads him down the corridor. He doesn't come back into the room until he has seen the ambassador sway down the wide, winding staircase, cross the tiled mosaic floor of the reception, and walk out of the building into his limousine.

We stand and stare at each other, waiting for Jean Claud to return. Adeline picks up the phone and orders a car to go to the embassy to collect her girls. I am in shock. What is going on here?

'Why didn't you tell me Linah was missing?' demands Adeline.

'I didn't know she was missing until just now. Her father rang me one hour ago and told me she hadn't arrived home last night, but I thought nothing of it. She is street wise and sensible. I told him I was expecting her and would ask her to call him. Good God! What am I going to tell him now?'

Jean Claud walks back into the office and reads the concern on my face.

'Bad news about Linah. I wasn't expecting that,' he mutters.

'If he has hurt my girls I will kill him,' chips in Adeline.

'Don't be silly. Your girls can take care of themselves. Nothing has changed from our original plan except that M'sieur Giger has to find a new assistant.'

'Is that all you have to say about Linah? She is my responsibility, and we Brits take our responsibilities very seriously.'

'Ah yes, I was forgetting you are British. I am convinced she will be taken care of. We will see to it that she returns as soon as possible.'

'As for you, Chapelle, I think you had better tell me the complete story.' My forceful manner amazed even me.

Adeline nods in agreement, and Lafleur simply shrugs his shoulders.

'Okay, Jacques. I will call you Jacques, as it appears you are now one of our family. The plan that we have explained to you is sound. The only fact we left out is the involvement of The Bear. I am sure you will understand why we have given him this name. We need his money and his influence and connections. It is our intention to have him removed from the equation at a later date so we can give control of Morocco's development back to the people – after making a considerable fortune for ourselves, of course.'

'Of course,' butts in Lafleur.

'I suggest we move forward with our plans, prepare the ground for the development of the new bank, and stay very focused on the future but watch our backs continuously.'

'Continuously,' butts in Lafleur again.

'Shut up, Lafleur. You are annoying me.'

Lafleur speaks up for the first time. 'This man is ruthless, Jean Claud. We must not underestimate him. He will want rid of us just as much as we want rid of him.'

As if on cue, the door opens and Adeline's two unfortunate girls stagger into the room with their clothes torn, their bodies battered and bruised, and their dignity in tatters.

'Good gracious,' Adeline screams, 'Whatever did they do to you?'

She helps them over to the sofa and pours two dry martinis. They refuse the olives; their mouths are too swollen to swallow.

'Does The Bear know this is what his men did to you?'

They nodded. 'Although he didn't touch us, he was plying them with drink and encouraging them.'

'Jean Claud, this must stop. He has gone too far this time.'

'Let us stay calm. We have time to plan. He will not be back in the kingdom for at least a month.'

'What of Linah?' I say. 'She is in great danger. Look at what he has done to these girls.' I can't take my eyes off them. My thoughts turn to Amelia. She should have been one of them. No wonder she was so scared.

'Linah. Yes, we should have taken greater care of Linah,' chimed in Lafleur.

'Where do you think he will have taken her?'

'My guess is Hong Kong, he owns an enormous sex empire there, I will make a few phone calls in the hope that we can locate her. She is not in danger just yet; he will want to see what we do first.'

'I have to go and get her. She is my main consideration, and—'

'And what?' snaps Adeline.

'And I like her. I have a lot of respect for her work.'

'You are stupid. She is Moroccan. She will use you and then drop you, and she won't care about your feelings.'

'That's enough of this bickering,' breaks in Jean Claud. 'If she is in trouble because of us, we will get her back. So just stop. Calm down, and let us first find out where she is. In the meantime, let's make some money. Jacques, speed up the advertising agency and bring the campaigns forward in time. Lafleur, find where Linah is and what her situation is. Adeline, take these two girls home safely and give them everything they need. I have a meeting at the Treasury in two hours.'

Tell It As It Is

I don't know if I should tell Linah's father what I know. There is a possibility that she will contact him, but I have to call.

I wait for the phone to connect; it takes forever.

'Hello, is that you, Linah?' asks a man on the end of it.

'Hi. I am sorry, it isn't Linah. I am M'sieur Giger. I was calling to ask if you have heard from Linah, as she –.'

He interrupts my sentence.

'M'sieur Giger, thank you for calling back. I am Linah's father. We have received a very strange call from her. We are concerned.'

'In that case, could I suggest we meet?'

'Yes! Of course, come round to the apartment.'

I didn't expect to be invited to her home but think this to be a good idea, as I don't have much time.

'I have a meeting at lunchtime. Could I come now?'

'We are waiting for you, M'sieur Giger. We look forward to meeting with you very soon.'

My petit taxi mounts the kerb outside her apartment. Forty dirham is displayed on the metre. I give him thirty.

'Sir, the metre says forty. You owe me another ten dirham.'

'Your metre also shows "Night Charges." It is ten o'clock in the morning, in case you hadn't noticed.'

I slam the door shut and leave him smouldering. I took an instant dislike to this guy the moment he stopped for me, and my opinion didn't improve as the ride progressed. We didn't come the shortest way, and his driving was erratic, to say the least. Funny, isn't it, how important first impressions are? It is essential to make a good first impression.

Just as I reach up to ring the top bell marked 'Apartment 19', the garage door to my left bursts into life and rolls itself up into the ceiling. A dirty, dusty red Renault Clio shoots out from the basement, across the pavement, and straight into the stream of traffic. The continuous stream of cars breaks formation to let it in, expressing only a toot of annoyance. Thank goodness no one was walking across the sidewalk; driving in Morocco is scary. I dive into the depths of the basement before the doors come shuttering back down. The basement is pitch black. I was hoping the lights would be back on, but this is downtown Casablanca, not the exclusive tourist area where I live. The only light is squeezing in through the gaps of each shutter. Most of the car spaces are vacant; I can just make out the names and apartment numbers hand painted on the end walls. The scribbled lettering seems to denote a second, more menacing message: 'Park in my space and I will destroy your car.' The one thing I know about Moroccans is that they are very possessive.

I grope my way past a dusty Ford, a motorcycle in a thousand pieces, and an old but well-maintained Mercedes. Eventually I can make out 'Linah 19' written neatly on the wall in white chalk. Parked beneath it is Linah's shining new BMW. Well, she made it safely into the car park. I can only guess what must have happened next. She would have taken the elevator, so I will do the same and follow her path. It isn't difficult to understand how easy it could be to kidnap a girl down here. The only clue I have to the location of the elevator is the whirling noise of its pulley and cranks as it goes up and down between the floors. At the stainless steel doors, a tiny red button glows in the dark to identify it. I presume I have to press; it turns green with a touch.

I wait in the dark, dusty, very scary concrete corridor. I can hear the elevator stop at the ground floor, the floor above me. There is muffled chatter as the people step out. I pray it will come down to the basement next and not go shooting back up to answer another call.

It does, and as I stand in this confined, pitch-black concrete box it occurs to me that the electricity must be on. The light isn't working, but the elevator is. So why is that? I can only assume the bulbs have been removed or stolen, which is always a possibility. Then it dawns on me that the electricity would have been off anyway due to the power cut, so Linah would have been forced to take the stairs. No wonder it took her so long to reach her apartment. Silly me, she didn't reach her apartment.

I have more success. It still takes an age, but I do reach door number 19 and knock.

A teenage girl opens it. 'M'sieur Giger, please come in.'

The man I saw on the balcony appears behind her. He is wearing the same clothes he had worn the day before.

'We saw you arrive, M'sieur Giger. Please make yourself comfortable. Would you care for a Moroccan tea?'

I accept and seat myself on the settee. Two young girls sit on the floor in front of me.

'My name is Jorge, and these are Linah's sisters, Kalima and Katrina. We have heard a lot about you. Linah likes you a lot and was very excited when she met you. In fact, she never stopped talking about you all that evening. You know what these young girls are like, M'sieur Giger.'

I nod. I don't know why I am nodding. I haven't a clue what these young girls are like.

A small, overweight woman places a tray of steaming hot mint tea on the table before me.

'Would you care to serve, M'sieur Giger? My husband has a terrible shake of his hands and spills it all over.'

I stir the tea in the pot, making sure the mint is being absorbed, add four teaspoons of sugar, and stir again. Then I pour it from a height of two feet into five small glass tumblers. You see, this is to get air into the tea; it is a Moroccan tradition and takes a certain amount of skill. It is definitely not to be attempted with shaking hands. Jorge sits next to me with a pile of home-baked scones.

'I believe you have heard from Linah,' I say.

'Yes; just after I spoke with you this morning the phone rang, and it was Linah. She was calm but a little hesitant. She told me she was working with you and that she would be out of the country for a few months. If we could not get in touch with her we could call you on your mobile. Is this true, M'sieur Giger?'

I don't know what to say. I have to think fast.

'Yes, this is true,' I answer. 'She is working for me, but at this moment in time she is with a client of ours, so I don't know exactly where she is and what she is doing. I intend to join her in a couple of days and possibly bring her home.'

I hope my lying is not evident on my face.

'You see, Fatima?' Jorge turns to his wife. 'I told you, M'sieur Giger is a good man and will take care of her.'

She smiles at me and beckons me to pour another round of teas. My hands are definitely shaking this time. I try to change the subject.

'I am very excited with Linah. We get on so well and understand each other.'

The two girls giggle.

We talk for an hour. Apart from two sisters, Linah has a brother, but he is attending an interview at the Intercontinental Hotel. They are in need of a waiter. Jorge tells me he was working on the new tram system. But now the track system is complete, the construction teams have been laid off. Fatima spends most of her time in the kitchen, making Jorge's modest income go as far as she can by baking and cooking the simplest of Moroccan dishes. I must admit, her scones are wonderful.

'We were delighted when you offered Linah this job. As you can see, life and times are very difficult for us. We want the best for our children, but opportunities are very rare. All four have been well educated, not only in languages and business matters but also in cooking and caring for their eventual husbands and families.'

The girls giggle again. Jorge continues to describe Linah's virtues, explaining how loyal she is, hardworking, and clever. 'Once she met an Iraqi government official. He asked consent to marry her and promised us the world. She begged me not to allow it, as she didn't love him.' Jorge went on to explain how a relationship like this would not only have solved Linah's future but theirs also.

'It was very difficult for me to say no, M'sieur Giger, but the happiness of my children is paramount.'

I nod and pat his hand. This man should be in advertising. If he could sell products as well as he is selling his daughter to me, he would make a fortune.

I come to the conclusion that they are a wonderful family. I am impressed and know they are really proud of their kids, especially Linah, who is the eldest and obviously their pride and joy.

I have to leave. Kalima insists on accompanying me down to the street and rushes over to the kerb to call a taxi. She questioned me consistently all the time we were in the elevator, which I must admit I found rather entertaining: Where was I born? Where do I live? Am I married? Do I have a girlfriend? What car do I drive? Would I like to live in Casablanca? Do I like her family? How much do I like her sister?

'I like you all very much, and I hope we can be friends.'

'I hope so too, M'sieur Giger. We like you very much.'

The pressure to find Linah and bring her home is even greater now that I have met her family. In fact, it is immense.

Banking Gone Mad

The director and his creative team are already sitting around the boardroom table; I am the last to arrive. I have been up all night, thinking out the strategy for the launch of the bank campaign. The opening of forty-six high street branches in the major cities, Rabat, Agadir, Casablanca, Fez, and Marrakech, is a mammoth task and a mammoth responsibility. This launch would both be a high-profile campaign introducing the bank to the people of Morocco and provide an important influx of cash to finance further developments. Behind this retail desk the main action of the bank will be taking place, but this will not be mentioned in the retail launch.

I congratulate them on the success of the image campaign and inform them that it has created amazing awareness and increased national pride in Morocco among ordinary, working-class people. It is essential that the Moroccan people have pride in themselves and an appetite for more. Future campaigns have to promise more than exciting projects and dreams; they have to promise security, and that means personal banking support and encouragement for small businesses. I need new accounts to flood into the bank, at the demise of the existing banks if necessary.

'Gentlemen, it is time to launch our second campaign. This involves the opening of a new bank for the working-class people of Morocco. The bank will be called "Your Bank", meaning the bank, which belongs to you. Our claim will be that ordinary men and woman are in control, not only of their own finances but of their futures, their careers, and the growth of their money. This will be the image part of our campaign and must be the corporate message in all the copy, slogans, and headlines. But gentlemen, this is not enough on its own.'

I look each one of them in turn and seriously wonder if they have a clue as to what I am talking about. 'We have to attract millions of new savers and investors, and we are going to do that with an offer they cannot refuse. The offer is: Open a current account with as little as ten dirham, and we will put a thousand dirham into your account. When the account has grown to five thousand dirham, interest will be added at 40 per cent. When the account has grown to ten thousand dirham, interest will be added at 50 per cent, as long as the account is in credit. Gentlemen, this is a limited-period offer for six months. Your target is to enrol half the earning population of Morocco as clients within three months. We have to make it happen – and quickly. Any questions?'

Silence reigns.

'Do you understand the message and what is required?'

'We understand,' responds the director. 'When would you like to see our presentation?'

'Mohammed, you know me. As soon as possible, so let's say this time next week. Is that okay?'

Mohammed nods in agreement. The rest of his staff sit in stony silence.

'But before that, Mohammed, I need your media proposals and the costs for a nationwide TV and poster campaign in the cities. Hit that offer hard in the local press. Also mail out to the wealthier people and to company directors, office workers, hotel staff, and shop assistants. I need that on my desk first thing Thursday morning. Is that possible?'

'Everything is possible for you, M'sieur Giger.'

'Great.' And with that, I stand, shake his hand, and leave.

I dare not look back; I know they are all shaking in their shoes.

My mobile chimes the French national anthem. Luckily I am cruising along the corniche, and it is safe for me to answer it.

'Yes, Jean Claud, what have you got for me?'

'We have found Linah. She is in Hong Kong. She was seen being hustled by two gorillas into a back-street brothel owned by, guess who? The Bear.' He tells me the answer before I have time to think, but

I would have guessed right. 'The good news is she is not one of the girls on offer – not yet, anyway. We believe she is being held in one of the top rooms. A light has appeared at one of the windows in the roof. We are guessing this is the room she is in.'

'So she is safe?'

'She is safe, but I doubt she will be enjoying it. I have given instruction that she has to be under surveillance 24/7.'

'Thanks for that, Jean Claud. I have actioned the agency. They are presenting next week, and hopefully we will be ready to roll the week after.'

'That's great news. Keep your head down. There is a lot happening behind the scenes. People are dying, and I don't want you hurt. I hope you are aware that you are our front man, so try to avoid being photographed. Avoid interviews from the press, and keep an eye on your rear-view mirror at all times.'

'Will do. Speak to you soon.'

I swing the car through the Marina Compound gate and screech to a standstill in my designated space. Kamal strides over to greet me.

'Welcome home, M'sieur Giger. I haven't seen you for some time.'

'I have been away on business,' I lie. 'What have I missed in Casablanca?'

'You have had the Moroccan police around to see you, but I told them exactly the same, that you are away on business.'

'Any idea why they called?'

'Some woman has gone missing. They seem to think she is with you.'

'If she is pretty she might be.' He laughs at my comment, not realising that I have turned the truth into a joke – which is exactly what I wanted to do.

'There is still trouble down at the port, another explosion last night on board a French tanker. And a Chinese port official was found dead at his desk – shot through the head, they say.'

'Goodness, this is awful?'

'Oh yes, and the electricity is back on. The new power station is up and running. Do you know these new stations are French-owned? I suppose all the profit goes back to France. Whatever is our government thinking of? Anyway, we can see our way across town again and watch our favourite TV programs.'

'Is that all the news?'

'That's all, M'sieur Giger. Oh, except Madame la Chapelle is in your apartment waiting for you.'

'I'd better go, then.'

'Do you want your car cleaned?' he shouts after me.

'No, don't bother. It's a hire car. I will take it back tonight.'

I pass him a thousand-dirham note. He doesn't really want to clean my car, but he does need the money.

'Did you see what that bastard did to my girls? The sooner we don't need him the better.'

'Calm down, Adeline. Don't forget there will come a time when he doesn't need you, so watch your back.'

'He even suggested that I go and service him myself. He touches me like a piece of meat and talks to me like ...'

I hand her a port and lemon. I don't know why I poured her a port and lemon; it is simply the first bottle I grabbed hold of. She takes a sip and bursts into tears. I feel sorry for her; she is so elegant and proud, yet so vulnerable and frightened. We must have lain together for over an hour before there is a loud tap on the door.

'It's me, M'sieur Giger, Kamal. You have a delivery.'

'Wait a minute, Kamal. I will be with you shortly.' I open the door slowly to check that he is alone, and he thrusts an envelope into my hand.

'Sorry to interrupt you, M'sieur Giger, but the man said it was urgent.'

'Who, the delivery man?'

'Yes, but he wasn't from DHL or FedEx. It was a taxi driver. He just pulled up, gave it to me, and told me to deliver it immediately.'

'Is it likely to blow up? Is it a bomb?'

'I don't think so. It feels like a CD or a DVD. I'm sorry, M'sieur Giger. I wasn't being nosey. I just held it.'

'You are all right, Kamal. I think it is a disc also.' I close the door as he turns to go.

'Who was it?' Adeline is sitting up in bed now, rubbing her eyes and fingering her lips. They are dry and tender. She reaches over for her makeup bag.

'A delivery, someone has sent me a disc. Are you in the mood to watch a DVD?'

'Of course. I love films.'

I slip the disc into the player and climb back into the bed beside her. The screen flickers into life, and Linah appears. She looks tired. Her hair is falling over her face, and her eyes are swollen and sore with crying.

'M'sieur Giger, I don't know where I am. It is horrible, and I am frightened. They grabbed me when I got out of my car, and the next thing I know, I am here in this stinking room. I don't even think I am in Morocco. I have a message for you.' She picks up a piece of paper off her knee and stares at it. 'It says, M'sieur Giger, as you can see I am alive and well, but remember who your boss is. Do as you are told and get on with your job or you will not see me again. I will be fed to the wolves. M'sieur Giger, what does that mean? Help me, please.' The screen goes blank.

Adeline wraps herself around me. 'Oh goodness, whatever have we got ourselves into?' she wails. 'I will call Jean Claud and see what he suggests.'

'No, not yet!' I beg her. 'Wait a minute. Let me think. I need time to think.'

Seven Smokes an Hour Can Kill You

Fung Ching pulls his collar tighter around his neck and taps another cigarette out of the pack. On the floor scattered around his feet are the stubs of two hours of surveillance. He inserts a grain of weed into the end of the cigarette and lights it. He takes the drug in with a long, deep breath, which fills his nose and lungs with the foul, sweet smell. The pain in his body eases as the drug seeps into his bloodstream. As he slowly lets out the smoke it obliterates his face. He watches it rise slowly in the cold night air. Unfortunately the glow from his nicotine stick is clearly visible from the windows of the house, and his every move is being watched.

Young girls are constantly tottering down the cobbles of the alley on their high heels, knocking on the door and entering the downbeat apartment block. The door is tired and stripped bare of paint. The only sign of more dignified days are the white faded numbers in the centre panel, which announce this home as number ten in a long row of similar homes along Zang Ting Straza. Fung Ching scribbles down every arrival in his notebook, and in the next column, he inserts the time. He has no idea who these girls are, let alone their names, and his writing is becoming more and more illegible by the minute due to the cold in his fingers and the swirling in his head. He presumes the girls are the hookers arriving for their shift. They will report in for duty, undress down to knickers and stockings, and then sit in the rose-coloured welcoming lounge hoping to be chosen by a respectable client of need. But the chances are he will be unsympathetic to the point of being brutal.

The positive of the job is the amount of money these girls can earn. It is enormous, especially for girls who cannot read or write. Yet to survive they need every dollar. They have to pay their rent and serve their habit as well as clothe and feed themselves. They are indeed hooked into a way of life from which they are unable to escape. Their clients are from all walks of society, from bankers to bus drivers, politicians, policemen, tourists, and criminals. All Fung Ching can see are their silhouettes as the door opens and closes. The light surrounds them for only a few seconds as they enter. He scribbles as quickly as he can. He has been told to record the time every man and woman enters, how long they stay, and at what time they leave, but this is proving to be impossible.

Unfortunately the gangster on the door doesn't know that Fung Ching's scribbles are totally unreadable. Had he known he would not have been concerned. After a further two hours and many more comings and goings, when Fung Ching's brain is in a total state of uselessness, the door opens, and a group of four men stagger out onto the cobbles. Fung Ching scribbles down 'three men' and then changes it to 'four' as his eyes focus. Then he thinks better of it and rewrites 'three'. He can't see clearly anymore, and he doesn't really care. They are making a lot of noise boasting of their sexual exploits to one another; their laughter is excessive for this time of night. Fung Ching checks his watch and jots down the time. Then he fills in the details:

Brief description: Businessmen.
Sex: Male.
Nationality: Jordanian.
Age: 30+.

His original confusion as to the number of men was justified. He fails to see a fourth man break away from the group and turn down the far side of the alley. Nor does he hear the rubber Nike trainers on the cobbles as the man crosses the street and comes up behind him. His throat is slit from ear to ear; his book is grabbed from his hand before he hits the floor. His crumpled body is dragged down the alley and rolled into the black, chilled waters of the harbour. It hits the water with a splash. There is nobody to hear. He will be found somewhere downstream later, by which time it will be impossible to identify him and all clues as to why and when have been obliterated.

It takes three days for news of his death to filter back to the office of Jean Claud. There has been no sighting of Linah since her arrival at the house. Girls her age and size are up and down the alley all day and night; distinguishing between them is impossible. She could have been any one of a hundred who come and go. Nor has any movement been seen through the top-floor window where it is thought she is being held. Jean Claud is angry that the surveillance team are still only guessing that she is in the building. And what was Fung Ching doing, letting someone catch him unawares? The death of Fung Ching passes in frustration. He must have been asleep, reports Jean Claud.

Fung Ching is replaced by Mai Chea Tong, a tall, slender man aged twenty-four. He knows this area like the back of his hand; he grew up here in the back streets of downtown Kowloon. He has ambition. He dreams of being the next James Bond and reads spy and espionage novels for inspiration. To reach his goal he is prepared to do anything and to risk everything. Time has been lost, and so too has the art of continuous surveillance. After only six hours on the pavement, watching, writing, scratching, and jumping up and down to keep his blood circulating, he gets it into his head that he can enter the house as a customer and look for Linah himself. Whether from boredom, inexperience, or stupidity, he rings the bell. A voice from behind the door recites a prepared script in both Mandarin and English. The first question is exactly that.

'Mandarin or English?' He hesitates for a second and decides English will be more impressive.

'English, please,' he responds. There is silence. He is expecting to be asked the password, but after ten seconds he decides he better recite it anyway. 'Obama is in town.' During the last hour Mai Chea Tong has heard several visitors recite the phrase. He is not as stupid as he looks. The door swings open, and he steps inside. Death, let alone danger, has never entered his head. He walks down the dimly lit corridor towards the red room at the far end. Curled-up photographs of scantily clad girls are pinned to the walls. He doesn't have time to focus on any one in particular, but he is pretty sure they are all Asian. Just as he is about to enter the lounge, where he can see several girls reclining on sofas and cushions, a mammoth of a man steps out in front of him, stopping him dead in his tracks.

'You are new. We do not know you.'

'And it must stay that way,' Tong responds. He is pleased with his quick thinking and even more pleased when the man softens his aggression and speaks to him as a friend and not as an interrogator.

'I have to search you and take your bank details. I hope you have proof of your identity and over five thousand dollars in your account, because that is the entry fee.'

'I didn't know I needed five thousand dollars. That is an outrageous amount of money for a membership.'

'Ha! That's not for you to become a member. That's for me. Your initial first year membership fee is one million dollars, but you can visit as many times as you like for that.' The Asian laughs at his unreserved wit. 'Call it what you want, but you go no further until your status has been approved.'

Mai Chea Tong is unceremoniously thrown out of the door and lies in the wet alley for several minutes until the cold of the street's cobbles penetrates through his Levi's and rudely brings him to his senses. His pride is hurt, his confidence is in tatters, and his left eye is swelling rapidly and turning a ripe plum colour. Thoughts of changing his profession are actually passing through his mind. Yet he is still alive, a fact he has previously overlooked, and he is grateful for that. A Mercedes pulls up, its wide Pirelli tyres screeching to a stop on the cobbles. He hears the car door open and then slam shut. Someone taps the house door with a cane, recites 'Obama is in town', and disappears inside.

Mai Chea Tong just catches a glimpse of the man's face. He is convinced he has seen him before. Maybe it was on TV or maybe in a documentary or interview program. He can't be totally sure where. The man was wearing a dark full-length raincoat, which seemed to hang from his large trilby hat. He was big, overweight, obnoxious, and extremely confident. Mai Chea Tong is jealous of the bank account this man must have. He is probably a banker, a judge, or a politician – definitely a member if not the leader of the Hong Kong underworld. Cruelty emanated from his stance. Yes, he was definitely a cruel man. Mai Chea Tong hides his face as the car speeds off.

Proof of Linah's whereabouts is still uncertain. We know she is alive, and we know she is in Hong Kong. Someone, somehow, will have to get inside the house, if not to rescue her then to ascertain that she is inside and okay.

Banking Has Become an Art

The advertising campaign was launched last night with a sixty-second TV commercial supported by full-page ads in the press. The agency has got the message just right. Building on the Past Achievements campaign, 'The Pride in Your Country' focuses on having pride in yourself, promoting a new start with great opportunities and the promise of new wealth. Posters in the cities are inviting new accounts with an offer previously unheard of. Thirty main street branches are already operational, and bank machines are sprouting on walls in every shopping mall, road junction, and communication hub like leaves on a tree in springtime.

The offer is such that no one can refuse. Outside every branch queues are stretching down the street. Headlines in the papers read 'Ten-dirham madness makes all the difference', 'Never has ten dirham created so much excitement', and 'People are going crazy for Your Bank'. TV news reports are showing happy, laughing people on the street waving ten-dirham notes in the air, and this is nothing compared to the response on the web. Thousands of people are opening accounts online. It takes only minutes to fill in their names and addresses, pay ten dirham, and receive an ID number and an account number. Gone are the days of plastic cards and chequebooks. Now your mobile, computer or tablet is all you need.

In only one week, two million Moroccans have opened accounts with Your Bank, and the number is increasing by the minute.

Adeline's pink phone bursts into life. It identifies the caller to be the ambassador. She hesitates before slowly picking it up and placing it against her ear.

'Bring your best five girls to the embassy tonight at nine,' he shouts. 'We are celebrating the success of Your Bank. And Adeline' – he pauses; she strains her ears, thinking there is a fault on the line – 'come yourself. I want to celebrate with you personally.'

Her phone goes silent. Adeline turns white. Her breathing becomes erratic, and her chest wrenches in spasms. She slumps into a chair as her face drains of blood and she is overcome with fear. It is fifteen minutes before she can speak and dial her brother; there is no answer. Jean Claud listens to his phone ringing. He knows the call is from Adeline and ignores it. He too has been invited to the party and decides his sister will have to cope with this on her own.

I have a five-day window before my next meeting with the ad agency. When my phone rings and Adeline's name appears on the screen, I like Jean Claud ignore her call. I am dashing to the airport; I have a mere thirty minutes to make the flight to Dubai before flying on to Hong Kong. I can't risk a delay just now; nothing must stop me.

Passengers are already boarding the Boeing 343 to Dubai. My phone rings again. This time it is Amelia. She is obviously in distress but tries to pass it off.

'Sorry to call you, M'sieur Giger. Can I talk with you?'

'Of course you can, but I only have a few minutes. What can I do for you?

'Oh! I just wanted to hear a friendly voice, so I thought of you.'

'That is very nice, but I do only have a matter of minutes. Are you in danger?'

'No more than usual in my line of business. Tonight I am working at the Chinese Villa for … you know who. I don't want to go. I am so scared of this man.'

'Don't go. You have suffered enough from him.'

'It is not as simple as that, M'sieur Giger. You see, Madame Adeline la Chapelle has also been summoned along with four other girls. If I don't go it puts more stress on them. It will be the end of my career.'

Goodness! First Linah and now Adeline and Amelia. This man must be stopped.

'Amelia, I understand your predicament. You must all stick together. Surely you have been in situations like this before.'

'Not like this, M'sieur Giger. During the early evening we can support each other, but later they will split us up to entertain various groups of guests. M'sieur Giger, sometimes there are four or five of them. They have no respect for us.'

'Adeline will be there. She will help you.'

'She also is very frightened. The ambassador has requested her personally. I think we are all stressed out.'

'I can't help you. I have to board my plane. Amelia, please be careful. I am back in four days. We will meet up and hopefully laugh about it.' That was a stupid thing to say.

Anyway, my thoughts turn to Linah locked up in a back-street Hong Kong brothel. She is totally innocent, and it is because of me she is locked up. At least these other girls have got themselves into their situation. Linah is totally innocent. She needs my help more than they do. I have to go and get her.

'Amelia! We will meet when I get back.' But she has already hung up.

I have no idea what I am going to do once I reach Hong Kong. Checking in to the Intercontinental Hotel and catching up with Mai Chea Tong is the only plan in my head.

Not all Parties Are Fun

Adeline calls her brother three, four, five times but still gets no response. She pulls her Donna Karen coat tight around shoulders, buttons it under her chin, and locks the apartment door behind her. On the street her chauffeur stands next to her big black Mercedes. He opens the rear door and positions himself so he might catch a glance of her long, slender legs as she swings them into the sumptuously soft furnishings of this beautiful 500SL. This is the only perk Tom gets, so he always makes the most of it. Adeline usually flashes a little too much leg for him. She likes him, but more than that, she depends on him to be there when she needs him, so she treats him to a little tease. He never lets her down, but this evening she isn't in a charitable mood. Monsieur Jon Thomas, Tom to his friends, is disappointed but can tell by the look on her face that her thoughts are elsewhere. When she tells him to take her to the Chinese Villa, he actually feels sorry for her.

He has just driven Jean Claud there. He had to queue for ten minutes in a line of cars snaking up the gravel drive leading to the front door. The cars ranged from Ferraris to Bentleys, each one delivering an obnoxious, overindulgent occupant. Gorilla-type bouncers stood on each side of the villa door as The Bear welcomed every guest with a handshake and a dirty laugh. There was not a woman in sight. Wives and girlfriends have all been dispatched to the theatre or persuaded to stay at home with their children and their knitting. Tonight is a night out for the lads at the expense of The Bear. Their intention is to sample good food and drink, and enjoy the entertainment, but this is the Bears way of controlling them. When he wants people to do his bidding in business it always helps if he has a little something to help them make up their mind, like an obscene photograph or the threat of a newspaper story.

As Adeline turns through the large, ornate cast-iron gates into the drive it is obvious the party is already in full swing. The cars this time are all parked under the avenue of trees. The drive is clear all the way to the front door. Tom jumps out and rushes around to open the car door for her.

'Can you wait for me, Tom? I don't want to stay very long.' He can see the fear in her eyes and feel the tremor in her voice. It is all too evident. She swallows in mid sentence, trying to hide her feelings, but fails.

'Sorry, Ma'am. I have been instructed to the airport. I am to collect a gentleman arriving from Peking. Anyway,' he says, trying to cheer her up, 'you will be having the time of your life amongst all these distinguished people. This looks like a very extravagant party.'

'I will, Tom. You are right.' Adeline stands up straight, adjusts her coat, and thanks him. The Bear has already been informed of her arrival and before she is halfway up the stone steps to the front door he appears in the doorway.

'You look amazing, Adeline. I don't know how you do it at your age.'

She pretends the insult doesn't hurt. He laughs as he unbuttons her coat, slipping it off her shoulders and handing it to his attendant. He checks out her dress and is pleased with what he sees.

'Stay on my arm all evening, Adeline. And take that hurt look off your face. I will take exceptional care of you.' He pats her rump as he wraps her arm into his and escorts her into the great hall to show her off to his friends.

Amelia and the other four girls are already at work. They are pleased to see her, and a brief smile is exchanged between them. Each is being plied with champagne whilst keeping several men at arm's length. The girls are laughing at jokes they don't think are funny and listening intently to some stories they don't understand. They really are true professionals.

The Bear is outrageous. He humiliates Adeline at every opportunity, referring to her breasts as puppets, making her turn to show his guests how beautiful she is, and ordering her to fetch more drinks as if she were a waitress. She even has to feed nibbles into the mouths of his ugly friends. She laughs and flirts, watching the clock all the time and keeping an eye on the other girls, who are being equally ill-respected. Sometimes they are prodded and squeezed and sometimes kissed and caressed by Asian, Arab, and African power brokers. Occasionally they have to remove a groping hand on its way up their dress. A laugh and shake of a finger with a 'behave yourself or I will tell your wife' usually stops its progress.

Adeline scans the guests for her brother, but he is nowhere to be seen. She can only hope he is there. Amelia is already being escorted up the wide, winding staircase by three drunken gorillas, each staggering on every step; one has his hand on her arse. At the top of the stairs she looks over her shoulder at Adeline. Adeline cannot respond; she, too, is fighting off uninvited attention.

It is getting late. The guests are thinning out, and the respectable ones are making their way home. The once-sophisticated dining room with its silver tableware is now a shambles. Broken glasses litter the floor. Champagne and whiskey puddles the polished teak floor, making it very slippery. It is difficult for even a sober girl to stay upright. The Bear calls for another round of drinks for his three hangers-on, excusing himself as he takes hold of Adeline's arm and ushers her up the stairs.

The bedroom suite is palatial. At its heart is the grandest of four-poster beds; white silk sheets shimmer over more silken pillows than she can count. To a romantic the place is paradise. To Adeline the bedroom is a horror chamber. Her eyes focus on the handcuffs just visible behind the hanging drapes. She freezes when she catches a glimpse of the mirrored ceiling and the iron bar bracketed across the top frames of the bed with two large hooks hanging from it. He taps her across her face and throws her onto the bed.

'Time for the entertainment, Adeline. Prepare yourself.' She feels his massive weight release her as he steps back and disappears into the bathroom. Her brain is racing. She raises herself up on her arms and scans the room, her face still stinging from his torment. The bedroom door is only ten feet away. She can easily reach it, but descending the staircase and crossing the lounge, where several guests are still lingering will not be so simple.

She has no alternative but to go for it. Staying in the bedroom is not an option. She makes a dash for the door and twists the handle. The door swings open. She is in the corridor in a trice, running for her life down the corridor and around the landing. She thinks of Amelia and the other three girls, wondering how they are coping, but her priority is to save herself. She throws off her shoes and speeds down the staircase. Halfway across the lounge she lets out a loud scream and crumples to the floor. Blood is pouring out from between her toes; a shard of glass from a broken bottle is deeply embedded into her foot. The pain is unbearable. She grabs her foot, intending to pull out the glass. But something – the sight of her own blood, the pounding in her head, or just the fear flooding her body brings her to a stop, and she falls helpless to the floor only meters away from the door to safety.

She is carried back to the bedroom by two of The Bear's camaraderie and thrown roughly onto the bed with blood still oozing from her foot. It soaks rapidly into the white silk sheets. Although she needs medical attention and obviously several stitches, a plaster is stuck over the cut and her shoes forced back onto her swollen foot. The Bear always insists that his girls wear shoes at all times; it is his little turn-on. He sits in a large, comfortable armchair in the corner of the room, angry and sadistically happy. He watches his henchmen fondle her limp body and pour neat vodka into her mouth. Even in her unconscious state, she splutters as her stomach heaves at the intake of the liquid.

'Enough,' orders The Bear. 'I don't want her dead. She is too beautiful. Spread her and hang her up. Then leave us. On your way out tell the others that the show is about to begin.

Jean Claud Chapelle arrived at the party before the main influx of guests. He was under the impression that this evening was in celebration of

the successful launch of Your Bank and that he was
the guest of honour. His agenda read:

Reception with the ambassador - 9.30 pm
Meeting to discuss the progress of the retail
banking - 10.00 pm
Discussions to plan stage three - 11.00 pm
Speeches and votes of thanks - 12.00 am
Acceptance and acknowledgements - 12.15 am
Entertainment - 12.30 am

The entertainment at previous parties usually
involved naked dancers, erotic pole dancing,
lap dancing on selected guests, and masses of
champagne. After that, Jean Claud usually called
Tom to take him home.

After instructing Tom to go back and collect
Adeline, Jean Claud climbed the steps leading to the
front door. The ambassador was waiting to welcome
him. After an introductory joke and handshake he
lead Jean Claud through the decorated hall and into
a large office at the rear of the building.

Apart from Jean Claud and the ambassador,
there were three other men in the room. Dressed in
dinner jackets, immaculately adorned in bow ties
with pocket handkerchiefs, and black shiny patent
leather shoes, they looked very presentable. Only
their black, pitted African skin gave a hint of their
true menacing presence. They were obviously not
businessmen, nor were they party guests; they could
only be the ambassador's heavy mob. Jean Claud, in

his naiveté, just thought they must be the normal accompaniment for such a rich man.

The ambassador and Jean Claud sat in facing armchairs positioned in front of a roaring coal fire. Their discussions were formal yet friendly. The ambassador had to keep leaving to welcome arriving guests, which made it very difficult for Jean Claud to maintain continuity with his report. But he knew the ambassador would be gracious as long as things were progressing in his favour, and they were definitely doing that.

'So far so good,' retorted the ambassador. 'Now I want to explain the next part of the plan.' He tapped his finger on the side table, stubbing out his cigar, and lent towards Jean Claud.

'There has been a slight shift in the plan.' His face lost its smile. 'To be honest, Jean, you and your sister are making an enormous amount of money out of this deal, and you are not putting enough effort and time into it. You are leaving everything to M'sieur Jacques Giger, who, luckily for you, is making things happen to my liking. The other thing, which is even more important: I don't trust you. So to secure your status, you will use your title and persuasive personality to establish my position as head of several French companies.'

Jean Claud tried to speak but was abruptly silenced.

'The first is the French automotive industry. I want you to persuade Citroen, Renault, and Peugeot to sign their North African trading rights to me. The new car specifications for North Africa will be lower than their existing European models, but I will sell them for the same price. You must make this happen within the next two weeks. The agencies and service networks are already in place due to an enormous investment from me.'

Jean Claud went pale, and his hands became cold and sweaty. 'That is impossible. These companies are the biggest and most powerful companies in the world. They are not going to hand over their North African businesses to you. I am very sorry, but there is absolutely nothing I can do that will make this happen. You will have to tender for the business against all the other interested parties.'

The Bear moved even closer. Now he was almost nose-to-nose with Jean Claud.

'You are failing to understand the situation, Jean Claud. I am losing patience. This is the plan and your task. You are too far into this takeover to go silly on me. Just do your job.'

Jean Claud did his best to stop his voice from shaking. 'I repeat, it is impossible. I will not be bullied into interfering with these companies.'

The ambassador was right not to trust him. In fact, it was Jean Claud's intention to own the North African trading rights himself. He could easily achieve this with his contacts in the French government, but to hand the business over to The Bear was unthinkable.

'I have to welcome some new guests. I will be back as soon as possible. Don't go away.' The ambassador left instructions with his cavalry that Jean Claud had not to leave the room.

'Think on my demands, Jean. I will be back soon.' With that he left Jean Claud with his thoughts. It was almost an hour before he returned.

'Let me help you change your mind,' growled the ambassador. He helped Jean Claud to his feet and walked towards the door. 'Come with me. I have something to show you.'

Jean Claud rose to his feet and followed him down the corridor and up the stairway. He could see the party guests talking, laughing, drinking, and flirting below in the reception lounge. No one even noticed them. He was angry and sweating as he followed the ambassador along the north corridor. He hated this man so much so, that he was already planning to have him removed from the plot. What he saw next took him completely by surprise.

The ambassador leads the way into the large, opulent bedroom and closes the door behind them. Walking over to the large four-poster bed, he draws back the drapes. Adeline is hanging by her wrists, handcuffed to the bar across the top bed beams. Her dress barely clings to her thin, stretched-out body. Her head is slumped sideways, and her face is deathly white. Her feet have been forced into her shoes, and her right foot is still oozing blood, which is dripping onto the bed. She is unconscious and totally unaware of what is happening.

The Bear laughs. 'Your sister runs a very dangerous service, Jean Claud. You know this, yet you not only allow her to continue but encourage her. There is no way I would let my sister do what she does. But then again, I am not as indecent as you.'

Jean Claud stands mouth open and in shock. He steps towards Adeline to cut her down but is held back by the firm grip of two enormous gorillas.

'Tonight your sister's future is in your hands. Do as I request and she will know nothing of our deal. Refuse and I will set my pack of wolves on her. They will rip her apart, along with the other whores she sent me tonight. And don't think you can save her now and retreat on the deal later. I own your sister, and if you do not produce the goods, you will be saying good-bye to Adeline. She will not be killed, simply … spoilt. Do I make myself clear?'

'Clear,' Jean Claud mutters.

'I can't hear you.'

'Clear,' Jean Claud repeats slightly louder.

'Good! Now go and enjoy the party. Tomorrow you have work to do. I will be waiting for your call. Oh yes! And don't worry about Adeline; she will know nothing of this evening. Of course she has to earn her keep. My men deserve some fun. But she will be in your office tomorrow. Now get out of my sight. I have guests to entertain.'

Jean Claud is ushered out of the bedroom, and he hears the door lock behind him. He is a proud man, cunning and clever, but he is not violent. He is far out of his depth.

The Hong Kong Whore House

My flight from Dubai to Hong Kong is via Singapore. It takes forever. I probably fall asleep three or four times, but only for a matter of minutes. My mind is racing and full of things I only thought happened in James Bond novels. Amelia and Adeline are servicing The Bear, possibly being abused to the point of torture. Then there is Linah, an innocent girl whose mistake was to be sitting on the corniche when I walked past. She certainly didn't deserve to be locked up in a Chinese brothel in Hong Kong. Then there is me, a creative ad man whose only skill is to make companies succeed by creating memorable slogans and TV commercials. Now I am racing across the world to rescue a girl I hardly know from the clutches of one of the most horrible men on the planet. I have no plans as to how to find Linah. My thoughts turn to how can I get myself out of this mess. I can't walk away from it; The Bear will hunt me down and devour me whole.

It is eleven thirty when I wake in my hotel bed. The sun is blazing into the room, and someone is knocking frantically on the door. It is the Chinese maid.

'Me clean room please, me do it now or me in big trouble,' she begs.

I step aside to let her in. It is then I realise I am completely naked. Oh goodness, and the poor girl hasn't even batted an eyelid. I pull on my jeans and wait for her to vacate the bathroom. She rolls down the bed, dusts the TV and the dressing table, and then curtsies as she leaves. I slip an English twenty-pound note into her hand.

'Tank u Serr.' Then she is gone.

I ring Mai Chea Tong to hear the latest update on Linah. He too is in bed. He is one of a team of seven men watching the house. He tells me there has been very little activity at the house during the day; food arrives from a nearby noodle bar, and clean sheets and pillowcases arrive from the laundry on the corner. A DHL truck calls once or twice every day with crates and parcels, and the driver seems to gain access into the building with ease. Only as the light falls does the area come to life with tourists, hawkers, prowlers, and drug addicts. Mai Chea Tong suggests we meet at eight that evening so I can watch the action for myself.

'I don't expect tonight's activities to be any different from any other night,' he tells me.

'Then I will gain access to the building tonight, get up to the top room, rescue Linah, and get out of there AQAP.'

I hear him laugh. 'Why are you laughing, Tong?'

'You are in dreamland, M'sieur Giger. You will be killed.'

The word takes me aback. Being killed has never entered my head. To be honest, the thought stops me in my tracks for a second or two.

'That is not your problem, Tong. Meet me in the hotel lobby at noon.' He isn't ecstatic, to say the least, but finally agrees when I tell him I will make it worth his while. I am interested in the DHL delivery van. Maybe, just maybe, this is the way into the house.

Tong arrives late at the hotel, but better late than never. I order two gin and tonics, which are served with a bowl of olives and crusty bread, and then I sit him in the corner of the lounge, where I can demand his full attention.

'Tong, get me a large crate, big enough for me to sit inside. You will need leather straps, a large, sharp knife – oh yes! And a gun.'

'A gun?'

'Yes, I will need a gun.'

'But do you know how to fire a gun, M'sieur Giger?'

'No! You are going to show me. Instruct DHL to collect the box from your apartment at six o'clock, and give them the delivery address as the house. Stress that it must be delivered this evening.'

'You are a very brave man, M'sieur Giger.'

'A stupid man,' I correct him.

'I didn't want to say that.' He laughs, wipes his bread around the olive bowl, and squeezes it into his mouth.

'I'll go and make it happen, M'sieur Giger.'

'Good! I will come to your apartment at five. We will send the case from your place. Sending it from the embassy is too obvious.' He leaves, choking on the dried bread and spitting the olive stone out as he steps into the street.

I must be mad. Oh, for the opportunity to go home or wake up to find it all to be a dream – no, a nightmare.

Crated And Delivered

I spend the afternoon shopping for soft shoes, easy clothes, and basic survival tools such as a long blade knife, a Swiss pocket knife, a torch, a book to read, and a packet of bandages. Maybe Linah will be bruised or even injured; maybe it will be me who needs them.

I arrive at Tong's apartment at five. He has done well. The crate measures four feet by three by three feet and is made from aluminium with reinforced corners. Two large locks hang down the front, grasping the appropriate hooks riveted to the front. He has instructed DHL to collect it at six, but they can't guarantee the van's arrival to thirty minutes. Tong has already printed out the address label and stuck it in the centre of the lid. On the four sides he has stuck big arrows with the words 'This way up' and under that in red 'Fragile - handle with care'. He has also purchased large pieces of industrial foam.

'I thought these would protect you from being knocked about inside,' he explains with pride.

'Good thinking, Tong. Did you get a leather strap?' He reaches inside the box and pulls out a two-inch-wide, dark brown leather strap with a large brass clip on the end.

'Perfect. What time is it now?'

'Five thirty.'

'Okay, let's do it.'

We practice the locking procedure and then repeat it again, explaining in detail the importance of the position of the strap; I have to be able to cut it with my knife from the inside, through the slit between the lid and the box. I think Tong understands, so I step inside and make myself as comfortable as possible. I want to place my weight centrally in the crate, but this is proving to be difficult. Tong pushes the foam pieces down the sides of the crate to protect my shoulders, and then he forces more pieces under my legs. The support is very comforting. He reaches in and shakes my hand.

'May God protect you, M'sieur Giger.'

'He may indeed,' I respond.

Tong runs across to the window. 'DHL are here, M'sieur Giger. It will take only five minutes for him to ride the elevator.'

'Hurry, Tong. He mustn't know that I am inside.'

Tong closes the lid.

'Tong! Tong! The gun.'

The lid is lifted. Tong hands me the gun, 'M'sieur Giger, you don't know how to fire it.'

'I'll work it out. Is it loaded?'

'Yes. The cartridge is full. You have twenty shots, and the cartridge slots into the bottom of the handle. Just press it in, and make sure it catches.'

'Thanks, Tong. Be waiting down the alley with a car, for God's sake.'

'I will be there. Trust me.' I hear him looping the locks over the hooks and feel him pulling the strap up tight.

I can clearly hear Tong moving about in the apartment.

'Can you hear me, M'sieur Giger?'

'I can, clearly. Thank you, Tong.'

This means that he can also hear every move I make. A cough, sigh, yawn, or cry will give my position away. I start to sweat; I am terrified.

The doorbell rings.

'DHL collection,' announces the visitor. Tong opens the door, revealing the crate to the driver.

'Oh, I didn't realise it was going to be that big. I will have to get the trolley from the van. I will be back in a minute.'

'Did you hear that, M'sieur Giger?'

'I did. Tell him the keys to open the crate have been posted to the delivery address and will arrive tomorrow.'

'Good thinking, M'sieur Giger. He's coming back. Be careful.'

'I will.'

I am tipped onto the trolley and wheeled down the corridor to the elevator. The driver has been given all the instructions: Keep upright, be gentle, the keys are in the post, and most important of all, it must be delivered this evening. The courier has checked the address and promises delivery around eleven. My mind is totally occupied on staying alive. I sit rigid with fear. My legs are already cramping, and in the pitch darkness I can see nothing. The book I bought was a waste of money. I can feel the gun in my hand, and the knife for cutting the strap is tied to my thigh.

As the van draws away from the front door Tong leaps into action. His first task is to report to the embassy, to explain what he is going to do this evening and get approval and clearance that it is legal and safe. Halfway there he decides this is not a good idea. It isn't safe, and it definitely isn't legal. Nor can he trust anyone in the operations department at the embassy; the embassy staff are traitors, spies, and liars. Even a job at the embassy doesn't pay enough for the rent; people in Hong Kong will do anything for extra cash.

Tong swings his car down the side street and then takes the first right, meeting the main drag that takes him out of town. No, he isn't going shopping, but the shopping mall car park is the ideal place for him to dump his car. He walks back to the three-lane highway and turns left down toward the Avis rent-a-car office. A hire car will hide his identity should anyone get sight of the number plate. Plus, he needs a faster car than his own Fiat 500. Tong signs the agreement papers and is shown the operation procedure of the new, black, four-door BMW 530 iS.

After filling the tank he takes it for a spin. He wants to know exactly how it will handle in a chase around the back streets of Kowloon district 5.

After one confrontation with a tramcar and the upheaval of two rickshaws, Tong squeals the car to a standstill in a westbound lay-by. He rings the embassy to inform them that he will be on duty in half an hour and apologises for not signing in. No one answers his call. He knows the office will be empty; they will all be at home or partying by now. Leaving a message is simpler than signing in.

If I twist my wrist towards my face I can see the illuminated hands of my Brietling. It is ten past eight. Every muscle in my body is screaming for help. The word 'pain' does not describe my discomfort. I guess I must be in the DHL distribution facility. Surely I will be loaded onto the delivery truck within the next hour. There is no way I can sustain sanity in this position much longer. I can hear men talking in Mandarin. They are coming closer. A sharp bang on the lid sends shock waves through my body.

'Just this one and then go home,' orders one to the other. 'Do you understand? Deliver this one and then go home. Do not go home and deliver it in the morning.'

The second man laughs and responds in Mandarin, but I get the impression that he does understand. Over goes the crate. It is only fear that stops me yelling out. Whatever happened to 'Fragile – handle with care'? I hear the van engine burst into life and feel every bump as we drive out of the warehouse. We swing left, then right, and then left again. We stop, start, and then repeat the sequence over and over again. My watch shows ten forty-five as I feel the cobbles of the alleyway leading to the rear of the brothel. The engine dies. and the rear doors are prised open. An onrush of cold air fills the truck. I shiver and at the same time cross my fingers. I can't think of anything better to do.

'Wang, it's me with a DHL special delivery. Let me in. I am in a hurry.'

'Hello, bro. Why are you working so late?'

'Delivering this bloody thing to you. Give me a hand. It's a big bugger. Are you expecting it?'

'Not that I know.'

'What is in it?'

'The document says bed parts.'

'Do you have the keys to open it?'

'Apparently the keys have been posted to you. They will arrive tomorrow.'

'Okay, let's put it in the office overnight.'

'Where has it come from?'

'I don't know. I didn't collect it. The paperwork says it was shipped from Morocco. It came into the warehouse this evening, and I was told to deliver it immediately. Hurry up. I want to go home.'

'Mmmm, probably from the ambassador,' utters Wang.

I am tipped off the trolley and laid on my side for what seems an age. I have no idea where I am. I can hear men's voices and women laughing. There are many long periods of jibber-jabber, which I think is a TV. I am pretty sure there is no one close to the crate. I wait until one in the morning before thrusting the knife through the gap, sawing slowly and deliberately at the leather strap.

Just Do As You Are Told

Jean Claud doesn't go home after leaving the party. He goes instead straight to his office. On the way he calls Lafleur.

'Meet me at the office in half an hour. There is no time to waste.'

'What has happened? I am still at the ambassador's party.'

'Say bye-bye to the girl you are with and get here straight away.'

'This better be important,' threatens Lafleur.

'It is.'

Jean Claud sits behind his desk and pours out a whiskey. He is just about to flood it with dry ginger when he thinks better of it and pours it straight down his throat. The second one he does flood with ginger. Then he pours one for Lafleur. He can already hear him walking down the corridor.

'What is it, Jean Claud? Has the ambassador ruffled your feathers again?'

'He has done more than that. He has us in checkmate.'

'Explain.'

Jean Claud goes through the evening's meeting, stopping his story at the bedroom door before seeing Adeline strung up.

'Jean Claud,' Lafleur, shows his exasperation. 'Surely we expected this. Are you trying to tell me we have no plans to counter his move?'

'Our plan was to disgrace him and have him thrown out of the country, leaving all the businesses to us.'

'So maybe we have to do this sooner rather than later.' Lafleur shrugs as though it were common business practice.

Jean Claud stands up and places both hands on his desk. 'One, the plan has not gone far enough for us to take over the businesses just yet. Two …' He pauses and takes a deep breath. 'He has Adeline.' Then continues his account of the evening's events.

'So where is Adeline now?'

Jean Claud sinks back into his chair. 'She is still there, at the party, entertaining three or four of his gorillas.'

Lafleur is astonished. 'You left her there?'

'What else could I do? This way she will know nothing of our situation. And anyway, she was out for the count. The only way I could have got her out was to carry her. As it stands, she is in a situation that she has found herself in several times, and she has always managed to talk her way through it.'

'And where are the other three girls? And Linah?' continues Lafleur. 'I do understand your anxiety.'

'Look, let's not rush into this. Send Tom to wait for Adeline outside the front door. If she has not appeared by five o'clock, he has to go in and search for her. If he can't find her, then he has to call us immediately.'

'And what then?'

'I will think of something.'

'And what of the ambassador?'

'He has to be killed, but only at the right time and in the right way. Make it look like an accident or a suicide.'

'Killed by whom?'

'I don't know. Geiger, possibly.' Jean Claud pauses with a smile on his face. 'That could work. That could actually work!'

Adeline regains consciousness to find herself intertwined between three men. Two more are standing on each side of the bed with video cameras filming every move and recording every squeal she makes. She is forced into every conceivable sexual position and penetrated time after time.

'Enough, I am bored with this,' shouts the ambassador. He rises from the armchair in the corner of the room and instructs the cameramen to give him the discs. He tells the other three to get dressed and to get out. He waits for the door to close behind them before leaning over Adeline.

'You were very good tonight, my pretty. Your brothers will be very pleased with your enthusiasm to our little project. You are a very valuable member of the team.'

She groans as she rolls over to find herself face to face with the brutish man. She has more hatred in her for this man than she thought humanly possible. She searches for a sheet to cover herself, to hide her battered and bruised body. There isn't one. She has to lie there naked and hurting, hoping her ordeal is over. He runs his hand up her leg and thrusts his finger into her. She barely moves.

'Now Adeline, don't tell your brother about our extra business agreement. You tell him you enjoyed every minute of the party. You tell him you had fun. And if he sees your bruises, tell him they were just part of a game. Do this and you will be a very rich woman. If he finds out, through you or your girls, that you are making extra money' – he squeezes her throat with his free hand – 'you definitely won't be rich, and God only knows what you will look like.'

Adeline didn't understand what he was talking about.

'What business agreement?' she croaks through her swollen throat.

'The two hundred thousand dollars I have put into your account for your work this evening. You can give the other girls whatever you want from it. They too have worked very hard. Now get dressed and get out of here. I have some film I want to download onto the Internet. You are a star. You are big business, Adeline. You will give me a big return on my investment. But this has to be our secret.'

She still doesn't totally comprehend what he is telling her, but something tells her that she should be horrified. He stands and watches with amusement at her feeble attempt to fasten the buttons on her dress. Her fingers are shaking, her head is spinning, and her eyes fail to focus on the delicate button holes. Her shoes are nowhere to be seen. She gets on all fours to search for them under the bed.

'You look as pretty in that position as you do stretched out,' he taunts her. 'God was in a generous mood when he made you.' She hardly hears what he is saying. She has found her shoes. When she bends to put them on and sees the bloodstained bandage around her foot, she starts to piece together the events of the evening.

Half way down the stairs leading into the reception lounge, she collapses into Tom's arms. He has been searching the house for her as instructed. It is 5.15 am.

Who The Hell Are You?

The strap eventually splits free, and the buckle falls to the floor with a crack. The crate is on its side. It is easy for me to step out, except my legs refuse to work and my back will not straighten. The room is lit with a single bulb hanging from a wire; it is an office come storeroom. Because of the two-ring cooker in the corner it must also be used as a kitchen. Trash fills every corner and litters every surface. Luckily the door, which leads out into the corridor, is fractionally open, so I can see into the corridor which leads down to the front door. There is no one to be seen, but I can hear the girls in the reception lounge chattering in Mandarin. No one is speaking English or Moroccan. I close the lid of my crate, and with the key Tong handed me I manage to fasten the two padlocks around the brackets on the front. I have to remove the split belt from around its middle and hide it. Behind the bookcase amongst a pile of trash seems to be a good place. I am hoping the guys who will have to break it open it in the morning to find it empty will not know that when it arrived, it had a strap around it.

The doorbell chimes, and Wang walks from the girls' lounge and down the corridor. He peers through a small lens in the door and asks the same sequence of questions he always asks – unless it is his brother the DHL man, thank goodness.

'Mandarin or English?'

'English please,' comes back the reply.

'Cameron is in town.' I think, *they must change the name every day,* the door opens.

Wang escorts three English men into the lounge.

'Your embassy said you would be here at midnight. Where have you been?'

'God knows,' answers the most sober of the three. 'But we are here now, so show us the girls.'

The girls are used to dealing with drunken men, and drunken Englishmen are the easiest to deal with. If they have wives and children back home they will be feeling very guilty about what they are doing, and they are usually completely naive about the art of sexual pleasure. It is going to be an easy and rewarding night for the girls. They all thrust themselves forward, crossing their legs, sucking their fingers, and pulling down their dress straps. Each man picks one, and the dominant guy decides he wants two.

'You will have to pay for the second girl yourself,' demands Wang. 'Your company has only paid for one girl each. That will be ten thousand dollars up front.'

This isn't true, of course; this is Wang on the make. But in this case he wins. The drunken guy pulls out a wad of notes and picks the youngest-looking girl in the room.

'How old is this one?'

'Sixteen,' answers Wang. 'Be gentle with her.'

'You must be joking. I always fancied a mother and daughter.'

The girls giggle. She looks sixteen, but actually she is thirty-four. This is not a problem for her. She will put him asleep in ten minutes.

Each man staggers up the steps with the girls leading them. Wang returns to the lounge and sits amongst the four remaining girls. The first night he worked here he fondled them and joked with them, but after two years as doorman and bouncer this has lost its appeal. He just sits and watches TV whilst the girls powder their faces and repaint their lips. He kicks off his shoes and places them neatly in front of him in readiness for the doorbell ringing again.

I have to make my way to the top of the house, find the room Linah is in, and get us both out as quickly as possible. I take a deep breath and dash across the open lounge door, praying Wang and the girls don't see me. I reach the first step of the heavily carpeted staircase and run up the first fifteen steps two at a time. The girls in the TV lounge are still giggling. Wang is scanning through the TV channels. Nobody saw me. The second flight of steps are at the end of the first-floor corridor, this is also heavily carpeted. Red wall lights flicker between the dark mahogany doors. On each door is a plaque displaying the name of the suite. I see The Lady Godiva Grotto, The Bohemian Boudoir, and The Cleopatra Chamber. Hanging from the handles are cheap hotel 'Do not disturb' signs. Three of the five suites are occupied. The smell is overwhelming. A mix of dust, musk, and stale perfume blows through each door.

The corridor is dank; I tiptoe its entire length in silence. The idea is that if anyone unexpectedly comes out of one of the rooms, they will simply think I am one of the clients. I race up the second flight of steps and make it halfway down the second corridor, when a toilet flushes. Standing petrified, I wonder which one of the doors in front of me will open. Luckily none of them are bathrooms. The third staircase is bare wood. One swinging electric lightbulb is all that illuminates the entire flight of steps. Not only is it difficult to see, it is impossible to ascend in silence. My footsteps surely can be heard throughout the house. The interior decoration has changed from a sumptuous house of pleasure to a back-street East End slum. Paint is peeling off the doors. The bare plaster walls are damp and mouldy. A window at the end of the corridor is broken, and the night sounds of Hong Kong are coming straight in. A bird perched on the windowsill takes flight as I pass. It isn't the only thing that takes fright. The top floor is indeed directly under the roof; there are only two doors along this corridor. One is halfway along, and the other is on the opposite side five metres farther along. I put my ear to the first door. I can hear nothing, nor is there any light squeezing out from under the door. I put my nose to the large keyhole. The only thing I can smell is dust and damp. If Linah is in here, then she is dead, and I doubt that. I turn my attention to the second door.

On first inspection this door is the same as the other, but through the keyhole there is a dim light. I can see two large crates pushed together with a thin mattress laid over them. I can't get an angle to see anything else. I tap lightly on the door with my finger.

'Linah, are you in there? It is M'sieur Giger. I have come to take you home.'

I expect her to rush to the door and confirm her presence, but there is nothing – no movement and no sound. Maybe she is tied up; maybe she has been drugged. I turn the door handle and put my weight to the frame. It is locked and secured; there is no give in it whatsoever. I do have the gun. I can try and blow the lock off, but that will bring Wang up here, making our escape impossible.

Apart from the sounds seeping up the stairs from the rooms below, I don't feel threatened. I sink to my knees and start prodding the lock with my Swiss Army knife. I have only ever seen a lock picked on TV drama programs. They make it look so easy. I don't appear to be making any progress at all. I am on the point of despair when the handle turns and the door swings open. Standing there is a small, bleary-eyed Chinese girl dressed in western PJs and smelling rather pungent. She moves away from the door and steps back into the room. I follow her in.

'Are you alone? Is there anyone with you?'

She shrugs and perches on the edge of a frail dining chair. On the table there is a plate with the remains of a noodle dinner sticking to it. She picks up a can of Coke and drinks from it.

'Do you live here? Do you know a girl called Linah? She is from Morocco. She arrived last week?'

The girl looks at me as if I am stupid; it is obvious she hasn't a clue what I am talking about. I start to search the room. Apart from boxes and wooden crates, a cushion or two, and lots and lots of trash, there is nothing of importance and definitely nowhere for Linah to be hiding. Linah isn't here.

I peer through the shattered window that looks down onto the cobbled alleyway. It is deserted except for a black BMW at the end of the alley, which I hope is Tong waiting for me. All I have to do is to get out alive. I leave the girl sitting on the dining chair; she doesn't move, speak, or make any gesture. I guess she is either drugged, scared to death, or mentally retarded. Probably she is happy living here, glad of the food and having somewhere to sleep, not knowing or even caring why they want her in this room. Their plan could be to make us think Linah is imprisoned here. If that is their plan, then it worked, but now we know she isn't. But where the hell is she?

I can't waste any more time thinking about that; I have to get out of here.

I slip down the top three flights of steps with ease. I am prepared to use the gun if I have to. I grip it tight in my hand and push the cartridge up into the handle. The front doorbell rings, and Wang hastily puts his shoes on and the four girls check their makeup. At the front door Wang goes into his usual routine but doesn't get the response he is expecting. The three men outside are practically bashing the door down.

'Let us in Wang, you stupid man, before we blow your head off.'

Wang recognises the voice. He knows the man as 'King Kong', the ambassador's local bully. Wang slips the lock, but before he can open it the three men burst in, practically knocking it off its hinges.

'Where is it, Wang? What have you done with it?'

'What have I done with what?' he squeals as one of the men presses him up against the wall.'

'The crate, you stupid oaf, the bloody crate that came this evening.'

'Oh, that. It's in the office.'

'How can you accept a delivery without any paperwork, without any knowledge of what is in it, without contacting us to get clearance?'

'It looks quite innocent.' He squeals as the grip around his throat is tightened even further. 'It is locked! The keys are in the post. They will arrive in the morning.'

Wang is dragged into the office as the three men stand around looking at it.

'See, it's quite safe and secure. There is nothing to worry about.'

King Kong rattles the locks. 'Give me the keys.'

'I have just told you, the keys are in the post. They will arrive in the morning.'

The bully hits him in the stomach. As Wong crumples up he undercuts him, knocking him senseless to the ground.

'I can't tolerate incompetence.' He turns to his henchmen. 'Break it open.'

It takes only seconds for the lid to be forced open, revealing nothing but large pieces of industrial foam. Several of them fall out onto the floor. Wang and the three men stand in silence. It doesn't make sense. Obviously nothing has arrived in the crate, because it was locked; the only possible explanation is that something is going to leave in it. King Kong reaches for his mobile and thrashes at the keypad.

'Ambassador, there is nothing in it. It is empty. Nothing makes any sense.'

'Search the entire house – every room, every cupboard. Start with the roof. Good God, someone is going to swing for this if it is what I think it is.'

The ambassador, who is still in Morocco, is furious. 'Book me a seat on the first flight to Hong Kong,' he shouts to his secretary.

'First class, Ambassador?'

'Of course first class.'

By the Skin of My Teeth

The arrival of the three men has created pandemonium in the house. The four girls awaiting their next clients are screaming and huddled together in the far corner of the TV lounge. The TV is showing a science fiction movie, which has just reached a climax with a pitch battle between the Googleites and the Fromans. The three Englishmen are hustled out of their rooms as King Kong's men search the building. Each man has a half-naked girl wrapped around him. They are demanding an explanation.

'You can't treat us like this! We are English,' they shout, but to no gain. They are pushed aside, and the rooms are ransacked. It certainly looks and sounds as if World War Three has broken out.

Talking of breaking out, this is my chance to escape through the chaos. I am just about to push my way past the Englishmen when my shirt is grasped from the back and a pair of arms wrap around me.

I swing round, raising the gun ready to blow away anyone who has me covered. It is the little Chinese girl from the upstairs room.

'Take me with you, sir. Please take me with you,' she begs.

I grab her arm and pull her through the melee. I use my weight to push through the Englishmen; they think I am another client and the girl is a hooker. We reach the open front door and run for our lives down the cobbles towards the black BMW. If this car isn't Tong waiting for me, then God protect us.

As we run towards it, the engine starts up and the rear door swings open. I dive onto the back seat, dragging the girl in behind me. I don't even have time to look up and check that it is Tong. For a second it flashes through my mind that this is King Kong's car. We race down the cobbles and straight out into the middle stream of traffic on the expressway. We travel more than a mile before we pull up at the roadside and Tong leans over the front seat.

'You got her then, M'sieur Giger. Well done.'

'Well, not exactly,' I gasp, but now isn't the time to explain.

'Your place or mine?' jokes Tong.

'Yours.'

Sitting on Tong's sofa I feel an incredible sense of relief.

'Linah wasn't there,' I tell Tong. 'We have been watching the wrong place.'

Tong looks at me, confused. 'Then who is this?' He points at the girl.

'I don't have a clue.'

'M'sieur Giger, I was told you were attracted by women, but you have exceeded your reputation.' We both laugh.

'Let's have a coffee, and I'll tell you what happened.'

The girl jumps to her feet and follows Tong into the kitchen.

'She stinks, M'sieur Giger,' he declares on his return. 'Anyway, she insisted on making the coffee, so I let her.'

We can hear her searching the cupboards for cups and sugar. 'She seems to be quite capable.'

'Bath her later. Then we will see what she scrubs up like.'

I go through the events of the evening with Tong. I can tell he is impressed with my planning and courage.

'I will question the girl later and find out who she is and what she is doing.'

'She can speak English,' I tell him. 'She just plays at being helpless.'

'They all do. That's why we love them so much.'

'Ask her about Linah. Then let her shower.'

Her coffee tastes okay. She seems quite at home taking care of us. She explains that she was living in the rear room; her task was to take care of the girls and get them anything they needed. Last week another woman moved into the front room at the top of the house, but she was only there one day. She left early the next morning in the ambassador's limousine. The girl has no idea where they took her. It was then they moved her into the front room and told her to leave the light on at all times and to leave the curtains open. She laughs at this point. 'I don't know what curtains they were talking about.'

'Tong, I have to get back to Morocco. I am on the midday Malaysian flight. It will take forever: three hours to Singapore, four hours in Dubai, and then six hours to Morocco. Wake me at nine and take me to the airport, please.'

'M'sieur Giger, what are we going to do with ...' He gestures in the direction of the bathroom just as she comes out wrapped in a big, white towel. Her hair is long, sweeping around her shoulders. She looks very pretty with the biggest of smiles on her face.

'Oh, you will think of something, Tong. Maybe start by asking her name.'

'I'll put my mind to it, M'sieur Giger.'

'I think you can put more than that to it, Tong.' We both laugh at a horrible sexist joke.

Just an Empty Crate

The ambassador stands in front of the empty crate. He has come straight from the airport to the house to see for himself the shambles of the previous evening. He is furious with Wang.

'Have the keys arrived in the post?'

'No, sir.'

'Where is the girl who was living upstairs?'

'I don't know, sir. She has gone.'

'Did it not enter your head that you should check out the delivery with me?'

'No, sir. There was nothing out of the ordinary. My brother brought it in the DHL van and told me it had been shipped from Morocco.'

'Your brother!' The ambassador stared in disbelief. 'Your brother?'

'Yes sir, I trust him implicitly.'

The ambassador is mystified. 'Why should anyone send a locked empty crate?' He thinks for a minute. 'Is this exactly as the crate arrived?'

Wang winces. 'Yes! Except for the strap around it.'

'There was a strap around it? Where is the strap now?'

'I don't know. I just remember it had a strap around it.'

'Find it. It must be in here somewhere.'

Wang and the other guys search the room; it doesn't take long for them to find it behind the bookcase. The ambassador looks at it in rage.

'It's been cut, Wang. Can you see? Someone was inside the crate, cut the strap from the inside, climbed out, and locked it behind him. Do you think that is what happened?'

'Yes sir!'

The ambassador turns to his bodyguard. 'Take him away and get rid of him. I don't want to see this idiot again.'

Wang is dragged out of the room protesting and begging for understanding. Wang will never be seen again.

The ambassador's mind is racing. Who was in the box? Where is he now? The only solution that fits the scenario is that someone came to rescue Linah and intended to take her back. As Linah wasn't here, he took the Chinese girl. Maybe he thought the Chinese girl was Linah. In that case he didn't know what Linah looked like. The ambassador gives instructions to his gofer.

'Check out if the embassy employed any lowlifes last night to do a trick. And check out flights and passenger lists returning to Morocco today.'

The gofer leaves immediately. When the ambassador is in this mood and asks for something, he gets it immediately!

My mind is also racing, if the ambassador checks out passenger flight lists he will see my name along with Linah, which will have a no-show against it. He will know I was in the box. I just hope all the money I am making for him in Casablanca is of greater importance than me searching for my secretary.

The Search Continues in Singapore

Her name is Fern, and in less than one hour Tong has offered her a job as his live-in housekeeper. She snaps up the offer even before any mention of wages or money. I can't sleep. There is so much going through my head and so many more questions to ask Fern.

'How long were you working in the house?'

'I was there eight months, sir. He put me into the back room on the top floor. I was very lonely except for the times I spent with the girls. I had to take care of them, go to the shops for them, press their clothes, tidy their hair, sooth their aches and pains, pamper them, and listen to their tales of woe.'

'Who was Wang?'

'He was a nice guy and very kind to me. The ambassador made his life a misery. Everything that went wrong he got the blame for. The girls thought he was an idiot, but he wasn't. They would tease him and get him excited and then laugh as they insulted him. He hated them and the job.'

'What of you?'

'I look after myself, sir. I had a small cooker, so I could boil rice or vegetables. I had a washing machine and used to do Tong's laundry for him. In the evenings I would sit with the girls and hide when clients came in. I was very lonely. I thought my life had changed for the better when this other woman came to stay in the next room.'

'Did you meet her or speak with her?'

'No, she came and left so quickly. I got the impression that she was also surprised to be leaving. I heard the guards talking about her. They said she was Moroccan and was being groomed to be one of the girls, but they said she wasn't that kind of girl. She was intelligent, smart, and refined.'

'Have you any ideas where they might have taken her?'

'Well, I have worked for the ambassador for three years. He has several places in Hong Kong as well as houses in Singapore, Bangkok, and Kuala Lumpur. Of course, I have not been to these places. I have only heard the girls talking about them.'

'And you have no idea where she might be?'

'I do know the ambassador was going to Singapore that day she left. So if she is not in one of his houses here in Hong Kong, I would guess he took her to Singapore with him.'

I look at Tong. He knows what I am going to ask.

'Okay, I will check out his houses here. You take your flight and get off in Singapore.'

'Good plan, Tong. I can find the addresses he owns in Singapore from my team in Morocco. You can check out his houses here.'

I trust Tong, He is the nearest Chinese guy to an Englishman I have ever met. He is also bright, brave, and intelligent. During the drive to the airport we make plans on how to stay in touch and pool our findings. My head is so full of plans I totally forget that The Bear will now know it was me who had broken into his house. Unknown to me, King Kong has four men waiting for me at the airport. I am photographed entering the building, collecting my ticket, buying a book, and having a quick nap whilst waiting for the plane. They stream my progress back to the ambassador from their computers every five minutes. It is only when I take my seat on the plane and try to make small talk with the guy in the next seat that it becomes obvious he is one of the ambassador's men.

Does This Guy Never Pee?

'**A**re you comfortable, M'sieur Giger?' asks the air hostess. 'Is there anything I can get you – a drink, an extra pillow maybe?'

'No thank you. I am very comfortable and very tired. I will be asleep in a matter of minutes.'

She smiles and moves on to my travel partner and asks the same questions. He totally ignores her. She gives me a glance and a shrug of annoyance before moving off. All I have gained from the incident is that his name is Gorbachev. I guess he must be Russian.

No sooner has the hostess moved away than he reaches into his pocket, takes out a folded piece of paper, and passes it to me.

'Is this for me? What is it?' Still there is no response from him.

I unfold it and read the message scribbled across it.

'M'sieur Jacques Giger, you are a very lucky man to still be alive. You are playing a dangerous game that you have no respect for its consequence. I strongly suggest you get on with your task and stop wasting time and my patience by chasing Linah. May I introduce Boris. He has been instructed to escort you back to Morocco. He speaks no English. His task is to stop your consistent pursuit of Linah and make sure you are not taking Fern off the island. I want her back. Should you not obey my simple request, I have given him instructions to kill you. Such is the seriousness of your situation.'

It is simply signed 'A'.

We fly all the way to Singapore in silence; there isn't anything I can say. As you know, we Brits do not take lightly to being threatened and told what to do, especially by a man whom I dislike as much as The Bear. I must admit, the thought of being killed keeps echoing around in my head. I look over at Boris. He looks respectable, well dressed in a black suit and polished shoes, but he is so big and slug-like. Watching him operate his knife and fork during lunch illustrates to me how slow and cumbersome he is. In fact, his eating habits are primeval. Surely it can't be that difficult to give this guy the slip. I make a decision that I hope I will not regret. I am going to lose this dummy in Singapore and continue my search for Linah. I am British, Linah's safety is my priority and responsibility, and I love her. Did I say love her? For the next two hours I plan how I can escape him.

Given that I do not know the layout of the airport in Singapore, it is going to be an opportune escape.

But if I can leave him on the plane bound for Dubai, arrested or even dead, that would be perfect. He will not be a threat to me any longer. Goodness, I am planning my escape in the same way I plan my advertising campaigns. Only the consequences are different.

My phone vibrates; it is a text from Jean Claud in response to my request for details of the ambassador's houses in Singapore.

It reads, 'On your arrival in Singapore, call at the French consulate. They are expecting you. They have the addresses you need.'

Boris is trying to read the screen. Hey! I thought he couldn't speak English. I'm not so sure anymore. I mustn't depend on that fact any longer. The pilot announces our arrival in Singapore and goes through the complete sequence for all eventualities. Luckily I am travelling light. My only bag is the one in the locker above my head. I wonder what Boris has brought.

I follow the other passengers along the gangways towards baggage collection. At the end of the longest transporter I turn right and follow the signs to the transfer lounge. Boris is directly behind me duplicating my every step. I have three hours in which to lose him before the Dubai flight departs. I position myself opposite the departure monitors. The Dubai flight is displayed, but no gate has been designated. It does say the flight is on time. Boris sits next to me. To relieve the boredom I search out the loos. Boris follows me in and stands by the exit whilst I perform my toilet. *Does this guy never pee?* I ask myself. *Of course he can't. If he does, I will escape.* I admit my latest plan has brought a smile to my face, which is very evident as I walk past him and search out the bar.

'Two pints of English bitter, please, and two packets of cheese and onion crisps.'

I carry the tray over to a table for two and make myself comfortable. I push the second drink in front of Boris and invite him to join me. As I expect, he refuses, but he does accept the crisps. Ha ha ha, it's only going to be a matter of time before he needs a drink. It is half an hour, to be precise. He lifts his glass and takes a sip. I hold my breath in the hope that he likes English bitter. He does. When he is halfway down his glass, I order a second round and two more packets of crisps. Not that I think it will make a lot of difference, but I pour a vodka into his beer. If this guy is Russian he will live off vodka, and with his bulk he can probably absorb gallons of the stuff.

I Have Never Been Shot at Before

After two hours there are four empty glasses on the table. The departure monitor shows that flight EM502 to Dubai will be departing on time at 15.40 from gate 12. But before I go, another trip to the loo is called for. We go through the same procedure as before. Boris stands by the exit and watches my every move. Is this guy inhuman or what? Does this guy never, ever pee?

I am starting to panic; my opportunities for losing him are running out.

He sticks to me like glue during the twenty minutes we sit outside gate 12, and then he follows me step for step onto the plane. The air hostess welcomes me aboard and points me to my seat, which is towards the rear of the plane, next to the window, 52H. A risky plan shoots into my head. With Boris still behind me I slip into the loo and lock the door. Outside I can hear people shouting. Boris is standing by the door and refusing to move. He is blocking the aisle and holding up the loading procedure. No one can get past him. The captain is summoned, and two airline officials manhandle him up the plane towards the rear. Other passengers hurriedly follow, searching for their seats, stuffing the overhead lockers with their bags and coats, blocking the aisle, and giving me the distance between us that I had hoped for; I doubt he can even see the loo door from so far back in the plane.

Loading is chaotic, as it always is until everyone is aboard and seated. Through the slightly opened loo door I can see the passengers pushing past each other along the gangway. I can't see Boris; I pray he is seated and his exit is blocked. Now is my chance. It is now or never.

As luck will have it, when I burst out of the loo the air hostess is totally occupied checking a passenger's ticket. There is a problem with his seat number; this has created a small gap in the flow of boarding passengers. I push past her and knock three passengers sideways as I squeeze through the door. The steps down to the tarmac are cluttered with queuing people, but I can't let that worry me. I scream, 'Clear the way! Clear the way!' as I push past. Some drop their bags. Oh dear, I can see an old lady falling backwards onto a group of guys. I hope they catch her. One guy throws a punch at me; luckily he misses. Once on the tarmac I run for my life towards the airport terminal. Over to my right is an empty baggage tractor also heading towards the terminal. I manage to grab the back trolley and hoist myself aboard. My heart is pumping and my breath exhausted. I lie flat on the trailer and cast a glance back at the plane. Boris is standing at the top of the steps. He must have been watching me all the time, yet in the crush of passengers it has taken him until now to push through the people and get out of the plane.

I am just thinking that there is no way he can stop me now and this must be my lucky day when the wire grill across the back of the trolley lights up with flashes and sparks. My God. Boris is shooting at me! He must be emptying his entire gun on me. He is bellowing like a rampant bull. The frightened passengers boarding the flight are all laid flat on the steps. Some are screaming and others crying with fright.

The shooting stops. Boris is being wrestled to the ground by several airport officials. I can already hear the sirens of police cars racing towards the plane. I am in shock. I have never been shot at before. Blown up in a restaurant, yes, but never shot at. The grill across the trolley is buckled and scarred, but it has saved my life. Boris's aim was straight and true. I lie on the trolley and breathe a sigh of relief.

The tractor driver is oblivious to the series of events. He doesn't even know anything out of the ordinary has happened. He is wearing a headset, possibly listening to his favourite music, which must be against the airport rules. Thank God for disobedient tractor drivers. I hop off as we pass the entrance to the terminal and make my way to arrivals. The queue at immigration is short; there must be a lull in arriving passengers.

'Your ticket is for a connection to Morocco, M'sieur Giger. Have you changed your plans?'

'I missed my connecting flight, so I have decided to stop over in Singapore for a few days. Is that okay?'

'Of course it is, M'sieur Giger. I hope you enjoy your stay.'

I need a drink. As I sit in silence with my shirt sticking to my back, I sip a Laphroaig 1977 single-malt Scotch whisky. A police van races out of the airport, its lights flashing and siren pounding. I can only hope it contains Boris on his way to the police cells.

The Plan to End All Plans

Abel Lafleur always has a calming effect on Jean Claud. He is, after all, the accountant and can make figures say whatever he wants them to say. He has a calculating mind that is organised to the point of being boring, yet he has a focus and determination that is appreciated by all his family. He controls all the family's stocks and shares; he is a master at making money. He buys and sells as if he knows in advance what the market is going to do. Maybe he does.

'Regarding the auto franchise, Jean Claud' – Lafleur pats him on his shoulder – 'it has to be fixed that the ambassador wins the contracts. But just before he signs, he has to disappear. Then we will sign on his behalf. We will become the owners of the biggest automotive company on the continent.'

Lafleur pauses. 'Come on, Jean Claud, give me a smile. You should be very happy.'

'I am happy. I will be even happier when it belongs to us.'

Lafleur continues. 'We have to double our shares in the power company. That will give us a 66 per cent holding. When the ambassador is out of the equation we will automatically become the management of Moroccan Power. I am already controlling the import of oil and the selling of electricity not only to Moroccan companies but Libya and Algeria as well.' Lafleur can't resist a little giggle. 'We will actually be signing the power business over to ourselves, which will give us control of the bank.'

Jean Claud looks puzzled.

'Because the oil and power revenue is 80 per cent of the bank's business,' Lafleur explains. 'So your task is to win the North African auto tenders and take care of The Bear. Leave everything else to me. And of course I don't have to tell you: say nothing to Adeline or to Jacques Giger.'

'Of course not.'

'If she starts complaining about last night, be nice to her, but she has to understand what is at stake here.'

Jean Claud sits at his desk until Adeline arrives. He will sit there all day if necessary; he wants to be sure she is all right. It is four thirty when she appears. She looks smart and poised; he is amazed that she has recovered so quickly.

'How was the party?' he asks.

'That man is outrageous. I can't work with him any longer. You have to do something about him.'

'Did he hurt you?'

'No, but he should be shot for what he put the girls through. I will have to give them an enormous payment to pacify them.'

'Just tell me how much. They deserve every Euro.'

'That is very kind of you, Jacques. They will appreciate that.'

In fact Adeline has not been in touch with her girls. She has not heard from them, nor has she tried to contact them. She knows the state they will be in, and it has taken her all afternoon to pull herself together and to hide the hurt. She is sore where girls should not be sore. The men had not only been rough with her but they were not clean. She has spent two hours in the bath scrubbing herself with disinfectants and taking double the dose of 'morning after' pills. The bruises will heal; infection and pregnancy will not. She also has vague memories of her ordeal being filmed and talks of it going on the Internet. This scares her, but there is no way she can discuss the matter with her brother.

'Adeline!' He puts his arm around her in a way a brother does when he is going to tell his sister something she might disapprove of. 'The ambassador will be taken care of this summer. Be patient. It will all be worth it in the end.'

Adeline looks back at her brother. 'What do you mean?'

'We are taking him out of the equation. I have spoken with Abel. I promise you, the ambassador will be out of your life before the end of the summer.'

Adeline wants to believe him, but she isn't convinced. The Bear will not walk away from a deal like this. 'How are you going to do that? He is not going to lie down and hand it all over to us.'

'If need be, he will meet with an accident. He is a disgusting man.'

'Kill him?' Adeline recoils in shock.

'Not exactly. We have it all taken care of. And don't let Lafleur know you know. He will be angry that I have told you.'

Adeline is in shock. Never before has her family been involved in violence of any kind. But The Bear is a terrible man, and she doesn't want to see him again.

The Singapore Lady

Having been born and brought up in the grimy North of England, the cleanliness of Singapore is inspiring. People chew gum, but there is no gum on the pavements. People drink alcohol, but there is no fighting, spitting, or antisocial behaviour. When the green man flashes, two hundred people cross the road in a safe, unhurried way. When the light turns red, they all stop and wait patiently. I am sure there must be a police force, but on the streets they are nowhere to be seen. The people of Singapore are kind, helpful, patient, and understanding. The bookshops are full of students reading and learning. They sit on the floor of the shop or on the pavement outside. When their thirst for knowledge is quenched, they put the books back on the shelves. This is so unlike Northern England; where teenagers hang around street corners, coffee shops, and pubs. Of course, Singapore isn't innocent to the desires of its people. Somewhere there are houses of ill repute, and I need to find them. But at this moment in time I haven't a clue where they are, and I need help to find them.

At the French consulate I am made very welcome. They have all the answers I need. They know every strip club and gin joint, and more important, they know every back-street house and brothel, including who owns it and the names of the girls working there. The only thing they don't know is which house Linah is being held in.

The French consulate works very closely with the police department, and when I explain the reason for my search they immediately call the police department for assistance. As expected, when the police hear of my concern for Linah they offer to help and designate an officer to accompany me. They say I need a guide to take me around the city, to take me places where ordinary people don't go, and most important of all, to protect me. I sit in my hotel room and wait for Sergeant Allulu to arrive.

The receptionist at the Orchard Palace Hotel announces that Sergeant Allulu has arrived. I ask her to send him up.

'M'sieur Jacques Giger, I am so pleased to meet you.'

I am in shock; it never entered my head that Sergeant Allulu would be a woman. She is sophisticated, intelligent, and sexy. She could be an international businesswoman, a film star, or even a princess.

Wearing a large-rimmed, floppy straw hat, which is held off her face by a pair of the biggest flowered sunglasses I have ever seen, she stands in the doorway like a sunflower reaching up for the sun. Her three-quarter-length cotton flowered dress swishes out as she pivots on a pair of white sandals, the strap slightly wrinkling a pair of pink cotton ankle socks which are caressing her thin, elegant ankles.

'Well, are you not going to invite me in?'

'Of course! Please come in. Ehh, thank you for helping me. I am sure we will make a great team. Ehh, what should I call you?'

'Marie will do. And what should I call you?'

'Ehh! Jacques will do.' Goodness, I must stop this spluttering.

I order dinner for two from room service, and we talk long into the evening. Marie is the police department's secret weapon. She does anything, goes anywhere, confronts anyone, and never fails; failure is not in her DNA. Her experience of Singapore's nightlife is definitely appreciated. She knows the ambassador well and doesn't think Linah will be in any of his whorehouses. She also likes the ambassador and has met him on several occasions. She believes that if Linah is in Singapore, she will be staying in one of his villas. She looks at her watch and jumps to her feet.

'Come on, let's go do some work,' she suggests.

'What, now? It's eleven thirty!'

'Yes, now. We will go interview the girls on Orchard Road and find out if Linah is in one of the houses.' She unzips her pleated flower dress and slips on a leather miniskirt. 'If I look like them, they will be more relaxed and tell me more.' A pair of very high-heeled shoes completes her lady-of-the-night look. The receptionist's face is a picture of disbelief as we walk past her through the lounge and out onto the street.

Orchard Road is even more beautiful at night than it is during the day. It combines the natural with the modern, hi-tech world. If you want to meet a partner, you sit under a sixty-foot tree. If you want to be entertained in other ways, you sit at a pavement bar under a forty-foot TV screen. I sit in front of one such screen; Marie heads for the trees. I can't take my eyes off her. I watch her as she moves from one pavement bench to the next. The girls sitting there talk and laugh easily with her. She moves from one girl to the next until she is almost out of sight. On several occasions men approach her. She laughs along with them. One even kisses her. Her refusal must be the nicest put-down ever. They all walk away laughing and I am sure much happier for their encounter. After one hour she returns to my table.

'Linah is not working in any of the houses. No one has seen or heard of her.'

'Where do we go from here?' I ask.

'I don't know about you, but I am going home to sleep. I will pick you up at the hotel in the morning.'

'At what time?'

'One hour after I wake up. In the meantime, check with your man in Kowloon. I don't want to be stirring this place up if she isn't here.'

She then taps three numbers into her mobile, and within seconds a police car pulls up at the curve.

'My squad are never far away.' She smiles and disappears into the back of the blacked-out car.

Am I impressed or am I impressed? My mind is absolutely blown with admiration.

During the night I receive a report from Tong. He is convinced that Linah is not in Hong Kong. He has personally searched all known locations and questioned everyone on his surveillance team. No one has seen or heard of her. If that was his bad news, then his good news is that the ambassador has booked ten seats on a flight this afternoon from Hong Kong to Singapore, maybe I have arrived before him. Will Linah be with him? I will soon know.

I have overslept, which is not surprising considering all I did yesterday. I was exhausted when my head hit the pillow. Anyway, I don't expect to hear from Marie until lunchtime. It is one thirty before she is knocking at my door.

'The ambassador will be flying into Singapore at 5.10 this afternoon,' she reports as she breezes in. 'He has ten seats booked on flight EM440. My team will be positioned at the airport to observe him. Maybe we will get a glimpse of your girlfriend.'

'She is not my girlfriend. She is my personal assistant.'

'Same thing. You are screwing her, aren't you?'

'Absolutely not. Do you think I screw every girl I meet?'

'I don't know whether to be relieved or disappointed,' she teases.

'Anyway, Tong is convinced that Linah is not in Hong Kong.'

'Just as I thought. Anyway, the ambassador is hosting a prestigious party tomorrow evening on Sentosa Island in celebration of his horse winning the Singapore steeplechase on Saturday afternoon.'

'That is tomorrow. What if his horse doesn't win?'

'It will. He has three horses running. One will win, trust me. Now listen. There will be over a thousand people at this party. It is on Sentosa, a beautiful island just south of the mainland, and will conclude with a firework display. Everyone who is anyone in Singapore has been invited, so you will need a formal suit.'

'Are we going to gate crash the party?'

'No.' She giggles. 'The only way onto the island is by the cable car, and we will have to pass by the guards on the gate to gain entry. The road across the bridge will be closed. I have received a formal invitation, and I can take a guest.'

'You mean an escort?'

'I mean a guest.'

'Are you always on the guest lists of the aristocracy?'

'Of course. I am Marie Allulu, a sergeant in the Singapore Police Force. We will look, watch, and listen. It is an opportunity not to missed. Now prepare yourself. I am taking you shopping.'

'Shopping! I don't do shopping.'

'Then you will be going to the party naked. It's your choice.'

I pretend to consider the option. She laughs at my indecision.

'You English have such a silly sense of humour.'

'Swiss!' I correct her.

'You, my darling, are Mr Tim Collinwood, an Englishman working in Saudi Arabia as a creative director of advertising. I have done my homework. But your secret is safe with me!'

I order tea and cakes from room service and listen to her stories of Singapore. She was born in Hong Kong and at the age of seven left with her parents when they moved to Miami. She attended school in Florida until the age of seventeen and graduated at St Petersburg University with a degree in psychology and criminology, after which she applied for police training.

'What attracted you to the police force?'

'My father was a pathologist and worked very closely with the police in the forensic laboratory. He made it sound very exciting and even dangerous at times. I was never a goody-goody little girl. I was cheeky and adventurous. And as I grew older, I became uncontrollable. I gave my parents a very hard time.'

'So why did you come to Singapore?'

'We had relatives living here and came to stay with them during the summer of 2003. I liked it so much I decided to stay, and given my training with the Miami police, these guys thought it was their birthday when I turned up for the interview. The rest is history. I just got promoted up the ladder because of my cheek, daring, and … and whatever other attributes you might think I have.'

'I am sure you have plenty. I am very impressed.'

She blushes but denies it. 'I don't do blushing. Anyway, police work here is much simpler than in Miami. The people are better behaved and respect each other, so we don't have the trivial domestic nonsense to sort out which wastes so much police time in America. Maybe the occasional kid racer needs pulling in and his Ferrari confiscating, but it is usually big crime, international crime, smuggling, kidnapping, forgery, and drug running that we are involved in. So you can see how it is so easy to get to the top.'

'But everyone treats you as someone special.'

'I am special. I am the only female police officer in Singapore. As most of my superiors would like to get inside my pants, I seem to get what I want. A girl has to use what a girl has got to get what she wants.'

'And do they get what they want?'

'Ha. I have sent a couple of them home happy, but only a couple.'

'Lucky guys. You are definitely someone very special.'

Surrounded

We continue our conversation at the Thai Palace restaurant on Clark Quay whilst eating a prawn curry in a red Thai sauce, which is to die for. This must be one of the most beautiful eating-places on the planet. Eighteenth-century bistros sit beneath magnificent twenty-first-century sky scraping glass towers. In the centre of this amazing architectural mix sits a traditional English pub. Marie will not be drawn towards such a Great British institution, so we sit on the quay surrounded by hot flaming BBQs grilling the largest prawns, steaks, and chicken breasts you have ever seen. Frothing beers and chilled wines are carried on trays held high above the heads of the waiters, who risk life and limb crossing the quay road from the bars and restaurants lining the road to the diners who are laughing and joking along the edge of the quay. They strut across in a continuous chain, entertaining the tourists and residents alike with silly gestures and funny dance steps. Everyone is laughing and is thoroughly enjoying this relaxed, beautiful place. Now I can understand why Marie chose to live here in Singapore.

We are sitting at a long table which seats five people along both sides. The end of the table overhangs the harbour, and the water gently swishes up the stonework with every passing boat. Above our heads there is a large rectangular umbrella stretching the entire length of the table. During the day it will shield the diners from the sun, which is essential, but now it is restricting our view of the laser light show streaking out into the heavens from the scraper tops. It also hides our view of the full moon, which is illuminating the street, forming dancing shadows which only add to the beauty of this romantic, stimulating environment. We are sitting on one long bench, so close to each other I am actually touching the people dining on both sides of me. They could have been beautiful Asian girls, but on this occasion one is a fat, sloppy American off one of the cruise ships, the other a young man engrossed in playing a game on his mobile. Marie is sitting opposite. The other diners on our table are coming and going all the time, so our table changes its personality every five minutes. I find it captivating, listening to tourists ordering from the selection of Thai meals in their different languages, most making a complete hash of it. Luckily for them the waiters can understand, and orders are delivered as requested.

My conversation with Marie has changed many times, from her work to our search for Linah and from places of interest to fashions, food, and the cost of living. The history of Singapore fascinates me; I could sit here and listen to her all night. It is Marie who first becomes aware of the three men sitting at the far end of our table. They are dressed in Arabian white *thobes* and red chequered *guttras*. They seem to be more interested in us than in their food, which was served earlier and is now going cold. Because of the umbrella their faces are in shadow. All we can see are their hands and the dishes of untouched food surrounding them.

The young couple at the quay end of the table, who I guess are on honeymoon, stand to leave, and immediately two more Arabian-dressed gentlemen take their seats. Marie scribbles a message on her napkin and passes it to me. The first word is written in large capitals: 'LAUGH'. Underneath she has written, 'Pretend this is a joke.'

The rest of her text is scribbled and almost illegible. 'I don't like the look of these Arabian guys. I think something is going down. I will visit the loo and call HQ.' I screw up the tissue and laugh.

'Very funny. You should be on the stage,' I respond, elaborating on her instruction.

'I'll be back in a minute. I must pay a visit to the ladies' room. Order the sweet, something cold and fresh, like a banana split loaded with toffee ice cream. Can I trust you to do that?'

'You can. But don't be too long, or I will be eating both portions.'

She laughs as she trips across the road, threading her way around the beer-carrying waiters coming and going from the bars.

Mistaken for a Drug Baron

'Hi, Marie. Are you enjoying your evening?' Marie's captain is not only her boss but also her best friend; he thinks the world of her.

'Very much. M'sieur Giger is great company. We are just catching a bite to eat on Clark Quay before I take him shopping for a suit. He must look the part at the ambassador's party tomorrow evening.'

'What can I do for you, Marie? Why are you calling me on your day off?'

'I was wondering if we have heard of anything going down tonight.'

'You take your work too seriously, Marie. Enjoy your evening.'

'I can't, you know that. So! Have we heard of anything?'

'There has been a drug heist. Two million dollars' worth of cocaine has gone missing, so our local Saudi godfather is very angry. He has his men out looking for the gang who robbed him.'

'And have we any idea who this gang is?'

'Apparently not. This is a new gang on our patch. All we have is a picture of its leader sent to us by the American FBI. He is the leader of an American gang operating in Chicago, and they believe he is now in Singapore.'

'What does he look like?'

'Well, looking at his picture I suppose he looks very much like M'sieur Giger: tall, fair, white-skinned, and—'

Marie freezes. 'Ron, I think we are in the middle of this gang war. We are eating at Clark Quay, and five Saudi guys have just encircled us. They are more interested in M'sieur Giger than in their meal. This is why I am ringing you.'

'You must get out of there. They have probably mistaken M'sieur Giger for the American gang leader.'

'They are not going to let us just walk away. Can you come and get us?'

'The boys are on their way to you. Which table are you sitting at?'

'Third one down on the left, overlooking the water.'

'Be prepared to make a sharp exit.'

I am relieved to see Marie walking back across the quay towards me. She sits at the table.

'Did you order dessert?'

'No, I couldn't catch the waiter's attention.'

'Good, let's give it a miss.' She reaches out across the table and opens her hands. Her palms are sweating, glistening in the lights; it is obvious she wants me to take hold of them. I didn't expect her to be so forward. She stares into my eyes and is trying to tell me something, but my male ego is not picking up her intended message.

I am excited at the prospect of her advance. It is a super summer evening. The warm air is blowing off the sea. The clanking of the yachts pulling at their anchors is hypnotising, and now romance could be in the air. Across the harbour I can see a speedboat weaving in and out of the hundreds of anchored boats. The patterns it is making in the water are spectacular as it loops and turns towards us.

The other guys on the table are unimpressed by the spectacle; it is Marie and I who seem to be captivating their attention. They are watching our every move. Now we have eight Saudis sitting around us.

The crowds scatter as three Jeeps force their way down the quay; tourists and strollers alike separate to let them through. Marie squeezes my hand tightly. Her hands are frozen, yet sweating. She is either stressing, anxious, scared, or excited. I wish I knew which.

The three vehicles squeak to a stop opposite our table, and nine men jump out and position themselves at the four corners of our table. The Arabs try to leave but are gently persuaded to stay seated by rifles being pushed into their backs. Marie pulls me to my feet and practically drags me to the edge of the quay. There is a flight of stone steps leading down to the surface of the water, where a small wooden platform floats up and down in the waves. Without letting loose of my hand, she guides me down the steps. The approaching speedboat swoops round, throwing up a spray of black, salty sea, and pulls alongside the now-heaving platform. Written clearly along its hull are the words 'SPF Harbour Patrol'. Two police officers help us aboard, and without a word being spoken we speed off into the darkness.

I glance over my shoulder and through the fine mist of spray thrown up from the launch's pair of powerful engines, I can see the armed police climbing back into their Jeeps. The Saudis are sitting like school children in detention, not moving and still not eating.

'We didn't pay for our meal' is all I can think of saying.

'Don't worry about it. The boys will pay our bill,' Marie reassures me.

She eventually lets go of my hands and pats my knee.

'I don't feel like shopping tonight. We will do it tomorrow.'

Back in my hotel room Marie explains that the Saudi guys had mistaken me for an American gang leader who had stolen cocaine from them. Her captain had made the decision to freeze the action and get us out of there.

'We don't usually get involved in gang warfare,' she explains. 'We are quite happy to watch them shoot each other. But tonight we were in the thick of it, far too close for comfort. We couldn't arrest them because we have no proof as to their intention. We don't want to kill them because they will declare war on us and turn on the police department and our families. So tonight you saw the Singapore police doing what they do best: simply defusing a situation. Are you impressed?'

I am impressed, but I suppose I am slightly disappointed that my hopes of a romantic evening have been dashed. But yes, I am definitely impressed. And I am still alive. There is always another evening for love.

How to Win the Steeplechase

Three TV channels are covering the steeplechase; it is one of the most prestigious and glamorous events in the city's calendar. The excitement it is creating is equivalent to an English royal wedding, the university boat race, and our New Year's celebration all thrown in together.

'So is the race fixed?' I ask.

'I doubt it. There are too many big players – Saudi princes, Chinese government officials, and Japanese businessmen. You don't cheat on these guys.'

'So how does the ambassador know his horse is going to win?'

She pats me on my knee, which is becoming slightly repetitive, and leans over to whisper in my ear. 'He has the fastest horses and the most experienced jockeys. That is all you need to know. Now enjoy the race.'

The ambassador's horses come in first, third, and fourth. He takes home three million dollars.

Before we ride the cable car at Mount Faber, our names are checked against the guest list by a young, diligent soldier.

'Miss M Allulu and guest.' The guard looks in my direction and asks me for my name.

'Sergeant Bolova, Thomas Bolova,' answers Marie before I have time to say the wrong thing. She slips a card into my hand. It is a police identification card to prove my new identity. The soldier recognises the badge immediately.

'Enjoy your evening.'

We join the queue for the cable car. There are ten guests in front of us; it will soon be our turn to fly.

'Thank Mr Bolova for his badge,' I whisper. 'Do you always think of everything?'

'One of us has to.'

Now it is our turn to enter the swinging capsule. Two obese Chinese guests climb in behind us, rocking the car to the limit of its swing. They are full of fun and can't resist a joke with Marie. One pulls out a mobile from his waistcoat pocket. They insist on a picture of us so they can remember our meeting. Marie plays at being shy and covers her face, but not me; I am as excited as they are.

The view over Keppel Harbour is amazing. As we fly over the cruise ships tied to the quay, I can see their passengers walking the decks, swimming in the pools, and even playing tennis at this time of night. Cruising is definitely an experience that appeals to me.

We say good-bye to our new Chinese friends as we walk up to Marina Park.

'Nice guys,' I remark.

Marie gives me a disgusted look. 'If they are who they say they are, then they are nice guys. If they aren't, then the ambassador will have a picture of you on his computer by now.'

'Oh my God, how stupid can I get? It never entered my head. What can we do?'

'Enjoy the evening and pray.'

This is the party of parties; there must be well over a thousand people on the hill. Several stages are lit with top groups singing their latest hits. High-wire artists are walking from treetop to treetop. There's bungee jumping and fairground rides, including a helter skelter and a waltzer just like the ones we had back home when I was a child. Beautiful half-naked girls are weaving in and around the crowds offering free cocktails from silver trays.

'The chances of finding Linah here are practically nil. I suggest we enjoy ourselves,' screams Marie in my ear making herself heard above the excited crowds.

'Where is the ambassador?'

'He might not even be here. This is his way of saying thank-you to all the people who support him.'

We walk around the park for two hours. Everyone knows Marie. She chats with several of the girls and flirts with a couple of local bankers who are much the worse for drink, but no one has any information about Linah's whereabouts.

Her mobile lights up with an incoming call.

'Who is it?' I ask her.

'It's my boss. There has been a murder in the city. I have to go. I am afraid you will have to find your own way back.'

'I will come with you.'

'So sorry, but you can't.'

'Why not?'

The helicopter hovering above my head answers the question for me.

'My chauffeur has arrived. I will call you tomorrow.'

She rushes off towards the helicopter, which has landed beyond the trees. The partygoers think it is another attraction; they shout and applaud as she runs over to it and clambers in. Then she is gone.

Buried Alive

I am lost without her. I know no one, and I definitely don't know my way back to the hotel. I can see the cable car station down the hill, so I decide to say farewell to the festivities and make my way home. I am not aware of anyone watching or following me. I am totally oblivious to a group of men walking down the slope behind me. A large, hairy hand grips my face, and a white cloth is held to my nose. The smell is appalling. I don't remember turning or struggling. All I do remember is coughing, gasping for air, and being lowered to the ground. My night on Sentosa ends very abruptly.

I regain consciousness with a headache beyond description. The room is dark and my vision blurred. From the little I can see, I am guessing I am in a warehouse or storeroom. Wooden crates and cardboard boxes surround me. My hands are tied behind my back and my ankles strapped together.

'Welcome back to reality, M'sieur Giger. I hope you enjoyed the party. I am so sorry you had to leave so early, but you have a flight to catch.'

I try to speak, but my mouth is gagged with packing tape. I can only see the silhouette of the man who is speaking to me, and I don't recognise his voice. He is calm and controlling. There is a click as a light switch is operated; a box at my feet is illuminated. It is a coffin.

'As you were so happy to arrive in Hong Kong in a box, M'sieur Giger, we thought it appropriate that you should leave in one. I am sure that will meet with your approval.' The coffin lid is raised to reveal a gas cylinder inside.

'You must be joking,' I try to say, but it comes out as a muffled grunt.

The man laughs.

'I knew you would approve. Lift him in.'

I have no idea how many people are manhandling me into the coffin. There is at least one on each limb, and another rips off the gag. A medical mask is placed over my nose and mouth. The oxygen cylinder is turned on. The air is cold and has a strange scent.

I am aware of the lid coming down on me.

'Wait!' shouts the man.

It flashes through my head that this is a joke and they are just trying to scare me. I am expecting to be lifted out. I can't believe anyone would lock me in a coffin. The thought of being buried alive is the most horrendous thing that I can imagine. I was once in an elevator that stopped between floors. The first five minutes I treated as a joke, laughing with one of the pretty secretaries from the management suite who was in with me. After thirty minutes I was a quivering wreck. The girl, whose name I cannot remember, was wiping my brow and explaining that the fire brigade had been summoned and we would be out of there in minutes. It was at this moment I recognised my fear of small spaces was something I would have to live with.

The man leans over me. He is so close all I can see are the whites of his eyes staring down at me.

'M'sieur Giger, the air in the canister will last for forty-eight hours. I suggest you breathe very slowly and lightly, just in case your flight is delayed. Now enjoy your trip. We don't want to see you again.'

I think at first he is The Bear, but his voice is too light, and he has a strong American lilt.

To my horror, the lid closes. I can hear hammering around the sides. I am absolutely scared to death and already drenched in sweat. My one saving grace is I am not totally aware of what is happening. My head is swirling, and my thoughts have gone all abstract. In this semiconscious state I recall a visit to the dentist when I was a child. On that occasion a pretty nurse was holding my hand and counting down from ten in my ear. This is not the case today. As the air in the coffin fills my lungs, I fall into a deep sleep.

Tricked

'Captain, I am airborne. What is going on, and where do you want me to go?' Marie speaks into the microphone attached to her head kit.

'Hi! Marie, sorry to spoil your night out. We have received a call for help from the captain of the *World Eclipse*, the White Star cruise liner tied up in the harbour. He says there has been a shooting at the swimming pool on the first-class deck at the rear of the ship. He reports three people are dead and a man with a handgun is hiding somewhere aboard his ship. He has sealed the exits and withdrawn the gangway, so the gunman is trapped. This makes him very dangerous, especially to anyone who might be trying to apprehend him. I have three patrol cars racing to the ship, but it might take them some time to get through the traffic. Armed dog teams have also been dispatched. I have got you clearance to land on the quay next to the ship. Chances are,

Sergeant Allulu, you will be the first officer on the scene. Seal the ship; wait for backup, and don't go it alone. Goodness, what am I saying? I don't have to tell you what to do.'

'Did you hear that, Dirk?' Marie pats her pilot on the shoulder. 'We have to go to the harbour.'

'Yes, Sarge. We are already on our way.'

As the helicopter circles above the luxury liner, Marie can only marvel at this beautiful vessel. Dirk is looking for a place to land but at the same time avoiding the cable car. It usually doesn't run after dark, but tonight is an exception because of the ambassador's party. Marie doesn't speak to him; she knows a distraction at this time could be fatal. She scans the rear of the ship. She can see the swimming pool but can't see any disturbance on or around the deck. The swimming pool area is brightly lit. There are a few swimmers, but most of the guests are relaxing on loungers, sitting at the bar, or dancing to a pop trio playing on a brightly coloured stage in the far corner of the deck.

On the bridge she can see the captain and several of his officers mulling over controls and charts. They all appear to be very relaxed.

'Fasten your seat belt, Sarge. We are landing between those two cranes. Can you see the three guys with the lights? They are guiding us down. Hold on. We will be secure in seconds.'

The helicopter gently touches down, and the rotor blades are turned off. Marie knows she has to wait for the pilot to give her clearance before clambering out.

'Okay, Sarge, out you go. Run in a straight line away from the copter so I can see you before you turn towards the ship.'

Marie knows how to get out of the police helicopter; she has done it many times. As she runs along the side of the ship two patrol cars come racing up behind her, lights flashing and sirens blaring. They all arrive at the gangway at the same time. The ship's steward, whose job it is to welcome passengers back on board from their night out in the city, is more amused than surprised.

'What's going on? I hope you have tickets,' he jokes.

The dogs, armed officers, and Marie rush past him and up the ramp. By the time they get to the top, the captain is waiting for them.

'Good evening, my name is Captain La Vinci. Welcome aboard the *World Eclipse*. What can I do for you?'

'You called us and reported a shooting at the top-deck swimming pool.'

The captain looks bemused and shakes his head.

'I didn't call you. There has not been a disturbance of any kind on my ship tonight.'

Marie reports back to her captain.

'You must search the ship. Check it out for yourself. Are you sure this guy is really the captain?'

'Leave it to me, boss. I'll get to the bottom of this.'

Marie turns to the captain.

'This is a very serious incident, Captain. I am afraid we will have to search your ship. And can you and I go to your office? I will have to read your log and check your staff and passenger lists.'

'I can't stop you, but please be as discreet as possible. My passengers have paid a lot of money for this amount of luxury. It's going to take you a long time. It's a big ship, and I have eight hundred staff and nearly two thousand passengers on board.'

Marie sighs. 'It has to be done.'

With computer printouts piled up in front of her, she suddenly thinks of me. She takes out her mobile and dials to check on my whereabouts but gets no response.

Off the Face of the Earth

'Sarge, we are wasting our time here. I am going to send the boys home. It must have been a hoax call.'

'Okay, Marie. It's your call. Send the guys back to patrol. Get back to your date, and enjoy the party.'

'Sarge, you must be joking. It's five in the morning.'

'Goodness, I am so sorry to have spoilt your evening. I have completely lost sense of time. It has been a crazy night. We have had a gang shootout down town resulting in three deaths. I haven't read the reports yet, but I am guessing the lost marijuana has turned up.'

'Have we heard from M'sieur Giger? I left him on Sentosa. I hope he found his way back to the hotel.'

'Marie, I don't have time to nursemaid your boyfriends! He is totally your responsibility. I hope for your sake nothing has happened to him. If it has we will have the French embassy on our backs.'

'I'll call at his hotel to make sure he is OK. And Sarge! He isn't my boyfriend. You are.'

'I wish.'

And he does wish. He has always had a crush on Marie, but so have all the other officers in the force.

Marie and the patrol team shake hands with the captain of the *World Eclipse* and thank him for his patience. The boat is still active with passengers swimming and drinking on all three decks.

'Your passengers never sleep. They must all be police officers,' jokes Marie.

'The ship never sleeps,' replies the captain.

'Well, I do. Thank you again for your help. We have to check out every report.'

'I was wondering,' said the captain hesitantly. 'Would you care to be my personal guest at the captain's dinner tomorrow evening? It is our last night in Singapore before we head for Hong Kong.'

Marie smiles politely. 'I would have enjoyed that very much. But unfortunately I am far too busy, and for me to take another night off would not be acceptable. Take care, Captain, and happy sailing.'

The patrol team stare at each other. They all have the same thought in their heads. If the captain of the *World Eclipse* can't pull her, what chance do they have?

'Where is my helicopter?' asks Marie, scanning the quay.

'It left hours ago. You will have to slum it in the back of the patrol car.'

'Come on, then. You can drop me at the Orchard Palace hotel.' Both men leap towards a door, opening both rear doors for her to enter.

'You're trying too hard, guys. I can open my own doors. You do the driving, okay?'

Marie is spoilt rotten by her fellow officers. They all think the world of her and she of them. With a quick ruffle of their hair, Marie slumps into the back seat of the squad car as they speed off towards Orchard Road.

Marie finds the receptionist fast asleep, her head laid on her hands over the counter. She is coming to the end of a double shift after agreeing to relieve her friend who is celebrating her wedding anniversary. But after twenty hours of monotony, she has finally succumbed to exhaustion. Marie taps her hand and shows her police ID.

'Oh! Good morning, Sergeant. I know who you are. You don't have to show me your ID. Are you alone? Where is M'sieur Giger?'

'I was just about to ask you the same question. Is he not in his room?'

The receptionist checks the key rack.

'His room key is still here. He has not come back yet. Anyway, I thought he was with you, so I wasn't concerned.'

'I have been calling his mobile every ten minutes. He doesn't answer, so I presumed he must be asleep.'

'Sorry, Sergeant. He is still out on the town.'

'Could I have the key to his room? I need to check.'

'It isn't hotel practice to hand out keys, but I suppose in this case he won't mind.'

'Thank you. I will bring it straight back.'

Marie rushes to the elevator just as the doors are closing. Luckily someone on the same floor has summoned the lift. She is on the fifth floor within seconds. Pushing past the waiting guest, she rushes down the corridor to suite 12. The room has been ransacked. The bed is overturned, and every drawer has been emptied onto the floor. Her experience tells her that the room was searched in a hurry. It is obvious to her that they were looking for something specific. It could be something as simple as money or valuables, but she doubts this. They were probably looking for an ID, a passport, or even a gun. And if they left the room in such a mess, they must not have expected anyone back in the near future. She checks in the bathroom and opens the remaining two wardrobe doors and is relieved not to find a body.

'Sarge, Giger is missing. He didn't make it back to the hotel. Have you any ideas? Did the boys explain to the gang at the wharf the other night that M'sieur Giger was one of us and had nothing to do with their stolen drugs?'

'As far as I know they cleared him from suspicion. I doubt the mafia has anything to do with him.'

'Sarge, I have a sneaky feeling that the hoax with the cruise ship last night was a plot to separate us, a way of getting M'sieur Giger on his own. Why should anyone want to do that? He is only a guy looking for his missing secretary.'

'Marie, calm down. I am pretty sure he will turn up when his hooker throws him out. But just in case, I will check the passenger lists of tonight's outbound flights, especially to Casablanca. Marie, I suggest you go directly to the airport. I know there is a flight to Morocco at nine thirty. You still have time to get there. Eyeball every passenger. He might be leaving under a different identity or leaving against his will, so look for people very close to each other, people who could be linking arms or tied together.'

Marie slams the bedroom door shut as she runs back to reception. Throwing the keys to the receptionist, she gives instructions that she has to be contacted should I arrive back.

'And don't let anyone into his room until I get back,' she shouts as she runs out to the waiting patrol car.

The passengers have just been called to board flight AM230 to Morocco when Marie arrives. She stands next to the ticket steward at gate 9 watching all three hundred passengers filter past onto the plane. There is no one acting peculiarly, nothing suspicious, and definitely no M'sieur Giger. It never enters Marie's head to check out the freight being loaded into the hold. If she had turned her head and looked out through the window behind her, she would have seen a coffin lifted on board addressed to a M'sieur Jean Claud Chapelle.

Death Is Scary

Will I survive the next forty-eight hours? I can't imagine anything that comes close to my predicament in terms of terror and torture. To be nailed into a coffin, unable to move, tied hand and foot will be the cause of many a sleepless night if I survive. I keep gaining consciousness; a few thoughts pass through my head. What is this gas I am breathing? It must be doped to keep me calm? What is the vibration I can feel? My body aches. I wish I were dead.

Having no sense of time is a nightmare in itself. How long have I been here? When will the gas run out? What do I do if I want to pee? I slip in and out of consciousness. I am oh so cold, so cold. My breath is crystallising on the inside of the facemask. I can hear voices. Is someone coming to release me? There is so little room in here I can't even bang on the side of the box or kick on the top to draw attention to myself. The coffin is padded. I can hear my mobile;

someone is sending me a text. Yes, my mobile is in my inside pocket. They must have overlooked it. I can't reach it. I have no idea who it is. It rings several times, just making matters worse. Every time it rings I wake up; I would rather sleep through this ordeal. Then it starts beeping. The battery is low. This is my only sense of time. It must be forty hours since I last charged it, and that was just before Marie came to the hotel. I must have been in this box for thirty-two hours. Oh my God!

I regain consciousness again. I can hear scratching on the wood. it sounds like a seagull walking along the roof of my holiday lodge in the Lake District. I can hear voices, French voices. The box is being rocked, and then light floods my eyes. I can't see a thing. I have to screw them up as tight as possible to stop the pain. Then I hear a voice.

'Welcome back, Jacques. You gave us quite a scare.'

It takes me several minutes before I can open my eyes and focus. Someone is removing my facemask. The air is clean and fresh. My head starts to clear almost immediately, but it still takes me ten minutes before I can sit up. My senses are coming back as oxygenated blood reaches my extremities. My fingers are working again. I can touch and feel, and my toes are slowly warming up. Jean Claud is staring down at me. I have never been so pleased to see anyone in my entire life.

There is a piece of notepaper clipped to my chest. Jean Claud picks it up and reads it. He laughs.

'It appears someone doesn't like you, Jacques. It says "Keep control of your boy … or else." Whatever have you been up to now?'

I don't want to report my last two days with Jean Claud just now. My complete obsession with Linah has nothing to do with him, and my mental and physical condition are off the scale. Just to concentrate and focus clearly is proving very difficult. I request a taxi home and promise to tell Jean Claud about my visit to Singapore later.

'I can't wait to hear your story. And the French embassy are calling me every hour. Apparently the Singapore police have activated a massive search for you. Shall I tell them you have arrived home safe and sound?'

My puddled mind spins round to Marie. She must be frantic with worry. I didn't want to leave her in this way. Maybe I can make contact with her later. I hope so.

'Yes! Please tell the embassy I have arrived in Casablanca. Make up a story that I had to get back immediately.'

'I'm not going to tell them how you arrived. First, they wouldn't believe me. And second, I am not spending the rest of the day filling in police reports.'

Thankfully Tom appears at the door. 'Tom! Just on cue. Take M'sieur Giger home in the limo and then come back for me.'

'Yes, sir.'

All I Want Is Time to Think

T om drops me in the car park, and Kamal helps me up to my apartment. I thank him and lock the door. I need time to think before blabbing about my time in Hong Kong and Singapore. The phone rings almost immediately. That is the last thing I need, but it says 'Amelia calling'. I think twice before answering, but eventually I pick it up and place it to my ear without saying a word.

'M'sieur Giger, it is me, Amelia. Are you there? I need to see you. Oh, please be there.'

'I am here, Amelia. I have just got home this minute. How are you? How was the party?'

'M'sieur Giger, it was a nightmare. I need your help. I don't know what to do. Can I come to you?'

'Of course you can come. I need to talk with you also.'

'I will come as soon as it is dark. You will understand why later.'

'Come whenever. I might be asleep. Text me when you arrive.'

'Yes. Oh, thank you, M'sieur Giger. I will be with you in about one hour.' The phone dies.

My head is filled with thoughts of Linah. I hardly know her, yet I could be in love with her. She is the only girl I have not had in my bed. Is that because I have so much respect for her? She has dignity, intelligence, and massive appeal. Her innocence is extremely provocative. Her heart-shaped lips and long black hair give her the appearance of a Walt Disney princess. She is far too young for me, but that doesn't seem to bother Moroccan girls. My caring for her is not only that of a boss towards his secretary but more of a father towards his daughter.

I drop my head into my hands. She is in danger because of me, held against her will by a tyrant, God only knows where. My scattered mind is incapable of thinking straight, let alone deciding what I should do next.

My mobile vibes. The text reads, 'In the car park, on my way up.'

It is Amelia. I must have fallen asleep. It is dark outside. I hold the door open when I hear her footsteps tripping down the corridor.

'Oh, you poor thing,' I say as she collapses into my arms. She has two black eyes and a three-inch cut down her right cheek. 'Have you been to the hospital with that?'

'You must be joking. They would call the police.'

'Let me take a look at you.' She screams as I grip her arm and press on a series of bruises.

'They used me like a rag doll, M'sieur Giger. I am black and blue all over.'

'Let me see to your face, and then I will run you a warm bath. Then you must tell me everything. Have you seen Adeline?'

'I haven't seen or spoken with her. I left the villa only two hours ago. I have been locked in a room there for two days. I didn't know what to do. I have been calling you every hour.'

'Goodness! You poor thing.'

'I can't go see Adeline looking like this. I am also too frightened to go to my apartment in case those guys follow me and find out where I live.'

She looks up at me and bursts out crying.

'Oh, M'sieur Giger.'

'Amelia, Amelia, you are safe now. Let me take care of you.'

I run a hot, soapy bath and then pick her off the bed and gently lay her in the water. I dribble the warm water over her bruised body and run my hands across her shoulders and around her neck. I can feel her muscles relaxing. The pain in her expression is easing, and her sobs are turning into sighs. It was my mother who told me I have a nice touch, and it has been a useful tool on many occasions.

Wrapped in a fur-lined woollen dressing gown, she curls up on my sofa and talks me through the events of the party. I am appalled at what she says. The cut on her face is not as deep as I first thought.

They were teasing her with a knife to spice up the filming, but she lurched forward, and the knife scratched her cheek. Now that the dried blood has been washed away, it is clear that the cut is only a scratch and will heal on its own. The wound can be disguised by make-up until then.

I warm up a tin of tomato soup and spoon-feed her like a baby. It is the only food I have in the cupboard, but she seems to be enjoying it. She talks until she falls asleep. I place a blanket over her and leave her on the sofa before going to bed myself. A man is the last thing Amelia needs right now. But when I awake in the morning she is curled up next to me. She feels good.

Over breakfast she brightens up. The pain in her body is easing, and after she performs a little paintwork on her eyes it is difficult to see they are bruised. She tells me there is no way she is going back to work for Adeline if it involves the ambassador. Adeline will have to find another girl to service this man. I ask after Adeline again, but Amelia has not heard from her.

'You like Adeline, don't you, M'sieur Giger?' She laughs. 'I can tell. You speak of her with passion. I know she likes you.'

'I don't think you should be telling me that. Anyway, it is Linah that I am worried about. And between you and me, it is Linah who means the most to me.'

'Linah is Moroccan. She can take care of herself. Adeline on the other hand is French. There is a big difference.'

I don't understand what she is trying to tell me. Adeline is part of the rich French aristocracy, way above my northern working-class childhood, whereas Linah is just a simple girl in trouble because of me. I can relate to Linah. Yes, maybe I am in love with her.

'I will speak with Adeline and tell her why you will not work with the ambassador anymore. I am sure she will understand. I will make everything all right for you. What are you doing today?'

'I should go to college.' She thinks for a minute. 'Yes, I will go to college.'

'Maybe I can pick you up after class and treat you to a fish dinner down on the harbour tonight. We can share a bottle of Blanc De Pinot Noir and take in the summer sea air.'

'I would like that, M'sieur Giger. I would like that very much.' She blushes as I kiss her.

When Passion and Despair
Take Control

My intercom beeps. 'Sorry to trouble you, M'sieur Giger, but I have a delivery for you.' It is Kamal. 'Shall I bring it up to you?'

'Yes please, as soon as possible Kamal.' It only takes him a couple of minutes before he is at my door handing me a small package wrapped in plain brown paper. The only words written on it are 'For the immediate attention of M'sieur Jacques Giger.'

'Who gave it to you, Kamal?'

'I have not seen him before, M'sieur Giger. He was Chinese. He just drove up in a large black car, thrust it through my office window, and drove off. He was gone in seconds. He said nothing.'

'Thank you, Kamal.' I slip him fifty dirham.

The package is tightly wrapped. I search for a knife with which to cut into it. Just as I snap the seal, my intercom beeps again.

'M'sieur Giger, Madame Adeline la Chapelle is here to see you. Can I send her to you?'

'Thank you, Kamal. Please send her up.' That is unusual; Adeline never waits to be announced. I peer out over the balcony into the car park. Yes, it is her car, and the cheeky bitch has parked in my space. I wonder what she wants. Anyway, it will give me an opportunity to discuss Amelia.

Adeline walks into my apartment and sits on the sofa. She is beautiful and elegant in her tight-fitting beige dress. As she crosses her legs her skirt tightens, as it always does. She sits in silence, head bowed, looking down at her feet as if in despair. I can't help but notice that her foot is bandaged. I don't want to race into an attack, demanding to know how she can allow her girls to risk their lives servicing such an evil man as the ambassador, whilst she is so distressed. It is only right that I give her the opportunity to explain the events of the party from her point of view. So I just sit opposite her and stare.

We stare at each other for what seems an age. Her dark brown eyes are wide open and her skin powder white. Her bottom lip starts to tremble. She looks like a child who has done something wrong and is wondering whether to confess or not. To be honest, her depression is even deeper than that. She has a look of complete surrender. A tear runs down her face as her breathing gets heavier. She starts gagging with each swallow, and suddenly with a rush of passion she bursts into tears, crying uncontrollably she buries her face into the cushions of the sofa. Her entire body is trembling, jerking in a spasmodic frenzy.

She is all played out; she is ruined. Her decline from a proud, elegant princess to a shaking, sobbing peasant girl has taken a mere three minutes. All her arrogance and confidence has gone. Her soul is bared; she is a simple woman suffering something that as yet I don't understand. My first reaction is to comfort her, but to be honest I haven't yet recovered from Amelia's outburst. I sit like a passionless man, which to Adeline right now I am. I feel sorry for her, yet in a funny, stupid way I also feel proud of her. She is human after all. She does have a heart, and she is still very beautiful. I wait for her breathing to calm down before lifting her head off the sofa and wiping her tears with the sleeve of my shirt. I kiss her and gently lay her head on my chest as I pull her beside me. She reaches out her hands towards my face and pulls herself up towards me. As she gets closer her lips find mine, and the salt of her tears tease my mouth. It is difficult to defend what I do next, but I do what comes naturally. With slow, caressing movements I run my fingers through her hair, round the nape of her neck, and find the tag holding the zip of her dress. As her dress drops away, she raises herself to her knees, reveals my body, and sinks slowly down onto me.

I finger her hair away from her face and run my thumbs along the top of her cheekbone, clearing away the tears that are running down her face. Her lips slowly part, and with her tongue she licks away the salt that is sticking to them. As though her blood is starting to flow through them again, her lips slowly return to a stronger shade of red. She is a master at using her tongue to draw attention to herself. She is saying, 'Look at me, I am beautiful. I bet you want me. Well, you will have to do a lot better than that if you want to succeed.'

She does it all the time when we are talking. At first I thought it was an unconscious habit, but I soon realized that she knows exactly what she is doing and the reaction it has on me. I must admit she does it in the most provocative way, leaving me speechless and helpless. I just have to marvel at her poise.

I can't help myself; I run my hands down her face, smoothing out every crease in her skin and exploring every dimple in her flesh. As they travel across her shoulders I slide the straps of her underclothes off her shoulders. Her bra falls forward to reveal the most perfect breasts I have ever seen: smooth, white, and firm, yet exotic. Her nipples are pert and proud. They too are talking to me: 'Take me. Love me. I am yours.' She is purring like a kitten, giving out little sighs of pleasure and encouraging me to run my finger around them. Her senses are screaming, though I am hardly touching them.

She is kind to me to start with, caring and caressing. But very soon she is writhing up and down on me like a demented goddess, her fingers ripping into my flesh, down my chest, and across my shoulders. She bites first my lips and then my ears, chanting and crying. Is this passion or anger?

Is it love or hatred? My body responds in nervous shock waves as her nails gouge into my back. I return her bite as her teeth sink into my cheek; I can feel blood running down my face. The room is spinning. When I open my eyes all I can see are flashing lights. My head is pounding with every surge of blood that gushes around my body. She too is reaching a climax. Her body is tensing, and her tummy muscles are tightening across her hips. Her legs become rigid against my thighs, squeezing me to the point of suffocation. Her breasts are ablaze in upturned supremacy. I totally lose control and explode inside her. She gives out a deafening scream and collapses on top of me, her body holding me down to the sofa. We lay love-locked together, panting and sweating, helpless to passion, devoid of any sense of respect, responsibility, or realisation of what we have just been through together.

Lifting her off is not easy. Still on top of me, she has fallen asleep. Not only is she a dead weight, but her grip on me is immense. I manage to throw several loose cushions onto the floor, and by rolling her over I manage to roll us both onto them. Adeline is out for the count. I cover her exposed body with her dress and then cover her with a duvet. She lies at peace, contented and warm.

It is four thirty. We must have slept for two hours or more. Goodness! What a day. Can I be in love with this girl as well as Linah? Of course not. My attentions have to be for Linah. Adeline will eventually rise back into the goddess she is. Linah will not. Adeline is in control of her fate; Linah is not. Linah is a simple Moroccan girl looking for a way to improve herself. She is in need of help and appreciation. Linah is my responsibility and the girl I want.

I lick my wounds. I am amazed at the number of bites and scratches I have sustained. I don't think for one minute that I won this battle. Dried blood sits in the scratch lines down my chest. Thankfully my nipples are intact. I thought she had twisted them off. I dab my battered body with whiskey-soaked cotton buds, first cleaning and then revealing the depth of the gashes, which sting like hell when the liquor meets my torn flesh. She lies motionless on the floor. Whatever brought that on? Whatever has turned this controlling, iconic woman into a ravishing sexual predator? I have no idea. Does she hate me or love me? The more important question is, does she hate or love herself?

She lies there all night. I sit on the sofa watching over her. She hardly moves. Only once does she groan and shout out. I can't make out her call, yet I can tell it is full of fear. I have no idea what is going through her head. It must be three o'clock in the morning before I lie down beside her to share her duvet. She wakes for a second.

'Did I hurt you? I'm sorry,' she mutters. Not giving me time to answer, she rolls towards me and places her arm across my chest. 'I have fallen in love with you,' she whispers.

Over breakfast Adeline gives nothing away. She passes the party off as 'Just the same as all the others.' She is sure that Amelia, Roxanne, and Marie will be all right and promises to contact them during the day. Her bandaged foot is due to a glass falling on it, and her exhaustion is simply attributed to two continuous days and nights of partying. It is just as I pour her a second coffee that I remember the package.

Found in Cairo

'The package,' I gasp. 'Goodness, I forgot. I received another package yesterday. I am guessing it is either from or about Linah. Where did I put it?'

'I thought you were going to Hong Kong to find her. Did you not go?'

I took time out from my search to report my adventure in Hong Kong.

'So she wasn't there?'

'She was there, but after only one day they took her out.'

I told her about the Chinese girl I found in Linah's room. 'She thought he had taken her to Singapore, so I stayed over in Singapore for a night to look for her there.'

I tell her about Boris and Marie but not about coming home in a coffin.

I search the room and find the package behind the sofa. 'Look, it's another disc. Let's play it and see if it throws any light on her whereabouts.'

We sit together on the sofa as the screen goes into a countdown mode. Then we hear Linah's voice.

'M'sieur Giger, please use your computer and go to www.fromragstoriches.egy.com. I am waiting to speak with you there.'

The address comes up on the screen. It only takes me a matter of seconds to type it into the address panel. Linah appears on the computer screen. She is sitting on the floor of a small van. Her ankles are tied, but her arms are free. Her face is smeared in grime, and her hair has not been groomed for days. The camera zooms onto her face.

'Where the hell have you been?' she screams. 'I have been in this bloody van for two days waiting to give you this live feed. They obviously think you need proof that I am still alive. It appears to me that you have already forgotten me.'

Unfortunately Adeline walks behind me, and my camera picks her up. Linah goes hysterical. 'Look! I knew it, another woman in your life.' She bursts into tears.

A paper is thrust into her hand, and a clock is held up to the camera. Someone shouts instructions to her in Arabic. She wipes her face and studies the paper before starting to read. 'M'sieur Jacques Giger, I am on this live feed to convince you that I am still alive and well. You can see from the clock that I am one hour ahead of you. That is because I am in Cairo.'

With that the camera pans to her right. The van's rear door opens, and the pyramids are clearly visible in the distance.

She continues speaking. 'They know it was you in the crate in Hong Kong, and they admire your courage and your determination. But I am to tell you to get on with your task. If you try to find me again before the task is completed, I will be killed.' She gasps. 'The sooner you complete your task, the sooner I will be returned to you.'

She drops the paper. 'Oh! M'sieur Giger, I don't know what to do. Please help me.' The feed goes dead and the screen blank. I click on the address again, but this time it simply says, 'No such address. Please check you are typing in your address correctly or contact your provider.'

'What are you going to do?' asks Adeline.

'I am going to find her. When Morocco is owned by this man, do you think he is going to let you, me, and her live to tell the tale? I have to find her. I know she is alive, I know she is in Cairo, and I know she has been sitting in a parked van overlooking the pyramids for the last two days. Can you contact the Egyptian police and persuade them to scan their CCTV cameras around that area? One of the cameras might have caught a parked van. Give them the time now, because I am guessing they will be moving away as we speak.'

'I will call them from the embassy as soon as I get back. But Jacques, we have to continue with the job at hand.'

'I agree. I am going to check on the progress of the advertising agency and action the next stage.'

'Please be careful, Jacques. I mean what I told you last night.'

That takes me by surprise; I thought she had just been ranting.

'Jacques, this man must be stopped. He must not get away with this.'

'One thing at a time, Adeline. Please, one thing at a time.' She kisses me, lifts her coat off the hanger, and walks out. 'I'll let you know what success I have with the Egyptian police.'

'As soon as possible,' I stress.

She promises.

I have to meet with Jean Claud. Then I need to visit the advertising agency, to strengthen the campaign in the areas of weakness and progress the stronger sections. Jean Claud is not available; I get through to Lafleur.

'What of Linah?' he asks.

'She wasn't there. It was a red herring. It was a Chinese girl living in the room. Your men thought it was Linah, but she was long gone.'

'You need to stop worrying about Linah. She is Moroccan. She can take care of herself.'

'Lafleur, I have heard that so many times I am tiring of it. I need to meet with you today. I need an update on our progress.'

'You are in luck. I can spare you one hour at two o'clock.'

'I will be there. Will Jean Claud be with you?'

'I doubt it. He has several tasks to take care of. But don't worry, I know everything that is happening, possibly even better than Jean Claud.'

With that I have to be satisfied. I zero my handset and call the advertising agency, making an appointment for four. It is one o'clock before Adeline gets back to me.

'Good and bad news,' she reports. 'CCTV footage is showing a van parked up in a car park less than a kilometre from the pyramids that departed at the time I gave them. The police noted the registration and later found the van abandoned on the highway leading to the Israeli border.'

'So from the registration we know who owns the van.'

'Yes. It is an Avis van rental, hired for three days and paid for in advance. Avis received a call one hour ago informing them of the whereabouts of the van and instructing them to collect it.'

'So who rented it?'

She does not answer.

'Come on, Adeline. Why do I have to work so hard to get information from you?'

'Well, that is the twenty-four-thousand-dollar question.'

'And the answer to my question is?'

'You hired it.'

'I did? How can that be? Someone must have got my name and bank card details to pay for a van rental.'

'That would be quite easy. In Morocco, nothing is sacred. Wave a dirham note under someone's nose and they will tell you everything.'

'So what of the Egyptian police?'

'They are not interested. No crime has been committed. No one has been reported missing, and the van has been returned in good condition.'

'I despair, Adeline. I really do.'

'I do have one piece of good news for you.'

'Tell me, please.'

'The police spoke with a man who parked next to the van. He told them there were three men and a girl in the van. He believed they were all Moroccan, not Egyptian.'

'So what is good about that?'

'Moroccan men will be kinder to a Moroccan woman than an Egyptian or Chinese gang. And let's be honest, being in Cairo brings her closer to home.'

Over the Target

Lafleur is sitting behind his antique ebony desk; he beckons me to sit across the room from him on a long leather settee.

'We have all done very well, especially you, Jacques. Now your job is practically complete. Within the next three or four weeks we will be in a position to continue on our own. The momentum is building so fast, Jean Claud is delighted.'

'And what of the ambassador?' I ask.

'He is of no consequence to us. He will soon be out of our lives forever.'

'And Linah?'

'I have told you what I think about Linah. Forget her. She will be okay.'

So many people have told me this. I don't understand why. Have they never been in love? There is no way I can forget her. I know Lafleur thinks I am stupid. Maybe I am. I am finding it very difficult to focus on what he is telling me. He commences to give me a rundown on our achievements and what will happen next.

'Can you remember the five pillars that I described at our first meeting?'

'I can. Oil, electricity, banking, trade, and sex.'

'Well, we have always supplied Morocco with oil, and now our market share is so vast that we can monitor and control the competition. Plus, we now sell 50 per cent of all the cars and vans sold in the kingdom. We intend building on this success by introducing a new 'people's car,' probably from the Peugeot range. This will be a small, reliable, efficient car that everyone can afford. The bank will devise a saving and borrowing scheme which will make it easily affordable for even the lowest-paid workers. If Hitler can do it to sell his Beetle, then I am sure we can.'

'But Hitler cheated his people.'

Lafleur ignores my remark.

'We have taken possession of the two power stations in Morocco and can guarantee supply to the entire kingdom for many years to come, even accounting for the massive increase in demand that we have forecast due to the expansion of the economy. Talking of which, we own the bank, which already has 80 per cent of working Moroccans banking with us. This gives us a 60 per cent control of the Kingdom's internal spending power. The bank is developing its corporate accounts and heavily investing in any Moroccan business which has international potential.'

A MOROCCAN AFFAIR

Lafleur continued, 'We are in total control of all imports and exports because we own not only the ports but also the ships. The Chinese consortium that was strangling our trade figures is no more. This gives us total discretion as to which products we allow into the kingdom. In support of this, we own fleets of trucks delivering right across North Africa, even as far as Egypt. We are in discussion to open new rail and road networks, especially high-speed rail links to the south and east. A new airport is being planned in the south to encourage growth in southern Morocco and Africa; this will be connected by tramways and monorail systems to all city centres and major transport hubs.

'The bank is financing our expansion in fruit and vegetable exports; distribution has been simplified and greater production stimulated. Beef and sheep farming will boom next year, and soon Moroccan horse will be served on every table across Africa and Asia. We are researching the possibility of farming llama, ostrich, and camel. Vast areas of new farmland are already being designated.

'In the city small businesses are springing up everywhere. There are Moroccan food shops, restaurants, fast food franchises, clothing stores, and material bars. Domestically produced carpets, bags, bedding, and house furnishings will soon rival Ikea. It is our intention that everything Moroccan will be admired, respected, and desired by the entire world.

'The construction business is taking off also; French companies are building exotic housing for

European, Asian, and Chinese businessmen. Hotels and apartments are springing up along the corniche encouraging tourism. Economical housing and apartments are being erected in the suburbs for city workers. This means more schools, hospitals, colleges, theatres, cinemas, sports stadiums, and shopping malls.

'You see, M'sieur Giger, the secret is to get everyone working. When people are working, they have money to spend. And as we own what they spend it on, it will all come to us.' He laughs. 'I don't know why countries like England, Spain, and Greece make such hard work of it.'

He laughs again even louder. 'How can anyone think that by putting people out of work is going to make the country rich?'

A chill runs up my spine. I can't fault his plan or question its success, but I am not growing any fonder of this man.

'We will be the most powerful family on the planet.' Then he corrects himself. 'When I say we, I mean France, of course.'

For some reason, I don't believe his correction.

'So what of me?' I ask.

'Your final task is to increase tourism. We need world currencies flooding into Morocco to finance our growth. Along with the tourists will be businessmen looking for opportunities to grow rich and fat. We have to give them what they need, what they want, and what they like. Your advertising task is to make Morocco the place to visit because of our culture, our weather, our history, and our hospitality. We need to see an enormous increase in tourism this summer. Can you make that happen, M'sieur Giger? We only have until October.'

'What of the fifth pillar?' I ask him.

'M'sieur Giger, you are a man of the world. Sex is the oldest and biggest business in the world. See how Holland makes money from it. See how Thailand attracts visitors with it. Have some fun, M'sieur Giger. Adeline is in charge of this industry. Work with her. Guide her. Inspire her. You deserve to have some fun and make us a lot of money.'

He can see the disapproval on my face. 'Control it, M'sieur Giger. Your task is to bring it above ground. That will keep the underworld out and the money coming our way.'

I let his phraseology go unchecked. This conversation isn't going anywhere, but he still has not answered several questions. What of the ambassador? What of Linah? And I suppose, apart from being rich, what of me?

Lafleur checks his watch, stands up, and leans forward to shake my hand. He wants me to leave. There is something bothering me. No, it isn't his plan. It is his attitude, his wording. There is definitely something I am not seeing. Right now I have a meeting with the advertising agency followed by another attempt at finding Linah. If I am to be rich, then she deserves a life of luxury for what she is going though. I am in for a few more sleepless nights.

The Final Countdown

The advertising agency is already aware of the success. They too are expanding due to more companies employing their services.

'Don't forget who you have to thank for this success,' I remind them. 'And don't go to sleep on me in favour of new business.'

'Definitely not, M'sieur Giger. You are *the man*.'

I am convinced that Mohammed Abdullah Chahid is a man of his word who knows what is best for him and his agency.

'Good. We have one, probably two more campaigns. I might combine them. I still have to decide. Anyway, the first of the two is easy. You have to sell Morocco to the world as a holiday location. It has to rival Spain for fun, Monaco for gaming, Egypt for history, and India for service. The airlines, the hotels, the bank, and every involved industry, from the taxis and the bus companies right down to the ice cream sellers, will be part of the campaign. They will all benefit from the increase in demand. The call to action will be: "Call now for the Magic of Morocco". If you can create the awareness, then Morocco will do the rest.'

I continue to brief Mohammed Abdullah Chahid on what sort of support he can expect. 'All bookings will be handled by the kingdom's travel agency, which is the central pin to the communication and bookings procedure. We want high-quality visitors: people with money to spend, not your common British beach lounger. The bank will finance every transaction and offer deals and incentive schemes. Booking bonuses will be unequalled anywhere in the world. I will give you a list of new activities after you have explored all Morocco's natural attractions. They will include events like Formula One racing, sea regattas along the coast, world sporting events, and original holidays such as desert experiences: become a French Foreign Legionnaire for a fortnight, experience the life of the Desert Panzer Corps, drive a tank.'

I laugh at what I am coming up with. Mohammed Abdullah Chahid is rocking with excitement. 'We will also breathe new life into the Atlas Mountains with nature tours, climbing activities, film extravaganzas, and mountain experiences.'

Chahid must know that long after I am gone, his agency will be at the forefront in promoting Morocco and enjoying its rise to fame. I call Adeline. If I am to get back to my search for Linah, I have to action plans for the sex industry immediately. She agrees to come back to my apartment later in this evening. This is ideal; it gives me a few hours to put my mind to the subject of sex. You might think this a dream of a job for a healthy, virile man like myself, but I just want it out of my head. My main concern is Linah. I have booked a seat on the six-thirty flight to Cairo in the morning.

Adeline smells wonderful and looks amazing in her new plum-coloured, pleated silk dress. Her matching high-heeled shoes restore her true grace and dignity. She really knows how to dress to excite. Well, she excites me, anyway. This is not going to be a meeting like the one this afternoon with the advertising agency. This meeting is going to be slow, sensuous, long, and passionate. It will be difficult for me to get away in time for my flight, but that is tomorrow's problem. Right now I hold her in my arms, press her against the wall, and run my hands all over her body. She wilts under my pressure, and we both crumple to the floor, where we make love. I do believe it is love, not sex. There is a difference.

It must be two in the morning. I have to bring up the business of the sex industry. Goodness, and she is sound asleep. I run my cold hand down her back.

She moans and turns to me. 'Okay, just one more time.'

'Adeline, wake up.'

'Now? What for?'

'Yes, now. I am on a flight to Agadir at six thirty with Mohammed Abdullah Chahid. You know who he is, the boss at the advertising agency.' This isn't the time to tell her I am going in search of Linah.

'Oh Jacques, slow down. Call him and delay your flight.'

I shake her, turn on the light, and make two strong coffees. By the time I get back to her she is sitting up in bed.

'We have to talk about sex.'

She smiles. 'I'd rather do it than talk about it.'

'Ha ha, funny girl.'

'Listen, before I go, you have to know what to do. Developing your little escort and hostess business into a national institution is not going to be easy, especially when we only have three months. I was talking with Lafleur. He says—'

'I know what he said to you,' she interrupts. 'He said the same to me just before I came to you.'

'Then you know what we have to do and why?'

'I do, but I have no idea how we are going to make it happen.'

'Well, I do. I have been thinking about it all day. I am going to tell you how to make it happen, and you have to start working on it first thing in the morning.'

She rolls over and sticks her butt into my stomach. 'Do you really have to tell me now.'

'Adeline, get a grip and listen.' I am starting to lose patience with her.

'The reason for controlling the sex business is to keep the mafia and underworld crooks out. Sex is how these guys make inroads into drugs, extortion, people trafficking, and protection.'

She looks at me as if I am stupid.

'Darling, you are so naive. It is to make money for us.'

'As well as, as well as,' I repeat angrily.'

'Okay, I am listening.'

I didn't mean to lose my temper, but to be honest I am not convinced my plan will work. It has never been done before, so my insecurity is showing through.

'Do I have your full attention?'

'You do.'

'All prostitution in the kingdom has to be ordered through the Internet. See it as the red light district in Amsterdam but on the Internet. We don't want girls trafficking themselves on the streets, in hotel lounges, or in shop windows. The girls will not be involved with money. All pricing will be done at the point of order. A price will be agreed and paid for through 'Discreet', a similar service to PayPal, which will be run by the bank. Then, like on eBay, we need feedback. If a girl cheats on the system or fails to supply what she has promised, she could be removed from the system. If a client abuses or hurts a girl, he has to be reported and arrested if the incident demands it. Do you understand so far?'

'Yes.'

'Any questions or queries so far?'

'No.'

She seems to understand what I am saying.

'We need web pages for static customers and mobile apps for clients on the move. Guys who just fancy a quick—'

'Yes, yes, I get the idea. You don't have to spell it out.' Adeline is fully awake now. I do have her full attention.

'You have to enrol the girls. Put the word about. If they don't enrol with us, they will not be allowed to operate in Morocco. Spell out the advantages: organisation, guaranteed payment, safety, hygiene, care, and support. You have to advertise the service to all the hotels. They will be delighted; they are losing a lot of revenue whilst the girls are littering their lounges. Check out the dating sites. See what they say on the web pages. Keep it clean and respectable. The service has to have an image of total respectability.'

I start to dress and pack my overnight bag.

'Morocco has got to be seen as being as proud of its liberated sex industry as it is in its heritage, climate, and culture. I will be back in a couple of days to help you and hopefully brief the advertising agency with what you have. And Adeline' – I hold her face in both hands and pull her towards me – 'this has got to be handled extremely discreetly and delicately.'

'I am aware of that.' She smiles. 'I will make it happen. I know the dangers and the risks the girls are taking at the moment. It has to stop. You can rely on me.'

I kiss her and nearly fall foul of her appeal. It is five o'clock. I have to go.

Cairo by Night

I have been warned about Cairo: stick to the tourist areas, don't drink the water, and keep tight hold of your bags and wallets. This still does not prepare me for my arrival at Cairo International Airport. I am just stepping out onto the concourse when my bag is snatched from my grasp and two burly Egyptians, one on each side, pick me up and carry me across the car park to a waiting black four-wheel-drive Shogun. Its engine is running, and the driver is leaning out through his window, directing the men to put my bag on the back seat. I am dropped unceremoniously at the rear door.

'Welcome to Cairo, sir. Thank you for choosing this taxi. Where would you like to go?' The driver is a dark, scorched-skinned Egyptian dressed in a brightly coloured shirt and bleached-out denim jeans. The bag carrier and his two henchmen saunter back to airport arrivals to collect their next unsuspecting client.

'I need a discreet, quality hotel, preferably not on the main drag. Can you recommend one?'

'Your wish is my command. I know the ideal hotel. It is just off Museum Square, close to everywhere but not a preserved artefact.' He laughs at his own joke.

'Sounds ideal. Let's go.'

I strap myself into the back seat. I have also been warned about Egyptian driving. I don't understand why we have to cross the river twice, but eventually we pull up outside The Cleopatra Palace. He asks for fifty Egyptian shillings and wants to know whether there is anything else he could help me with. Not only is he prepared to make himself available twenty-four hours a day, but he also knows Cairo inside out. He has heard of the Moroccan ambassador to Paris, and he knows the location of his villa.

'Sir, he has an enormous villa on the west bank of the Nile, ten to fifteen kilometres up the river. Would you like me to take you there?'

'Later. I will call you. Do you know if he is in residence?'

He laughs again. 'No, I don't know that, sir. But I can find out for you.'

'Please find out, and collect me here at seven thirty tonight.'

'Yes, sir!' He is delighted to be my designated driver for my stay. I like him. His English is nigh-on perfect. It is a shame about the slight Americanism, which I will forgive. He carries my bag up to reception, negotiates his commission with the receptionist, and then waves with a promise to be back at seven thirty.

The Cleopatra Palace is not a cheap hotel. My room is well upholstered, with a massive mahogany four-poster bed dominating the bedroom. The thick brocade curtains open onto a small balcony from which, if I lean right out, I can see the front of the museum. I arrange my few things, close the balcony windows to keep out the smell of car exhausts, and take rest on the thick, woven counterpane.

I have only the barest of plans. If the ambassador is in residence, I will sit outside his villa, wait for him to leave, and then follow him in the hope he might take me to Linah. It even crosses my mind that Linah might be held captive inside the villa. In this case I will have to get inside and search the building from cellar to roof. Even the grounds and gardens. Hopefully I might just find an obvious clue as to her whereabouts.

My room phone rings. 'Good evening, M'sieur Giger. This is reception. I hope everything meets with your approval.'

'Yes it does,' I groan, half asleep. 'Thank you very much.'

'Your driver has arrived and is waiting for you in reception.'

I look at my watch; it is seven thirty. Oh goodness, I must have fallen asleep!

'Thank you. I will be down shortly.'

An Exciting Night Out

I hurriedly pull on my clean jeans and button up a loose-fitting shirt. My black jacket adds a hint of respectability. I still don't have a plan, but I am determined to find Linah and save her from this wicked man.

My driver informs me that his name is Mohammed.

'Is every man in Egypt called Mohammed?' I ask him.

'Practically. A few are called Nasser.' We both laugh.

'So did you discover if the ambassador is at home?'

'He is expected home tonight. He left Singapore two days ago and stopped off in Dubai. From there he will probably drive to Bahrain. He usually does, he has a villa in Manama.'

'How many villas does he own? He is doing very well for himself, isn't he?'

Mohammed looks puzzled. 'These villas are not his. He just has the use of them.'

Now it is my turn to look puzzled. 'But he is very rich, isn't he?'

'It is said that he is bankrupt and it is only his friendship with the king and his job with the Moroccan government that keeps him afloat.'

I am in shock. If this is true, the guy is a complete fake, a high-class con artist. It is my duty to inform Jean Claud as soon as I can.

We bully our way down the East Bank, honking and swerving as Egyptian drivers do. Mohammed tells me that he has been a taxi driver in Cairo all his life; his father was a taxi driver before him. During the last forty years, he has learnt everything that there is to know about Cairo, and he knows everything that is going on.

'The only thing I don't know is the name of the ambassador,' he tells me. 'We just call him the ambassador.'

'Me too. Sometimes we refer to him as The Bear.'

'I have not heard that name before. Nobody in Egypt would insult him by calling him The Bear.' Mohammed says this with sincerity in his voice. He appears to have a lot of respect for the man.'

'So what do you know about him?' The air freshens as we speed across the Nile bridge and approach its centre point. The waters of the cool river offer a respite from the suffocating traffic fumes, but it only lasts for a few seconds. We plunge back into the traffic smog on the western exit.

'He is a very powerful man because he represents the king of Morocco and his forceful personality, of course. When he is staying in Cairo he entertains the rich and the famous, from film stars to royalty. If he isn't entertaining he will be partying the night away at a club called The Pharaoh. They make a big fuss of him there, probably because of his generous nature. He throws hundreds of pounds onto the stage in appreciation of the singers and dancers. This is very important to them, as they play for free. The waiters hover over him like bees around a honey pot. He tips them well. His brother usually accompanies him, sometimes his two cousins and always many girls. There are always many girls – five, six, sometimes as many as ten. He likes to surround himself with girls. He sits at the best table in the house, right at the front, next to the stage. Meat, fruit, and whiskey are served to him continuously, sometimes until seven or eight in the morning.'

'So are you saying everyone likes him?'

'Yes. In Cairo he is admired, but we don't say that about a man of his status.'

'What status is this?'

'He is the godfather.'

We pull off the main drag and turn into a beautiful, tree-lined avenue. The street lights are glistening like stars through the leaves. Each light has attracted a host of circling insects. Theirs is the only activity in the avenue. At ground level there is nothing. Behind the high, beige perimeter walls that border the avenue I assume the villas are very impressive, surrounded with manicured lawns, gardens, flowers, and swimming pools. Probably enormous dogs will be protecting the properties, lurking under the bushes awaiting the command to attack. Mohammed confirms my thoughts. We pull up opposite a golden cast-iron gate with lanterns flickering on the top of both supporting pillars. Around the top of the wall, decorative searchlights are in evidence.

'The ambassador's villa.'

'There is not a lot to see, Mohammed. Have you ever been through the gate?'

'Infact I went through last week for the first time. I was instructed to collect two guys and a girl at the airport, and I brought them here.'

'Was she Moroccan by any chance?'

'I couldn't really tell. She was completely covered. But she was definitely more Arab than African. I suppose she could have been Asian.'

I am puzzled.

'How did you know that?'

'She had style. It was the way she moved, the way she sat in the back of the cab – yes, now I remember. I heard her speak. She was definitely Arabian.'

I open the taxi door with the intention of walking over to the gate to peer through. Mohammed reaches over and stops me.

'Sir! There are cameras on every tree. If you want the ambassador to know you are here, go ahead.'

I hurriedly sit back inside the car. Being filmed is the last thing I want right now. He will recognise me immediately.

'Thanks for that, Mohammed. I wasn't thinking.'

I continue to tell him the bare bones of my story and why I am here. He isn't surprised.

'I told you, he loves women. But I doubt he will hurt her, especially if she is pretty.'

'I wish I could believe you, but unfortunately I know different. So, Mohammed, I have to get inside. I have to know if she is in there.'

'I don't advise you to go in. You will never get out.'

He stares straight through me. 'Sir, I have a suggestion. I have hundreds of taxi drivers as friends. We could put a twenty-four-hour watch on the house and follow every car that leaves. But I will have to pay these guys.'

'That's a great idea. Please do it.'

As I speak, the lights along the tops of the walls brighten as three large Mercedes limousines trundle past. The golden gates swing open and swallow the cars. I just manage to catch a glimpse of the passenger in the back seat of the leading car; it is the ambassador. In the following two cars are seated several women. Some are covered in *abayas*. Two if not three are white and fair. The gates close as quickly as they had separated, and I hear the electric lock shut tight.

'Sir, many women live in this villa. I doubt you will be able to find Linah.'

'I agree. Employ your friends, and let's start the surveillance as soon as possible.'

We drive slowly around the villa wall; there is nothing to see. Only one gate allows entry, and I can't see one single clue as to what is inside. The wall lights dim, and the avenue returns to normality. The moths and mosquitoes continue their circling, chasing flies and devouring them whole.

'Take me to this nightclub you mentioned. I will check it out.' Mohammed looks me up and down.

'Sir, they will not let you in dressed in jeans, and you must have a woman with you.'

'Okay, Mr Know-it-all. Fix it for me.'

'Yes, sir. I will contact my two youngest daughters and tell them to dress for a night out. But first we must dress you appropriately.'

'Youngest daughters! How young?'

'Young enough to be beautiful, old enough to know the score. Just don't put them into any danger.'

'I promise. Let's go, or the night will be over.'

Mohammed laughs out loud. 'The nightclub doesn't open for another three hours. We have plenty of time.'

My naiveté is showing; I feel so stupid.

The Queen Of Clubs

'So what should I wear?'

Mohammed tuts. An Egyptian tut sounds just the same as an English tut, so I understand his meaning.

'You must look rich. You must look powerful.' He thinks for a minute. 'Like the ambassador, I suppose. And you must act' – he pauses again – 'like Al Capone. Yes, like Al Capone. You must walk in and never look behind you. My daughters will be following you obediently. Forget that you are an English gentleman. Treat the girls as your slaves. You must be arrogant, full of self-importance. Then the waiters will treat you with respect and serve you well.'

'That's not easy for a nice guy like me.'

'It doesn't mean you are not a nice guy, sir. The ambassador is a nice guy.'

I sigh; I have no idea how he has come by this opinion.

Mohammed changes the subject. 'Do you have a black double-breasted suit? A white shirt with a big collar? Black leather shoes?'

'No! I have another pair of jeans, three T-shirts, and a pale blue cotton jacket.'

He laughs. 'And I thought you were a man of the world, a man of means. I hope I am not wasting my time on you.'

I assure him that he isn't and thank him for what he is doing. 'You see, Mohammed, I am inherently an artist. This means that money and status are not high on my priority list.'

'I don't understand that, sir. Money is life. I will have a word with the commissionaire at your hotel, and he will send you the required garments. And do I have to keep calling you sir?'

Now it is my turn to laugh. 'According to you, you should, but according to me, you can call me Jacques.'

'Mr Jacques it is then.'

He drops me at the door of my hotel, and after a few words with the commissionaire he promises to return with his daughters in two hours.

Soon my room's doorbell rings. Looking through the small magnifying lens in the central panel, I see a short, white-haired gentleman of Jewish origin standing next to a mobile rack of suits and shirts. A tell-tale trail down the blue carpet shows the wriggly path he has taken as he dragged the rack along the corridor from the elevator.

'You require a suit, sir. Will you be hiring it or buying it?'

Yes he is a tailor, but first he is a businessman. Now I know where I have been going wrong all these years, putting artistic values before money.

'I don't know yet. Can I decide later?'

'You may, sir, but I need a deposit of four hundred Egyptian pounds. You understand why, don't you?'

'Because you think I might steal it.'

He smiles. Just having this little man fuss all over me is worth four hundred pounds; nothing is too much trouble for him. I select a suit, but the jacket is a fraction too long, according to my suitor. So whilst I try on several shirts, he rolls up his sleeves, sits on the window seat, and threads a strand of cotton through a needle.

'Do you require a tie, sir? Most of my English and American clients insist on a tie.'

'Tonight I feel Egyptian. I will stay open-necked.'

'Then could I suggest a hint of gold?' He reaches up and clips a gold chain around my neck.

'It's not real gold. Neither are these rings,' he says as he slips three onto the fingers of my left hand. 'It's just the way it is here in Cairo.'

I pay him four hundred pounds, and he slips his card into the top pocket of the jacket. I have no idea if I have bought the suit or not. I don't have time to dwell on it. My room phone rings, and the girl on reception announces the arrival of Mohammed with two young ladies. Mohammed is impressed when he sees me. I return the compliment on the beauty of his daughters and shake their hands.

'Mr Jacques,' he whispers in my ear, 'that must be the last time you touch the girls. You must stay aloof. They will touch you, but you must remain distant and uninterested.'

'It appears I have a lot to learn, Mohammed.'

'You must learn very quickly if you want to be treated with respect in Cairo. It is a jungle out there.'

I climb into the back of the large limousine that Mohammed has swapped for his taxi. His two daughters sit one on either side of me talking excitedly in Arabic. 'They will do anything you instruct, Mr Jacques. But they are Egyptian women and, like their mother, only stop talking when you tell them to stop.'

I want Mohammed to come into the nightclub with us. I feel secure when he is around. But chauffeurs wait in their cars at the rear of the club. The two girls grab an arm each and march me up the red carpet to the front door. I pause to speak to the sentries on the door, but the girls practically lift me off my feet and carry me inside.

'They are lowlife, Mr Jacques. You don't speak with the likes of them. Just request a dinner table for four at the rear of the club and walk to the area where we want to sit. They will run like flies to prepare a table in the direction we are heading.'

And that is what happens. I sit overlooking the stage, and the waiters scurry around the girls, easing back their chairs until they are comfortable.

A bottle of whiskey, gin, and vodka are presented for my inspection, which I have no difficulty in approving. Plates of bites, nibbles, nuts, and Egyptian things, which I have never seen before, are scattered on to the table. Napkins are placed across our knees and a dinner menu thrust into my hands. It is obvious that I am in a world of male domination; I am expected to order the food for the three of us. We have four waiters in attendance, waiting for my instruction. I am finding it all a little overpowering. The girls come to my rescue. They both know the menu off by heart and choose the chicken. They speak aggressively in Arabic to the waiters, who withdraw.

'We told them to serve dinner in one hour. Until then they have to leave us alone,' explains Charlotte – I think she is Charlotte. I have now established their names to be Cleopatra and Charlotte. Who is which I still have to learn.

From where I am sitting I have a full view of the lounge and the semi-circular stage. Six long tables radiate from the stage like the rays of the sun. Two of these tables are already occupied, one by a Japanese business convention and the other by a party of foreign tourists, probably Jordanian or Iraqi. As these tables spread away from the stage the space between them increases, so tables for six and then eight fill the gap until right at the back of the lounge, against the wall, where we are sitting the tables seat four. On stage an Egyptian band is proving to be very popular. They aren't playing any notes that I recognise, but the other guests seem to be enjoying the music. Centre stage three slightly overweight girls belly dance, but I believe chunky is fashionable in Egypt. They are writhing and shaking everything they have and occasionally showing a little too much, especially when they pick up the money thrown to them. I can't help thinking the money is more an encouragement for them to bend over than to dance.

The band closes their act with a final display of boobs from the girls as money rains down. This gives us a time to chatter and for me to be educated into the etiquette of Egyptian nightlife. A second band with even more players and even more dancing girls prepare to troop onto the stage.

We are halfway through eating when Charlotte's mobile rings. It is Mohammed, who is still sitting outside in the car park.

'My father says the ambassador has arrived at the front door with his two cousins and ten girls. He can't see who the girls are.'

I nod. 'Thank your father for the information.' She does and slips her phone back into her bag.

We try to focus on the door, but a squad of waiters rush to clear away our soup dishes, I think it was fish soup, but I am not quite sure. A second squad of waiters stand in front of us proudly displaying three roasted chickens – yes, one whole chicken each. Rice and vegetables are squeezed onto the table between our glasses of fruit juice and sparkling water. As our dinner is artistically presented, the

Ambassador's grand entrance is totally obscured. I wanted to observe each girl as they walked in. They are chatting and laughing together. Their entrance far out performs that of the Arabian band and the dancers, who are shaking even more daringly to impress the ambassador and invite a generous shower of coins.

The ambassador's two cousins are seated closest to the stage with a girl between them. Next to them another girl, then the Ambassador, then three more girls complete the far side of the table facing me. On the near side of the table with their backs to me, there are six girls and recognition is impossible. They all have long black hair cascading over brightly coloured dresses embroidered in gold-coloured threads. Only two have bare backs, but they all have low-cut dresses boasting the famous monumental breasts that Egyptian women are so famous for.

'Are all the girls Egyptian?' I ask.

Cleopatra points to one of the girls with her back to us. 'See the girl third from the left? She is shorter than the others. She is not Egyptian, and she could be European. She is too precise and refined to be Egyptian.'

I pretend to understand what she is talking about. The game we are playing, 'Spot the Moroccan Girl', comes to an abrupt end when the small girl turns towards us and reveals her face. She is Malaysian.

Charlotte grabs my arm. 'Look!'

She points in the direction of the entrance. Another girl has just entered the lounge and is walking towards the table. She is dressed in an Arabic black *abaya*. Long black hair drapes over her shoulders, and dark sunglasses hide her face.

'Sunglasses in a night club!' remarks Charlotte. 'That's a bit eccentric, isn't it?'

We both nod in agreement.

'Definitely not Egyptian. Now she could be Moroccan.'

'I think she is Indian,' suggests Cleopatra.

'Linah is regularly mistaken for being Indian. Do you still think she is Indian?'

'Do Moroccans have breeding and style like that?' asks Charlotte.

'Of course.'

'Then she is Moroccan, an Arab Moroccan.'

We watch her brush past the seated girls, not even throwing a glance at them. The girl sitting between the Ambassador and his cousin is ushered to her feet. Obviously she is no longer required. She is shunted to the end of the table. The new girl takes her place.

'If that isn't Linah I will eat my hat.'

I can't take my eyes off her. Damn the lighting in here! Only occasionally does a shard of light from the revolving glitter ball flash across her face. Both the ambassador and his cousins are trying desperately to draw her into conversation, but she is playing hard to get. Only once do I see her answer them with a smile. As for the other girls, she is having nothing to do with them. She is drinking fruit juice. She does not appear to be enjoying her food, picking at it rather than eating, cutting her chicken into very small pieces and pushing them around her plate.

She could be a princess, Charlotte thinks. She calls her father and asks his opinion. He says he isn't aware of a princess being invited.

Cleopatra and Charlotte have totally lost the plot. They are absorbed in discussing the dresses and refinery of the women.

'How can such energetic dancers remain so plump?' I ask.

'They eat a lot and sleep a lot,' both girls answer in unison, then laugh.

'Oh!'

The drinking, the laughter, and the money throwing goes on and on. I have completely forgotten that Mohammed is still waiting in the car. My mobile vibrates.

It is Mohammed. 'If nothing is happening I suggest we go.'

I describe the scene around the ambassador's table and explain that we are convinced one of the girls is Linah.

'You won't get close to her at the table. Your only hope is that she—'

I interrupt his suggestion. 'Wait, something is happening. I will get back to you.'

I kill the phone and draw the two girls closer to me. Two waiters have walked up to the ambassador and are taking instruction. They ease back the chair of our Moroccan princess, who stands up and excuses herself. She glides towards the powder room escorted by the two waiters.

'Where is she going?' I whisper.

'She's going for a pee,' answers Cleopatra. Both girls giggle.

'Time you girls also went for a pee. Get down there and ask her name. If she is Linah, get her out to the car. I will warn your father to be ready.'

Both girls jump to their feet, and I watch them slip past the two waiters on guard at the loo door and disappear into the powder room. My heart is racing. I call our waiter and pay him for the evening, giving him the biggest tip he has received in a long time. Then I rush to the exit, hoping the three girls will already be there. I can see Mohammed sitting in the car outside the main door. I stand and wait. It seems an age, but it is probably only ten minutes. The powder room door opens. Out steps our princess, followed by Charlotte and Cleopatra. The two waiters step between them. Charlotte and Cleopatra come rushing over to me.

'I take it she isn't Linah?' I ask, disappointed.

'Oh, she is Linah, but she wouldn't come with us. She says the ambassador is watching her all the time and we would be dead before we got to the car park. She did say you have to stop worrying about her. She isn't in danger. In fact, she is being very well cared for. Her biggest threat is from the other girls, but she can cope with them. She knows the project you are working on is coming to a close and suggests that you finish your work and then come to find her. She also tells you to be careful and to trust no one, do your job, and leave Morocco immediately.'

I am puzzled. I am trying to save her, and she thinks she is saving me.

'Let's go home.'

Mohammed agrees. 'There is nothing more we can do here tonight. At least we know where she is and that she is safe.'

Mohammed is frozen and tired. He swings the car out of the drive and into the stream of night taxis and limousines. My mind is totally occupied, Charlotte and Cleopatra are in deep discussion in the back of the car and I try to explain the events to Mohammed, which have brought me to Cairo. I tell him how Linah was kidnapped; I describe the sex parties to him, the abuse including the torture and the intimidation and my fear for her safety.

It is six thirty before I get back to the hotel. I pour myself a large gin and tonic and split open a packet of peanuts from the mini bar. I lie back on my bed and try to piece together the events of the evening.

Advice is coming at me from all quarters. Mohammed thinks that I should finish the project then come back to Cairo for her. Charlotte and Cleopatra want me to stay in Cairo so they can take care of me. Adeline needs me in Casablanca to help her promote the escort business. Lafleur still sticks to his belief that Linah is not worth worrying about.

I can't sleep. Charlotte is in and out of the room bringing me coffee, wiping my brow, folding my trousers, and arranging my wardrobe. I don't know why she has stayed. I am not in the mood to entertain. All I can think about is Linah. Why, oh why, couldn't I have spoken with her? I might have persuaded her to come back with me.

Do It or Die

C leopatra and Mohammed continue to discuss the events during their drive home. So when the big black Jaguar starts behaving chaotically behind them, neither of them takes much notice of it.

Driving in Cairo is a nightmare. It is pointless checking your rear-view mirror; there is so much going on it is impossible to make sense of it. Fumes, horns, shouts, screams, crunching metal, and breaking glass are an every-minute occurrence. Yet Mohammed is experiencing a sixth sense. He has no proof that they are being followed, but he is sure they are.

Cleopatra is slumped in the rear seat with her eyes closed. She too wanted to stay with me; she didn't want to go home. Her younger sister had been so persistent, and Cleopatra didn't think it right that they both stayed. They have on several occasions shared the same man and on one occasion had a threesome, but neither had enjoyed competing against each other. Cleopatra is angry with herself. Isn't she the eldest? Should she not have priority? Should her younger sister not be the one going home with her father?

Mohammed breaks Cleopatra's line of thought. 'Do you recognise the car behind us darling? Take a look out of the rear window and see if you can identify it?'

She turns and stares out through the dust-covered glass; there are thousands of headlights shining back at her. 'Which one should I look at? They all look the same.'

'I am going to turn right at the next junction. Watch and see if a car turns with me. If it does, that is the one. I want you to check it out.'

Mohammed swings a sharp right straight across the path of cars on both sides, causing chaos and anger from other drivers. Cleopatra is thrown off balance for a second but sits up just in time to see a black Jaguar in the next lane turn with them.

'Is that the car?'

'Yes, he has been following us since we dropped off Charlotte and Mr Jacques.'

Cleopatra has been followed many times by male admirers. It is all part of life's rich tapestry when you are a pretty girl in Cairo. She knows what her father needs to know about the pursuing vehicle, and she goes into recognition mode.

'It's a black Jaguar with French plates. It seems to have a badge on the front grill. It could be an embassy car or a police car. There are three men inside, one driving and two in the back. They are smartly dressed in white shirts and black ties. They are gaining on us and will overtake in less than a minute.'

'I am going to let them overtake,' responds Mohammed. 'I prefer to have them in front rather than behind. Then I can see them properly.'

'They are coming past now.' She turns to get a closer look as they pass.

'They have guns! They all have guns!' she screams.

Mohammed slams the limo onto the sidewalk to avoid the car as it swings in front of him and screeches to a halt. Several tables and chairs are demolished in one swipe. The men sitting there are scattered like a set of bowling pins. They were just sipping coffee and playing dominoes; now they are laid on the pavement surrounded by cascading chairs and tables. One table crashes through the café window, smashing it to pieces. Shards of glass explode over everything and everybody. Passers-by, tourists, and shoeshine boys take whatever cover they can.

All three doors of the limousine are forced open simultaneously. A gun is stuck into Mohammed's face. Cleopatra screams with fright and tries to fight off the man climbing into the back with her. Thoughts of being kidnapped, raped, and put to work in a Hong Kong brothel flash through her mind, but only when she sees the gun at her father's head is she sure they are going to die.

Outside on the street there is panic. A police car is screaming up the street. Traffic on the road has come to a standstill. There are cars riding up on each other and drivers screaming in rage, pounding steaming bonnets with their fists.

Cleopatra feels a sharp slap across her face and a hand cover her mouth. The guy is strong. Just his hand spanning her face is enough to pin her into the seat. His face is in hers, too close for her to recognise him. Identifying him later will be impossible. He slightly releases his grip, thrusts an envelope into her mouth, and orders her to grip it with her teeth. Then he sprays her with an air canister. The car fills with a red fog, making it impossible for her to see. The cellulose fumes are in her throat, nose, and mouth.

'Give this letter to Jacques Giger, and then have nothing to do with him. He is a dangerous man and now your lives are in danger.'

He pulls away and watches her collapse across the back seat. 'Do what I tell you. You are too pretty to die.'

All three doors slam shut, and the men run back to their car and speed off. The entire incident has lasted only twenty seconds, but the scene they leave is one of devastation.

Mohammed and Cleopatra sit in silence; shocked, yet pleased they are still alive.

'What do we do now?' Mohammed asks her.

'Take this letter to Mr Jacques,' she suggests, reading the words on the front of the envelope: 'For the immediate attention of M'sieur Jacques Giger.'

Written in red spray paint across the front of her dress are the letters DIOD.

'What does DIOD mean?' she questions.

'I have seen this before,' answers Mohammed. 'It means "Do it or die".'

'I think we'd better do it.'

'So do I.'

My house phone rings and wakes me. I check my watch. It is eight in the morning. Charlotte is lying next to me fast asleep. I can't remember making it with her. In fact I am pretty sure I didn't as she is fully clothed. *Maybe another time?*

'Mr Giger, this is reception. You have guests. They are coming straight up to you.'

I dash to the door, checking that it is locked. Bang, bang, bang! Wow, that is a desperate hand on my door.

'Mr Giger, it's Mohammed. Let us in.' I can hear Cleopatra crying behind him.

'Good God, whatever happened to you?' They are in a terrible state. Mohammed is trembling and Cleopatra is covered in red spray paint. Some of it is on her face, and at first I think it is blood. 'Have you been in an accident?'

Charlotte takes Cleopatra to the bathroom. She is sobbing hysterically. Mohammed sits on the end of my bed and sips an orange juice from my fridge. He is as white as an Egyptian can be, and his eyes are wide open as if he has seen a ghost.

'Whatever are you into, Mr Giger?' he keeps repeating. 'For someone to resort to so much violence just to deliver a letter is beyond belief.'

'What letter?'

Mohammed pulls the letter from his *Djellaba*. 'For the immediate attention of M'sieur Jacques Giger.' It is written in good English and spelt correctly, a rare thing in Egypt. An educated person has written it. I tear it open. It has been written by hand but is easy to read and even easier to understand.

'Go back to Casablanca, finish your task, and then go home. Forget about Linah. I have lost my patience with you. This is your last warning.'

It is signed, 'A'.

'What are you going to do? These guys mean business. I don't think you know how dangerous these men are,' stutters Mohammed.

'I think you are right. Anyway, I can't expect you to risk your life on my account. I will obey their demand.'

Charlotte and Cleopatra step out of the bathroom, both draped in large white hotel towels. 'Maybe I will come back and visit you when this is all over.'

Mohammed laughs for the first time today.

'You are most welcome, Mr Giger. I do believe Charlotte and Cleopatra will approve.'

I order breakfast to be brought to the room. Hams, cheeses, stick bread, croissants, preserves, marmalades, hot coffee, and pastries soon arrive. We deserve a treat after the night out we have just experienced in Cairo.

Safe, Clean Sex

A deline is waiting for me at the airport. She rushes over and throws her arms around me.

'Darling, cool it. You will have us arrested. This is Casablanca, not Paris.'

'I don't care. I was so worried about you and why did you tell me you were going to Agadir when you were searching for Linah in Cairo.' She pulls back from me and looks me in the face. 'I take it you didn't find Her?'

'I did, actually.'

Her face changes.

'But she is not with me. I will tell you about my trip at the apartment. What have you been up to?'

Her face brightens as I pick up my overnight bag and put my free arm around her.

'Are you happy?'

'I am now.'

'I mean with the project.'

She jumps up and kisses me. 'Let's forget about the project for a while. We have better things to do.'

I slap her arse as she climbs into the taxi. Not many men have done that and got away with it.

My apartment is a shambles. My first thought is that it has been broken into. Drawers are open, clothes are scattered everywhere, dishes are piled high on the kitchen tops, and takeaway food trays litter the floor.

'Oh my God, what is going on here?'

Adeline jumps up and kisses me again.

'Don't worry, we'll clean it up. We have been using your place as our headquarters.'

'I don't mind you living here, but what a mess!'

'Well, we have been so busy, we haven't had time to clean up. I promise we will do it today.'

I remove three bras and a pair of pants from my sofa and sit down.

'Hey! Who's this "we" you keep talking about? If you have been entertaining a guy in my bed, you have a big problem.'

'Would you be jealous?'

'No, I just don't rent my bed out to guys.'

Her look turns to one of disappointment. There is indeed someone in my bedroom; I can hear them moving about. I rush to the door and throw it open before Adeline can stop me. Sure enough there is a body in my bed. Adeline grabs my arm, pulling me back before I can rip the sheets off.

'May I introduce my personal assistant?'

'Assisting in what?' I am not pleased.

Two hands appear from under the duvet, and a very sleepy Amelia pulls herself up into a sitting position.

'Bonjour, M'sieur Giger. Welcome home. I am so pleased to see you.'

'Amelia.' I am surprised to say the least. 'I am so pleased you are feeling better. Now get up, make a coffee, and tell me what the hell is going on.'

She jumps out of bed wearing only a shirt – one of my shirts, to be exact. She still shows evidence of her beating, with several large bruises slowly turning yellow down her legs, but it doesn't distract from her beauty.

The two girls sit one on either side of me. They are full of fun and eager to share their progress with me. It is nice to be surrounded by so much energy and enthusiasm. Adeline starts the presentation.

'We have enrolled 1,245 girls through word of mouth. Most are in Casablanca, Rabat, and Agadir. We estimate this to be 80 per cent of the hookers in these cities. We have also researched a similar number of girls who are scattered across the kingdom. We have their names and addresses and will contact them during the next two weeks.'

'We have also employed nine experienced johns,' interrupts Adeline. 'Men who regularly seek out girls. They are touring the streets at night, reading cards in telephone kiosks and speaking to the girls who hang out on the street on a one-on-one basis. The reports coming back to us are encouraging. The girls love the system, but we do stress that if they don't enrol they will be arrested. That might be the most compelling reason.'

Amelia continues the story. 'All these girls are on our computer along with their status, description, and services they are willing to offer. They have all been given code names, special e-mail addresses, and a free mobile, which they must only use for business. Should we get an enquiry that gives the wrong code name, we will assume the phone has been stolen and the girl is in trouble. Alarm bells will be sounded, and we will race to her assistance. One more month should see this part of the project complete. If a girl has not enrolled by the end of the month, she will not be able to do the business.'

'That is great news. You have done very well.' I patted the knees of both girls.

'Oh, that is not all, M'sieur Giger.' Amelia jumps to her feet. 'I have been enrolling the clients. We have nearly 15,000 clients across the world already. Each has downloaded the app, so they have a direct link to the girls and to us. They too are on our database with information about their names, employer, nationality, age, and preferences. Each client' – she pauses.– 'and M'sieur Giger, some clients are women – they have all paid a thousand dirham for the app along with a deposit of five thousand dirham, which they have to top up as they go.'

'I believe the mobile companies call this "Pay as you go",' butts in Adeline. 'But we call it "pay as you cum".' Both girls burst out laughing. They had been saving that joke for just this occasion.'

'Have you got a start date for the service?'

'M'sieur Giger, we are already in business. We are using Linah's office in the Twin Towers. We have three full-time girls watching and listening, answering questions from interested recruits and filing every contact made with our girls and every transaction. We are linked to the bank; they keep all the statements, and the accounts up to date. Money is rolling in.'

'This is beyond all expectation. And you have done this all by yourselves?'

'Well, not quite on our own. Amelia's cousin is a web designer for the government, so she set up the online communication system and activated the mobile apps. She knew the head of the government IT department who put the computer system in for us. They are both on our payroll, as we will need their continuing skills.'

I am a little concerned. 'Can we trust them to keep their mouths shut? Working for the government is a little too close for comfort?'

'For what we are paying them they will keep mum.' The girls sit back with big smiles on their faces.

'What do Jean Claud and Lafleur have to say about it?'

'They don't know yet. We wanted to be sure the system works before we tell them.'

'And does it work?'

'Like a dream.'

'Then let's go tell them. It looks as if our work is done.'

Is this wishful thinking? Am I going to get Linah back in the very near future? Would Cleopatra and Charlotte get the opportunity to take care of me so soon? I throw my clothes onto the pile of dresses and knickers already on the bedroom floor, and we all climb into a still warm bed. I can't think of a nicer way of celebrating our success.

The Job Is Done

September and October are probably the nicest months to be in Casablanca. The tourists have gone home. It is quiet and civilised. The air is clean, clear, and warm. The sea and the sky are still bright blue. I love watching the waves break against the quay and crash down over the open swimming pools. The pools are closed now, as the season is over. That means no more screaming children and no more crazy dives from young men showing off their skills and their prowess – not until next year, anyway.

Adeline and I walk the corniche, taking coffee at the very same cafe where Linah and I met. Sometimes we will share a burger or an exotic ice if we are feeling more exotic. Amelia is busy running the escort business and enjoying every minute. The company has moved into bigger offices and now has fifteen girls manning the computers. We have been told that several other countries want to install similar operations. Amelia spends a lot of her time touring the world, explaining and promoting the service, selling its attributes, and of course making sure she takes a percentage for her trouble.

Adeline and I sit watching the sea roll in, enjoying hot coffees to keep the fresh sea breeze at bay. She looks as sophisticated in her long, pale green buttoned-down over coat as she did during the summer in her fitted summer dresses. A limousine pulls up outside the cafe. It is very rare that such an imposing car appears on this side of town. It is causing quite a stir amongst the visitors along the corniche. The Moroccan flags fluttering from both front wings identify it as an embassy car.

The driver steps out. He is a tall, upright young man and looks very impressive in his military uniform. He pauses at the counter and has a word with the cafe owner. They share a joke and laugh then the proprietor points him in our direction.

'He might be coming for me,' mutters Adeline. 'I have to attend many civic receptions and parties, not as an escort anymore but as a representative of the French government, usually with Jean Claud. We are both very popular you know, for our role in the turnaround of Morocco's fortune, we are invited to impress the guests and inspire businessmen and politicians. But I am not aware of an engagement this afternoon.' Adeline is in her relaxed mood and doesn't want it to be any other way. The driver stands over us.

'M'sieur Jacques Giger?'

I am taken by surprise.

'Yes, I am M'sieur Jacques Giger. What can I do for you?'

He smiles. It is obvious I wasn't expecting him to address me, and he seems to find it very amusing. 'A letter for you, sir.' He hands me a large beige envelope sealed with a waxed emblem.

Adeline leans over to investigate and takes it out of my hands.

'It must be from the palace. Why is the king sending you a letter?'

'I don't know.' I grab it back off her.

'Do I need to respond?' I ask him.

'I am not aware that I have to return with anything, M'sieur Giger. My task was to find you and deliver the letter into your hands.'

I put my hand into my pocket and draw out a fifty-dirham note.

'M'sieur Giger, please do not embarrass me. I am very well paid as a dignitary of the kingdom.' I apologise sincerely as he turns and marches back to his car.

'What can it be, an invitation?' I hold up the envelope to the sun and try to see through it.

'Stop playing about. Just open it!' Adeline is far more excited than I am. She sits in silence as I break the seal and slide out a sheet of Moroccan palace notepaper.

'Well! What does it say?'

'It is an invitation to holiday in the Bahamas as a thank-you for my contribution to the kingdom's successful development.'

'From whom? Can you take a friend? When?'

'Whoa! Stop just there. It is from the ambassador and his wife. I have to be at the VIP lounge in the airport at ten thirty on Friday morning.'

'Just you?'

'Apparently, just me. Look.' I show her the bottom line. It reads, 'A refusal will not be accepted.' Under that is a big swishing 'A'.

'I suppose that is A for ambassador.'

'I suppose so,' she mutters indignantly.

I look straight into Adeline's eyes. 'What do you know about this guy? Is he still up to his tricks? Are you still working for him? Are you going to jump out of a large cake on the beach and entertain us?'

'I am not. I have had nothing to do with him since' – she pauses – 'since that last time. But he is still employing girls through the escort system. I don't know how he treats them, but we have had no complaints. The girls will be well paid for their services, so maybe they think it is worth the trick.'

'So Friday afternoon I will be sipping coconut cocktails in Jamaica or somewhere similar. Are you jealous?' I tease her.

'I wish I was going with you. I don't trust you with those fleshy girls.' She stops mid sentence. 'I didn't know he was married.'

'Neither did I.'

The Big Reveal

I t is eight o'clock on Friday, 8 October. Adeline's phone bursts into life. It is her brother.

'Hi, sis. The ambassador has requested the latest sales figures for the escort company. Is it today Giger meets him at the airport?'

'Yes, why?'

'Can he take them to him? The ambassador wants to study them during his vacation.'

'I suppose so.'

'Okay. Slip around to the office now, and you can take them to the airport. I suppose you are going to wave him off?'

'Yes, just to wave him off.'

'You are not going with him?'

'No, I am not going with him.'

'See you soon then.'

When Adeline arrives at the office, Jean Claud and Lafleur are in disagreement. As she walks in they both stand back in silence.

'Is anything the matter?'

Jean Claud comes forward and gives her a brotherly squeeze. 'Nothing for you to worry about. It is just a difference of opinion between Lafleur and me.' It is obvious that Lafleur is not happy.

'Come on, tell your baby sister what is troubling you.'

Jean Claud stutters whilst he makes up an explanation. 'Lafleur does not want to give the ambassador all the figures.'

'He has done nothing towards this project other than humiliate us and bully us,' chimes in Lafleur.

Jean Claud jumps to his defence. 'Without his money we could have done nothing. Look at us now! We must be the richest men on the planet … and woman.'

Lafleur is not converted. 'I hate this man. He has to be got rid of, or else he will be bullying us for the rest of our lives.'

'That is being taken care of.' Jean Claud picks up a brown leather briefcase and hands it to Adeline. 'You are definitely not going with him on the plane, are you?'

'No, I have not been invited.' Adeline looks deep into his eyes. She senses something sinister.

'You must not go with him. In fact, come straight back here. We have many things to discuss.'

'You worry too much about me. I am a big girl now.' And with that she grasps the briefcase and strides out of the office.

'You should have told her what is going to happen,' snaps Lafleur.

'I don't trust her. She has a soft spot for Giger. She might go with him.'

'Look, we do nothing until she gets back to the office.'

'If she doesn't come back, we do not detonate the bomb.'

'But he will find it in the briefcase, and it will be us who are dead.'

'She will come back.'

I must admit I feel a bit stupid standing here outside the VIP lounge holding my tatty overnight bag. Everyone else has exotic matching Louis Vuitton leather bags, but this is all I have, and this is the way I live. There is no sign of the ambassador. I look at my watch; it is 10.05. Adeline comes rushing up to me, gasping for breath.

'I thought I was going to miss you. The traffic is grid locked.' She jumps up and gives me a big hug. 'Has the ambassador arrived yet?'

'Not yet. There is no sight or sound of him. Let's go and wait in the lounge.'

We are stopped at the big glass doors to the VIP suite by an airport security guard; he requests to see our travel documents.

'I don't have a ticket. I am meeting the ambassador,' I tell him, feeling even sillier having to admit I don't know the ambassador's name. The guard scans down a list of names on his iPad.

'M'sieur Jacques Giger?'

'Yes, I am M'sieur Jacques Giger.'

'There is a slight delay, M'sieur Giger. Please help yourself to a free drink from the bar. Would you like a morning paper?' I refuse his offer.

He then turns to Adeline. 'There is no mention of your wife sir.'

'Oh! I am so sorry. May I introduce Madame Adeline la Chapelle, the sister of Jean Claud Chapelle, the French foreign ambassador. She is here only to wave me off and will not be flying today.'

The guard looks at Adeline. 'Madame, my sincere apologies. I did not recognise you. But Madame, I am afraid you are not allowed in the lounge if you are not flying.'

Adeline raises herself up onto her toes and whispers in his ear. I have no idea what she is saying to him, but whatever it is, it does the trick.

'Just this time, Madame.' He steps back and beckons us through. We find a vacant sofa in the far corner of the lounge, which has a view of the airport apron; I can hold her hand and caress her face, hidden from view by the large, soft, over-embroidered cushions. She looks very at ease in such an elaborate setting.

'Oh, before I forget, the ambassador has requested the latest sales figures from Abel. He asked me to call at the office first thing this morning so I could give them to him. As he is not here, can you see he gets them?'

I take the briefcase from her and place it on the floor against my overnight bag. The one good thing about traveling with embassy status is the ease of immigration; there are no baggage checks and embarrassing body searches.

Adeline bombards me with a list of instructions. 'You have to text me every hour and call me at least once a day.'

'Yes of course.'

'You can have fun but must not sleep around. You must watch your diet, not get drunk, and come home safe.' She is worried that I will not come back, and the thought of me coming back with Linah is a nightmare for her.

'M'sieur Giger, your plane is ready to depart.' A very distinguished official introduces himself and picks up my bag and briefcase.

'But where is the ambassador?' I ask.

'He is already on the plane, sir. He is awaiting your arrival.'

Adeline climbs all over me and nearly crushes me to death.

'I love you,' she whispers as her lips fold around mine.

I must admit I don't want to release my grip on her. She feels absolutely wonderful, but I have to take control of my emotions and push her off. The official is already leaving the lounge, and I don't know which way to go. I wave at her until she is out of sight. She looked as elegant and as dignified as she did that first morning I saw her, struggling with her breakfast in the Sheraton dining room. I jog down the corridor, trying to keep up with the steward until he shows me into the belly of the plane.

This is no ordinary Royal Air Maroc plane. It's like walking into the lounge of the Savoy Hotel. Leather sofas have replaced rows of seats. On the walls are hung original paintings by the Pre-Raphaelite Brotherhood, long drapes adorn the small windows, vases of flowers sit on coffee tables, and the floor is covered with a deep-pile crimson carpet.

'Make yourself at home, M'sieur Giger.' The pilot introduces himself. 'The ambassador will be with you shortly. We will depart in five minutes. You don't need a seat belt, but we ask you to stay seated until we are airborne.'

I do as I am told. *So this is how the other half live,* I think to myself. *I like it.*

The earth very quickly disappears beneath us. I feel the plane flatten and gain the confidence to walk over to the window. I love it when the sun beams down onto the white, woolly clouds. I can see another plane flying in the opposite direction, possibly on a path to Madrid or Paris. We bank slightly left and leave it behind as we head out towards the blue waters of the Atlantic.

The door dividing the lounge from the rear of the plane swings open, and the ambassador walks in wearing a very elaborate caftan. He no longer looks like the intimidating bear that inspired his nickname. He is laughing and obviously very happy and pleased to see me.

'Welcome to my world, M'sieur Giger. I am so pleased you could make it.'

'I thought I didn't have a choice.'

He laughs out loud and invites me to sit. 'How was your summer?'

Now it is my turn to laugh. 'Challenging, yet very rewarding. I hope you are pleased with what I have achieved.'

'I am delighted, and so is the king, so much so that he has instructed me to offer you a gift of your choice – only one gift, mind you. He is forever in your debt.'

'I don't understand. Where does the king come into the equation?'

'I understand why you must be confused, M'sieur Giger. Let us relax over a mint tea, and I will explain.'

He claps his hands, and three waiters enter the lounge to serve us tea.

'This Moroccan tea even beats the tea at Raffles, the world-famous hotel in Singapore.' The ambassador laughs.

'Thank you very much, now are you sitting comfortably, M'sieur Giger?'

I nod.

'Then I will begin.' He laughs. 'I too listened with my Mother in the 1950s. I was brought up in Britain and went to university in Cambridge.'

He sipped calmly on his tea for a couple of minutes and then sat back in his large leather chair. 'Two years ago, Jean Claud Chapelle and his cousin, Monsieur Abel Lafleur, advertised for a financial backer to enable a project that they believed would rock the world. They stated the investment would make three billion dollars' profit in the first two years alone. As you can imagine, it was the talk of the financial world. It created interest from the richest men on the planet, from China, Saudi Arabia, Hong Kong, and America. News of the project reached the ears of the king of Morocco. At first he thought it was a joke. Then he read that it involved re-marketing the biggest companies in Morocco, so he watched the developments very closely with a personal interest.

'Two factors were against Chapelle and Lafleur finding a backer. One was the location. No one expected Morocco to be the centre of such an ambitious project. The second was that Chapelle and Lafleur insisted on total control and freedom to do whatever they thought necessary. In other words, the financier would only be a sleeping partner. Of course, no backer would invest that amount of money without some reserve – except one man that is. That man was our king. He had faith in the Moroccan people. If these two Frenchmen could turn his kingdom into a world-leading market, then he was happy for them to do so.

'So as not to reveal his identity as the backer, he suggested that I present myself as a very rich man with unlimited deposits and introduce myself as an interested party. All we insisted on was a daily progress report and the understanding that we would not release money for the next stage until the previous stage had proven to be a success. Apart from that, they could have a free hand. They jumped at the offer, and it didn't seem to bother them who I was. They didn't even bother to check if I had the money and where it might be coming from. Their ignorance played into our hands. If they failed, then they would take the fall. I would admit to being bankrupt and go down in history as the biggest con artist ever. The king would never be named or involved. Ideal! You know the rest of the story.'

'But they told me the French government was backing the project and went to great pains to explain why and how.'

'That was all lies. The only people involved were Chapelle, Lafleur, me, and you: Chapelle for his business skills, Lafleur for his accountancy experience, me for the finance, and you for the practical, on-ground action.'

'Wow, you took a risk.'

'Not really. We did our homework on you all very thoroughly. We had every move you all made continuously covered. We only had one slight problem with you.'

'And what was that?'

'You were falling in love with Linah. We couldn't allow you to be distracted with so much money involved. You had to be totally focused and dedicated. So we took her out of the equation and used her to speed your progress. I am sorry if we caused you pain.'

'How did you know I was falling in love with Linah?'

'That one was easy. She was the only girl you didn't sleep with.'

'You must have known I was in love with her before I did.'

'As I told you, we knew everything.'

Nothing Hurts More Than Love

'Talking of Linah, if I have a gift, I pick the freedom of Linah and the opportunity to meet her again.'

'Wahoo, M'sieur Giger, wait until you know the full story before selecting your gift. This is an offer you must think carefully about'

He claps his hands again. The dividing door opens, and Linah walks in.

'M'sieur Giger, may I introduce my wife? Linah and I were married three weeks ago in Cairo.'

I am lost for words. I don't know whether to be angry or happy. My first reaction is one of shock; my second is that I feel sick. My love for this girl has built up inside me until I can hardly think of anything else. The entire campaign to develop Morocco has been a professional function, I was simply doing a job that I have done so many times. My inner passion has been spent on finding Linah.

She walks over and stands next to him. He holds out his hand to her, and she gently accepts it. She looks beautiful. No, she looks magnificent – and very happy.

'If Lafleur only told the truth once, it was that Linah would be okay and that I shouldn't worry about her.'

'He was right. She is a bright, beautiful woman. She will, in the words of Lafleur, be okay. I know you were in love with her, and it is not for me to tell you who to fall in love with. But we hope it is all in your head, your English head, a head that trusts everyone and believes all you are told. I am afraid you English are very naïve and gullible even when it comes to your own desires. Anyway! We hope that very soon you will agree and recover and begin to love again.'

I catch my breath and try to relax. This has taken me by surprise, and it must be showing. Maybe I was fooling myself. Let's be honest, I hardly knew her. But she is a very pretty, appealing woman, and she definitely knows which buttons to press when she wants something. I am sure the ambassador will be able to cope with her. He reaches over and hands me a stiff drink. I haven't a clue what it is, but it is just what I need. I have to confess that I am very happy for her, in fact for both of them.

'I will recover. I wish you lots of happiness,' I manage to say.

'Thank you. So all is forgiven?'

'All is forgiven.'

The ambassador squeezes her hand and asks her to sit in the corner of the lounge, as we have a lot to talk about before our holiday can begin.

'Before we talk business, I have a few questions I would like to ask you, Mr Ambassador.'

He looks at me with a questioning eye. 'Okay! Go ahead. I will answer if I can.'

I pluck up the courage to bring up the subject of his sexual depravation. 'Mr Ambassador, it appears that my first impressions of you were wrong, but there are still a few things that I do not understand.'

'Okay.'

'Why were you so rough on Adeline and her girls?'

'Em! I thought you might ask that.'

Excuses, Excuses

'I have a weakness. My weakness is very much like your own, M'sieur Giger. I love pretty women. Adeline was at the top of my list; she is very beautiful but arrogant, self-assured, rich, and extremely good in bed. She serviced both my hormonal needs and my business needs admirably.'

'But why so rough?'

'I must be honest. I do not have a lot of respect for women who prostitute themselves. But maybe in Adeline's case I got carried away. Tell her I am very sorry if my guests hurt her. At first I didn't know what they were putting her through. When I did find out, it was my intention to put a stop to it, and I spoke with her about it. She didn't seem concerned. She said her girls could cope and they needed the money, I took this to mean she also was up for it, so I let it continue. I know I scared her once or twice, but I never hurt her. Anyway, I am delighted at the success of her online hostess business. I can now employ girls knowing they are professional and that they will be safe. I hope I am given the opportunity to show Adeline how sorry I am for any hurt.'

I must admit a smile crosses my face. He talked himself out of that like the true bureaucrat that he is.

'So what do you think of Jean Claud and Monsieur Lafleur?'

He scratches his head and looks around the room before staring back at me.

'I have to confess, I have misgivings about both of them.'

I wait for him to catch his breath.

'I have no respect for men who not only allow but encourage their sister to do such things. They knew what she was doing and what she had to do, and they let her. I think these two men should be held responsible for the hurt she suffered. He shakes his head both in anger and despair.

'So did this lack of respect for them create any doubt in your mind as to their capability towards the project?'

'You are a very deep man, M'sieur Giger. Now I understand why you are so good at your job.'

'You are too kind, Mr Ambassador. Yes, I love advertising, but I also love the knowledge of why people do what they do. Every action is preceded by habit, understanding, need, greed, and love. Know those facts about someone and you know the whole person.'

'So you claim to be a psychologist as well as an ad man?'

'To be an ad man, you need to be a psychologist.'

'So! Did you trust these guys?'

'During its operation I did. They didn't put a foot wrong, but I have doubts now. They have been exceptionally well paid for their work. They are both multimillionaires. But now we expect them to walk away and to leave the future of Morocco to its people. I have recently received information that they have alternative plans. Men who will prostitute their sister are capable of doing anything.'

'What plans might they be?'

'They want full rights to all the industries, and to get that, they think all they have to do is to get rid of me. You now know that is not possible, but they still think I am a simple, bullying businessman.'

'Have they tried to buy you out?'

'Of course not. They wouldn't pay to gain control of what they believe is already theirs. They would have me killed.'

'I can't believe that. They are loyal to you. Goodness! Here in this very briefcase are the latest accounts that you asked for. I am sure you will be delighted with the figures.'

The ambassador looks down at the briefcase next to his chair.

'You say these are the figures that I asked for?' He lifts the case up onto his knees, and then he looks back at me. 'I didn't ask for any figures.'

Have You Any Idea What You Have Done?

'So have you two made up?' jokes Adeline as she walks back into Jean Claud's office.

'Of course. Did everything go to plan? Did you give the briefcase to the ambassador?' asks Lafleur.

'Not exactly. The ambassador was already on the plane, and they weren't even going to let me into the VIP lounge because I didn't have a ticket to fly. Can you believe that?'

'I'm sure you talked your way in,' answers Jean Claud.

'I did, but I should not have had to beg like I did.'

'I agree,' retorts Lafleur. 'Anyway, the streets of Morocco are paved with gold. From today even the sea will open up for us. If anyone fails to treat us with the highest form of respect we will have them put into prison.'

'Don't be silly, Abel. I don't like you talking like that.'

'So what did you do with the briefcase?'

'I gave it to Jacques. He promised to give it to the ambassador for me.'

'Ideal! You are a very clever woman, Adeline. Did anyone see M'sieur Giger with the case?'

'I suppose the steward did. Why?'

'Enough,' interrupts Jean Claud. 'Let me take you both through the accounts of our empire.' He turns to Lafleur. 'Put the TV on, Abel. Let's keep an eye on Sky News.'

The figures are indeed impressive; the amount of money that came into the bank during the first few months is in the billions of dollars. Jean Claud cracks open the second bottle of Champagne. The cork bounces off the ceiling and disappears behind the sixty-inch TV screen in the corner of the office. The giggles and the bubbles are getting the better of them all. Even Adeline is enjoying their success.

'Wait! What is this on the news?' Lafleur stops the merriment. A news bulletin featuring the ambassador is being reported. They all stare at the screen.

'Oh, it's nothing. It's just that stupid man opening the new distribution centre in Marrakech yesterday.'

'What did you think it was?' asks Adeline.

Lafleur starts to laugh under the influence of celebration. 'I thought it was the climax of our brilliant campaign, the end of the man who deserves to die.'

'I don't understand.' Adeline looks puzzled.

'That man whom you hate, that man who caused you so much pain and humiliation – well, we have taken care of him,' boasts Lafleur.

'Taken care of him? Have you got him to sign all the assets over to us?'

'We have done better than that. We have had him killed. In that briefcase you gave to Giger is a bomb. It will blow the ambassador out of the sky. And do you know what is even better? Giger is going to take the blame for it. He has been seen taking the case onto the plane, thanks to you. He has the motive to kill him. Everyone knows he has been totally focused on saving his lovely Linah. Nobody hates The Bear more than he does. It will be reported as an unfortunate mistake by Giger that he went up with the plane.'

Lafleur laughs with such emotion he knocks his champagne glass over, and it crashes to the floor. 'Nothing and no-one can stop us now.'

Adeline is in shock. She is shaking so hard she can't stand up. Then she realizes. 'And the news you are waiting for is the explosion of the plane?'

Her screams can be heard all the way to the street. She runs out of the office, down the corridor, and locks herself in the loo. Crying hysterically she tries to ring me on her mobile, but her fingers just won't operate. Time after time she tries, but her phone will not connect. Through her tears she tries to type me a warning text. Her hysteria makes it impossible for her to concentrate on what she is writing. She finally presses 'send' just before fainting to the floor.

There Is a Bomb on Board

My mobile vibes. A glance tells me it is Adeline.

'Answer it,' instructs the ambassador. 'It might be important.'

'It's not important. It's from Adeline. She is probably telling me that she is missing me already.'

'If you love her, you should respond.'

'Who says I love her? I have only had eyes for Linah.' I pause. 'But do you know, you might be right. I think I do love her.'

'Then answer it.' I click on her message. 'THERSABONINBCASE CUNBAK QIK.'

I stare at the message; it isn't like Adeline to send me a silly text.

'What's the matter?' asks the ambassador. 'Is she asking you to marry her?' He laughs.

I show him the message. 'What do you make of that?'

He stares at it for what seems an age.

'I think it reads, "There's a bomb in the briefcase, come back quick." If that is what she is telling you, we have a bomb on board.'

He looks at the briefcase and then dashes up to the cockpit. I sit frozen to my seat, unable to take it all in.

'Don't touch the case,' he screams back at me.

What is Adeline doing, handing me a case with a bomb in it? Surely she didn't know. Oh God, I hope she didn't know. And if Adeline has sent this message, then she is in danger also. She is always so precise.

The captain immediately tries to contact ground control to inform them of our situation. There is no response.

'Damn, just when we need them. What is our exact location?'

The co-pilot reads off the longitude and latitude figures from the compass in front of him.

'Why can't you reach ground control?

'You see, we are in the middle of the Atlantic. We have twenty minutes of flying time during which we are out of voice contact with ground control. We were in touch with air traffic control over Portugal, and soon we will be in touch with Maine air traffic control. Just at the moment we are out of sight from both of them.'

'Out of sight?' screams the ambassador. 'Do you mean no one knows where we are?'

'They know where we are. Everyone can see us on their computer screens. The plane is sending out a signal every minute. We just can't talk to them. We are on our own for another nineteen minutes and ten seconds.'

'All I can do is send out a mayday. Every ship, plane, boat, and train will hear a mayday call.'

'But they can't do anything to help us.' Reiterates the ambassador.

'This is flight RAM001 bound for Barbados calling ground control. We need help. Can anyone hear me?' The pilot tries again. Again there is silence.

The co-pilot is busy scanning his computer screen for the nearest landing strips.

'Captain, we have the Canary Islands, Bermuda, Haiti, and St Lucia. If we turn back we have Portugal or Southern Ireland.' The co-pilot's voice is quavering; he is scared.

'For God's sake! We are in the middle of the Atlantic. I doubt we have time to make any of those places. We will have to ditch into the sea.'

'You can't bring a perfectly good plane down into the sea. What is the sense of that?'

'So we wait until we are blown out of the sky? How do I bring it down then, in a million pieces?'

From where I am sitting in the lounge I can hear the argument in the cabin. Their voices are shrill. They are angry and very frightened. Arguing is not going to save us.

'Do we have any idea what will trigger this bomb? Will it blow at a designated height? At a specified time? When the case is opened?'

The ambassador rushes back to join us and looks at me for an answer.

'I have no idea what will make it explode. Can we throw the case out of the plane?' I know it is a stupid suggestion, but it is all I can think of.

'You mean just open the door and throw it out of the plane?'

'Of course that's what I mean. I am pretty sure we don't have time to land this damn plane. You have just told me we are in the middle of the Atlantic.'

The ambassador rushes back into the cabin.

The pilot looks at him. 'That might not be as silly as it sounds. We might be able to open the door if we can get below twenty thousand feet. The doors can be released when the pressure outside is the same as the pressure inside. But I need permission from ground control before I can reduce height. We might collide with another aircraft.'

The ambassador is outraged. 'Get the damn plane to twenty thousand feet. I don't care a toss about any other plane.'

The pilot pushes the joysticks forward, and the plane starts to lose height.'

'This is flight RAM001 bound for Barbados. We need help. Can anyone hear me?' The co-pilot takes up the chant, trying to make contact with control.

The speakers eventually crackle into life. 'This is Ground Control Maine, hearing you loud and clear. Welcome to America, RAM001.'

The co-pilot breathes a sigh of relief. 'This is RAM001. We believe we have a bomb on board. We are taking evasive action and lowering our flight path to twenty thousand feet. We can't think of anything else to do.'

'Did I hear you correctly, RAM001? You say you have a bomb on board?'

'That is correct. Can you get us to the nearest airport?'

'I will be back with you in seconds, RAM001. In the meantime you have clearance to lose height to twenty thousand feet.

Nobody Can Help Us Now

The ambassador comes back into the lounge and reports on events. 'The co-pilot is talking to air control. They will designate an airport and prepare all safety and rescue procedures. But in my opinion this is going to be too late.'

The ambassador is right. Ground control starts suggesting landing strips hours away. They even suggest we return to Casablanca. And then to add insult to injury, they want the names of everybody on board and details of what we are doing. What a waste of time! We are trying to save our lives up here, not write our obituaries. The only useful thing they have done – which, thinking about it, still does not help us – is to scramble two fighter aircraft to fly along side us. What can they can do, apart from watch us die? The truth is, we are on our own. We have to think and act fast.

'Any ideas?' asks the ambassador.

The plane is plunging earthwards; the steward is already standing by the door, ready to release the door lock at twenty thousand feet.

'We can't just throw it out,' he screams. 'The turbulence will explode any device inside it before it clears the wing.'

The ambassador throws in an idea. 'I know this might sound stupid, but do we have a parachute on board that we can tie to it?'

'Yes, in the steward's cabin. But they are too big for a small case. They are designed for the weight of a person.'

'Okay, can we make one? Can we make a parachute out of bed sheeting, for example, so it will drop gently into the air stream?'

Linah rushes into the bedroom to search for some sheeting. First she thinks of a pillowcase but on inspection decides they are far too small. *Maybe a duvet cover?* Yes, this is a possibility, but the one on her king-sized bed is far too large. A single off one of the crew's beds might do the trick. She dashes into the crew's quarters at the back of the plane.

She has no idea what type of fabric makes a good parachute. She has seen men throwing themselves out of planes and floating to earth in old war movies. The chutes are usually white and seem to be made of silk. She wonders if cotton will do. Anyway, the duvets on the single beds are cotton. She drags one off the mattress and rips the cover off it. As for tying it to the briefcase, maybe a curtain pull from the bathroom will do.

Linah sits at the desk and starts to thread the cord around the edge of the duvet case. She is by far the most composed and clearest thinker of us all; she deserves a medal if we survive.

'Do you know what you are doing, Linah?'

'Not a clue. Does it matter?'

'Not really, but what you are doing looks great to me.'

All the time we know the case can explode at any time, blowing us all to Kingdom Come. Life and death don't seem to have any meaning anymore. If it blows it blows. All we can do is act as fast as we can. Linah turns the sheet into a balloon shape and ties the strings around the handle of the case, trying not to move it.

'26,000 feet, 25,500 feet.' The captain's voice is booming through the PA system, counting us down.

Two American fighter planes have now joined us, one on either side; we can see the faces of the pilots watching our every move. They are talking to the pilot, asking what state we are in and what action we are taking. Contact with ground control has been abandoned. They are still requesting a passenger and crew list, and this is not our priority at this time. If we can get within one hundred miles of the American coast we will have all the helicopter and search ships the Coast Guard has available. They are already standing by to pick us out of the water should we choose to crash into the sea. But this means another ninety minutes of fast flying.

The senior steward steps forward. 'Excuse me, Mister Ambassador, but I have some parachute experience.'

'Do you think you can make a chute better than Linah?' There is a slight grin across his face.

'No, I don't mean in the making of them. I couldn't even thread a needle. I mean in parachute jumping.'

'So speak up. Tell us what is on your mind.'

'Well! Mister Ambassador, I could jump out of the plane with the briefcase, open the chute once I have cleared the plane, and then release the briefcase a safe distance away. The case will fall faster than me. And anyway, I could steer the chute away from it in case it explodes.'

The ambassador looks in my direction. I can tell from his face that he thinks this is a good idea.

'I take it we have proper chutes aboard the plane.'

'Yes, sir, we have five. As I said earlier, they are too big to be attached to the case. They are designed for people weighing 70 to 120 kilograms.'

I have many misgivings about this plan. 'Mr Ambassador, I appreciate this man's offer, but he will probably not survive. The bomb might go off as soon as he steps out of the plane or whilst he is free falling. Plus, he is going to land in the middle of the Atlantic. He will survive only minutes in the cold water. We have no protective clothing for him and no floats or dinghy to climb into. If by some miracle he does survive the fall it will take at least thirty minutes for help of any kind to get to him. He will not survive.'

'Sir! I think we are all dead anyway. At least the ambassador will be safe.'

'Thank you for your offer, steward, but we are not sacrificing anyone. If the plane blows, we all go. If it doesn't blow, we will all come out of this together.' The ambassador pats him on his shoulder. 'If we survive I will remember your dedication. You are a great man.'

The steward looks slightly disappointed, but I am sure inside he must be relieved. The pilot's voice comes booming over the PA system. We have just been informed by ground control that the king is watching our every move. He has sent us a message. There is a click as the pilot connects up the incoming message.

'This is your king. My prayers and the prayers of every Moroccan are for your safe return. May Allah be with you.'

'23,500 feet, 23,000 feet. Three more minutes.'

As we fly lower and lower we can feel the cold air of the surface of the Atlantic buffeting the plane. It is almost impossible to stand up.

'21,000 feet, 20,500 feet. Prepare to open the door.'

The two accompanying fighter pilots have been briefed as to our plan. Each aircraft pulls away. The pilot on the port side has a clear view of the fuselage door. The pilot on our starboard has positioned himself above us so he can watch the jettison and hopefully report on its safe disposal. Both fighters are flying slightly forward of us to be clear of an explosion should one occur.

The steward pulls hard down on the door handle. Nothing happens.

'Not yet! Stay calm,' shouts the pilot. 'We are not at twenty thousand feet yet.'

The steward turns to look at us all. His face is as white as the sheet he holds, and he is shaking vigorously. Perspiration is running down his face. We are all devoid of expression; there is nothing we can say. The rope we have tied around him and secured to the seats is straining as he presses down on the handle again.

'Okay, this time it should open.' This time the door unlocks. He only just manages to let go before it swings outward, caught by the 300-mph air stream, and breaks off its hinges, crashing into the tail fin. We stare in horror; we didn't expect that.

Being blown up and dying in a second is one thing. Being dragged out of a plane at twenty thousand feet and floating in space for God knows how long seems far more terrifying. I hand him the case and folded-up duvet. As he holds it out into the air stream, it is snatched from his hands. The parachute billows open, flapping crazily as it disappears. We pull the steward back into the safety of the plane and hold our breaths. One second, two seconds, three, four – surely it must be far behind us by now.

'Has it gone?' screams Linah.

The steward tries to look back through the gaping door, but the fighter pilot watching on the port side answers her question.

'The chute has caught on the tail fin. The bag is flying behind the aircraft but it is still held to the plane by the ropes.'

The second pilot confirms his report. 'The chute has got caught on the tail. I can see the case streaming out behind the plane fastened by the ropes.'

Now at fifteen thousand feet we are far too low to stay stable. We are in danger of touching the water with a wing tip. The pilot pulls back on the throttle, and the plane lurches into a climb back up to twenty thousand feet. The steep accent might just shake the parachute clear.

With the sudden climb and the force of the air rushing around inside the cabin we are thrown to the floor, rolling into and over each other, crashing into chairs and tables. I can hear Linah reciting her prayers and chanting the Koran.

'Back up to twenty thousand feet. Release oxygen masks and try to strap in.' commands the pilot.

Then the inevitable happens: an almighty explosion.

Dead or Alive

B reaking news: An unidentified plane has exploded over the mid-Atlantic.

Ten minutes later

Breaking news: A Royal Air Maroc plane has exploded over the mid-Atlantic.

Twenty minutes later

Breaking news: Sabotage has not been ruled out for the loss of the Moroccan royal flight in the mid-Atlantic one hour ago.

Jean Claud and Lafleur shake hands and raise their glasses to a job well done.

'It's all ours now,' says Jean Claud.

'I'll drink to that,' adds Lafleur.

They scan up and down the news channels for further information. CNN is filling in a few more details. 'A bomb on board an Air Maroc 747 plane of the royal fleet has exploded in the mid-Atlantic. Ten people including the crew are thought to have perished. It has been reported that the bomb was smuggled aboard the plane by a M'sieur Jacques Giger, a Swiss banker. The king was not on board the plane.'

A statement from the Moroccan royal household reads, 'We are awaiting further details of the explosion before we come to any conclusions as to what happened. We are aware that a M'sieur Jacques Giger was on board the plane, but we have no reason at this time to believe he played any part in the blowing up of the plane. M'sieur Giger is one of the missing passengers.'

Jean Claud looks at Lafleur. 'Royal flight? What do they mean, aboard a royal flight?'

'My own thoughts exactly,' queries Lafleur. 'What has the king got to do with this? Does Adeline know anything?'

'Where is she?'

Adeline is still unconscious on the bathroom floor. They have to break down the door to get to her. Desperate as they are to talk with her, it is three hours before she regains consciousness. She stares up into their faces.

'What have you done?' she croaks through her dried, broken lips. 'What the bloody hell have you done? You promised me that no one would get hurt. I didn't want the ambassador dead. I did what you told me to do. You said to keep him happy and keep the money coming, and that is what I did. All I went through, I went through for you, not for the ambassador. It was you who left me to suffer. Your stupid greed for wealth and fame has found you out.

You are murderers, and you have also killed the man I love, the only man who cared about me. How can you do this to me?'

'The man you love?' Lafleur recoils. 'Adeline, you must be out of your mind. You are the daughter of one of the wealthiest and most respected families in France. You can't fall in love with an English commoner who is having to work in Saudi Arabia to make a living. Forget him. He is a nobody.'

Jean Claud agrees. 'Lafleur is right. Giger was not the man for you. And anyway, you are so rich now you don't need a man to take care of you.'

'I need a man to love me, not to take care of me.' She breaks down in tears and buries her face in the sofa. Jean Claud and Lafleur are lost for words, totally failing to understand what could have possessed their sister to fall in love with an English ad man.

They are stunned at the news that the plane was a royal flight. What was the ambassador doing in a royal plane? Who was the ambassador? Jean Claud looks Lafleur straight in the eyes.

'Are we stupid or what? We have no idea who that guy was, what companies he owned, and whether he was working alone or with others.'

'His money was good.' Lafleur is adamant; his cool, calculating brain has no give in it whatsoever. 'He delivered all he promised, and so did we. So stop worrying.'

It is eight in the morning when the Moroccan police knock on the office door of Jean Claud. Their questions are simple and direct. Does a M'sieur

Jacques Giger work for you? Did you know he was on board the plane? Did he have any reason to blow up the plane? Did you know Giger was planning this massacre? Why was Adeline at the airport that morning?

The questions continue for over two hours. Lafleur is awakened at the same time at his home and asked similar questions. The questions are easy, and they both respond with exactly the same answers until they are asked if Adeline and Giger are having a relationship. Lafleur answers no. Jean Claud answers that he believes his sister to be in love. One of them is lying. What they do agree on is Adeline's innocence. Both state that she knows nothing and has nothing to do with it.

Adeline is still arrested that afternoon as an accomplice to blowing up the plane. She has no defence. She was seen handing me the briefcase, which contained the bomb. Her arrest makes the ten o'clock news and is spread all over the morning newspapers. 'Woman plants bomb on royal plane.' 'Daughter of French aristocrat tries to kill the king.' The stories are frightening and so untrue.

During the next two days the story unravels. The question of Adeline's involvement seems to be paramount. Both Jean Claud and Lafleur state quite categorically that she had nothing to do with it, and they cast the blame on me. I alone wanted the Ambassador dead because he had kidnapped the girl I was in love with. The press are having a field day. 'Jealous lover blows up royal plane.'

It takes the police another day to get Jean Claud and Lafleur to confess and admit they tricked her into giving me the bomb. They claim they had no idea that the ambassador was working for the King and their intention was only to scare the ambassador for his bullying and evil ways. They never intended to detonate the bomb.

Jean Claud and Lafleur are arrested, and their case will be heard in the near future. Adeline is allowed bail and advised to seek psychological help. She walks along the corniche every day, speaking to no one, with her head bowed and her eyes to the ground. Amelia sometimes walks with her, stopping for a coffee and staring out to sea in silence. Sometimes they buy an ice cream sundae topped with swirls of whipped cream, but Amelia usually ends up eating both and making herself sick.

Adeline cannot come to terms with what her brothers have done. How could they kill the man she loved – and trick her into handing him a bomb? The memory of me leaving her at the airport, turning, and waving, remains in her head. She re-runs the memory of those last few minutes together over and over again.

It is exactly one week after the explosion. Adeline and Amelia are sitting at their usual table on the corniche. It is a beautiful day. The sky is blue, the sun is hot, and the sea breeze is refreshing. The sound of the sea and the seagulls is stimulating. Amelia tries to find the waiter to pay for their coffees, but he is nowhere to be seen. She has to pay at the counter. I have been watching them for over an hour, wanting to rush over to them but not daring. They haven't spoken, smiled, or even drunk their coffee, just sat. I wait until Amelia is at the counter before approaching her. She looks straight at me, not recognizing me at first and then not believing what she sees.

'Is that really you, Jacques?' she croaks. 'I thought you were dead. What is going on?'

'Yes, it really is me. The plane did not crash. As the aircraft climbed, it shook the bomb free of the tail fin. The bomb did explode, almost immediately, but the air stream forced the explosion backwards and away from the plane. We thought the plane would break up, but it didn't. We all survived.'

'But where have you been? Why didn't you come back to us? Adeline has been close to killing herself.'

'Oh dear, I didn't realise she thought so much of me. She can have any man on the planet.'

'Thought so much of you! Jacques, she is crazy about you. She always has been, from the first day you met. You were too infatuated with your Moroccan to see it.'

'I thought she was just doing her job.'

'You men are stupid. You have no idea. So where have you been?'

'We landed in Maine under fighter escort, where we were questioned for two days. Thanks to the generosity of the king, we stayed in the Intercontinental Hotel and were pampered every minute of the day. The Moroccan police came over to question us. They knew Adeline was innocent, but they wanted the story to run, hoping to get a confession out of Jean Claud and Lafleur. You see, they had no proof of their involvement. The witnesses only saw Adeline and me with the briefcase.'

'Come on, let's tell Adeline.'

I grab her and pull her back. 'Wait a minute. Is it going to be too much of a shock for her? Maybe she should learn the truth gently.'

Amelia stops in her tracks and looks over at Adeline, who is still staring out over the ocean.

'You are right. Let me go and break it to her. You stay here.'

'Okay.'

I watch as Amelia sits down next to her. 'Adeline, what are you thinking about?'

Adeline sighs. 'Oh, not a lot. Just dreaming about how nice it would be to have Jacques sit here with me. It was me who killed him. How can I live with that?'

'You didn't kill him. You know that. Anyway, to kill someone they have to be dead.'

'What are you talking about? I know he will always be alive in my heart, but that is all.'

'That isn't true. The plane didn't blow up. It didn't crash. They are all still alive.'

'Stop it, Amelia. I can't take this.'

'Wait, calm down. What I am telling you is true.'

'Come on, let's go home before I slap you.'

'Adeline, it is true. He has just told me.'

'Told you, how? In a dream?'

'No, he has just spoken to me. He said they wouldn't let him come to you until your brother and

Jacques confessed. He is over there, at the counter, waiting for you. He wanted you to learn the truth gently. He was frightened the shock might be too great for you.

I watch her head turn towards me. All I can think of doing is to give her a wave. How stupid is that? She slowly raises her hand and waves back. I can see that Amelia is speaking to her. She looks at me, back at Amelia, and then back at me again.

I hear Amelia say, 'Go to him, you silly cow. What are you waiting for?'

Adeline pushes her chair away and starts towards me. She moves slowly and shakily at first but gathers strength with every step.

That embrace was the most beautiful feeling in the world. If you are in love, you will know what I am experiencing. If you haven't yet been in love, you have one of the wonders of the world to look forward to.

Back to the Beginning

My mind is fully activated. My body is still fired with passion, with lust, with desire, and I have nowhere to release it. Here I am, lying next to this smooth, tanned body twenty years my junior yet unable to make contact with her. She tosses and turns in her sleep. I move to the edge of the bed, saved from falling out by a thin, twisting yarn that circumnavigates the mattress edge. I turn just in time to narrowly avoid being cracked across my face by her flailing arms responding to yet another nervous twitch. Finally she lies still. I know she is awake; she can only lie still when she is awake. The cold air rushes in as she throws back the duvet and inconsiderately leaves me cold and coverless. I listen to her groping her way down the unlit corridor towards the kitchen. *I would love a cup of tea,* I think, *but experience has taught me that she will only make one cup, one cup without sugar for herself.*

We row about nothing. The most insignificant discussions turn into anger and frustration – man's logic versus woman's passion. We are both stubborn people and refuse to give in. Eventually she starts insulting my manhood, my hygiene standards, my cooking ability, and my age. I have no answer for this kind of onslaught. So I shut up; she chalks this up as a win and adds it to her list of insults. What is the point? We used to make mad, passionate love every night. After an argument, it was tremendous; it made the argument worth having. But now she turns her back on me and pretends to be asleep. I can hear the kettle boiling, and now she is stirring in the milk. There is silence. What is she doing now? I don't have a clue.

It seems like an age passes. Maybe I fall asleep for a few minutes, Or was it an hour? Now there is a single shaft of light breaking through the curtains; the sun is coming up. I can hear her coming back to bed. She will be cold; maybe she will cuddle up to me for warmth. That would be nice. I sense her enter the bedroom and through half-open eyes watch her walk towards the bed. She is holding something out towards me. Has she brought me a cup of tea? Should I speak or pretend to be asleep? As she raises her arm, I realise it isn't a cup in her hand but a knife – a kitchen knife. Its long blade flashes in the dawning light as she kneels on the bed beside me and thrusts it down towards my chest.

'Oh my God! Adeline,' I scream, 'what do you think you are doing?'

I grab her arm and force her over onto her back. She lies there beneath me, panting and sweating, trying to raise her head so she can bite my nose.

'Oh! So you are awake. Do you know we have not made love for nearly four nights?'

'Yes, actually, I am aware.'

'And you weren't going to do anything about it?'

'I thought it was you who had gone cold.'

'Well, I haven't. I thought you needed some excitement in your life. You seem to thrive on danger, so I thought I would kill you.'

She is laughing, and I feel her body give under me.

'You are right. I do thrive on danger, and you are in for the pounding of your life.'

'About time.'

I release her mouth from my bite.

'Adeline, would you really have stabbed me?'

She laughs. 'Of course I would.'

Congratulations

J ean Claud and Lafleur were given a pardon by the king. They hadn't actually killed anyone, and the success they had achieved in turning around the economy of Morocco was unbelievable. The king gave them a pardon and let them keep their newfound wealth, but he banned them from entering Morocco ever again.

Oh! By the way, I bet you are wondering what gift I chose. Well, what would a simple man with ten million dollars in his bank account need? I asked the ambassador to be my best man at our wedding and the king to be godfather to our baby. Adeline has just told me I am to be a father.

About the Author

T im Dickinson is a Yorkshire man, born and bred in this rugged part of England only two miles from the home of the Bronte sisters. His upbringing in the 1950s was simple; it was a place where values were true and morals were upheld. His artistic career took him to London to work as an advertising creative, where he wrote campaigns for Porsche cars, breakfast cereals and chocolate bars. It also took him to the Middle East, to Saudi Arabia, where he worked with some of the richest men in the world on the most prestigious advertising accounts. He launched DHL into the kingdom, introduced Arabia to Persil, opened shopping malls, schools, and banks, and promoted tourism. He has been involved in life at many levels. During those twelve years the world was his oyster; in his office alone nine different languages were spoken. Tim has the ability to bond with everyone, whatever their nationality;

he absorbed their cultures, tried to understand their religions, and embraced their traditions.

But not everything was so rich. Bullying and bribery were rife, and every day was spent under the threat of terrorist activity. He was forced out of his home and held at gunpoint on more than one occasion. But his core values saw him through, enabling him to lead one of the most creative advertising agencies in the Middle East. He says he has seen the most beautiful and experienced the most terrifying aspects of our modern world.

Tim is very much a family man, with two sons who are equally creative. One is a world-acclaimed musician; the other is renowned for innovation in product design. His family keep his feet on the ground. He is a proud father and grandfather. Watching his family grow up is his greatest joy.

'A Moroccan Affair' is the first of a series of Ad-man adventures. They are totally fictitious and any similarity to characters alive or dead is purely co-incidental. After saying that, some of the incidents have been inspired by my own experiences but considerably embroidered upon. Forced from my comfort zone and plunged into a new world, the shock to my system and psyche was considerable and I felt I just had to capture the reality of my situation. 'A Moroccan Affair' is a series of parables and has appeal on many levels: adventure, love, deceit, and betrayal, all linked with a sprinkling of Yorkshire humour. The foundation of the story illustrates the power of advertising and marketing as a medium for change, be it for good or bad.

I write in the first person and in the present tense so you can be involved in the action as it happens, be in the room when decisions are made and to share the excitement or despair of the moment. I have never known what was going to happen next. My life has been lived on the edge, sometimes very rewarding but sometimes scary. The language is bold and simple, as you would expect from the pen of a Yorkshire man. No punches are pulled and no emotions withheld.

Read the story as it happens, and I hope you enjoy it.

Printed in the United States
By Bookmasters